# REMEMBER ME

# REMEMBER ME

## SANDRA L. TATARA

**FIVE STAR**

*An imprint of Thomson Gale, a part of The Thomson Corporation*

THOMSON

GALE™

Detroit • New York • San Francisco • New Haven, Conn. • Waterville, Maine • London

THOMSON
GALE

**LIBRARY OF CONGRESS CATALOGING-IN-PUBLICATION DATA**

Tatara, Sandra L.
    Remember me / Sandra L. Tatara. — 1st ed.
       p. cm.
    ISBN-13: 978-1-59414-582-7 (hardcover : alk. paper)
    ISBN-10: 1-59414-582-2 (hardcover : alk. paper)
       1. Married women—Fiction. 2. Older men—Fiction. 3. Alzheimer's disease—Patients—Fiction. 4. Man-woman relationships—Fiction. 5. Ranch life—Fiction. I. Title.
    PS3620.A88R46 2007
    813'.6—dc22                                                 2007000468

First Edition. First Printing: May 2007.

Published in 2005 in conjunction with Tekno Books.

Printed in the United States of America on permanent paper
10 9 8 7 6 5 4 3 2 1

Dedicated in loving memory to:
My mother, Annabelle E. Hill
and dear friend, W. R. (Bill) Merritt

# ACKNOWLEDGMENTS

As I began to be serious about writing, and learned I enjoyed "Open Mic" nights, I was encouraged by the Feminist Writer's Guild, especially Whitney Scott, Toby Fox, Linda Cochran and Ellen Nordberg.

Thanks to the good friends in my writer's group, the Southland Scribes: Linda Cochran, Sherry Scarpaci, Jane Andringa, Joan Poninski, Lydia Ponczak, Ralph Horner, Ryan O'Reilly, George Kulles, Nancy Conley, Helen Osterman, and especially Julie Hyzy and Michael Black for all their help with the publishing process. Thanks to Earl Merkel, former group member, who urged me to work to get *Remember Me* published.

I would like to thank John Helfers at Tekno Books, and a very special thanks to my editor, Alice Duncan, who worked so hard against a very tight editing schedule.

Most of all, to my family, Frank, Michael, Mark, Kaye, Helen, my sweethearts John and Lily, and Andy and Paula. All of you make my life so truly blessed. Thank you.

★ ★ ★ ★ ★

# PART ONE

★ ★ ★ ★ ★

# CHAPTER ONE

Dani Monroe felt as empty as the old red barn around her. In spite of the early April sunshine, the packed ground of the walkway was cold beneath her boots. Between the two rows of stalls ran an indoor riding arena, its corners concealed in shadows. Flecks of dust danced in the shaft of light shining through the large doorway at the end of the barn. Dani strolled along the aisle, peering into the stalls as she passed. An aged and frail white mare stood alone in the end stall. She rarely went out to pasture with the other horses anymore. The mare raised her head and nickered at Dani's approach.

"Hi there, girl. How's Bella today?" Dani rubbed the mare's muzzle and stroked her neck before continuing on toward the back of the barn.

Pushing a wheelbarrow full of wood shavings, a ranch hand burst through the service door. He nodded to Dani and smiled around a wad of chewing tobacco. A dribble oozed past crooked teeth and over his discolored lip. He brushed his chin against the shoulder of his faded flannel shirt and shuffled on his way.

The sliding service door squeaked as Dani pushed against it and paused in the shadows to watch a rider working an impressive-looking buckskin in a round training pen. Under a black Stetson hat, the rider's dark hair, brushed with silver, framed a faded tan and remarkably unlined face. Dressed in jeans, black western shirt and denim jacket, a lean and fit physique belied his sixty-two years. His forehead creased in

11

concentration above steel-blue eyes. Charcoal-gray roper boots pressed hard in the stirrups as he cued the stocky buckskin into a canter, spun him around, and changed leads. "Dammit," he muttered and pulled the gelding to a stop.

Dani edged from the shadows and stood closer to the training pen. "Hi. Mind if I watch?"

The rider scowled. "It's okay. Almost done for today anyway." He backed his horse across the pen and put him into a trot. The horse gave a series of small bucks, moved twice around the circle, and stopped.

"You ornery son-of-a-bitch," he snapped, cued the horse into a canter and pushed him hard around the circle. The buckskin obeyed for several minutes before starting to slow. The rider barked a command, prodded with his spurs, and continued working for twenty minutes before pulling the lathered, hard-breathing horse to a walk to cool him down.

Dani leaned against the red iron gate with her boot propped against the bottom rail of the pen.

"Having a rough day with him?" she asked.

"Always have it rough with him. He's ornery," he said curtly, barely looking in her direction.

"Well, I won't bother you then." She turned toward the barn.

"You might as well open the gate for me as long as you're there," he called to her. "If you don't mind."

Dani gave him a small grin. "Sure."

Eyes flashing, the horse snorted, pawed at the damp ground, and nipped at her on his way through the gate. Dani made a face at him and followed at a safe distance.

The buckskin danced around in the crossties. "Dammit. Stand still." His owner loosened the cinch, eased the dusty Billy Cook saddle to the floor and yanked off the saddle pad. He worked a soft bristled brush over the sweaty horse.

Dani brushed dust from her jeans and sat on an empty milk

crate. He half glanced in her direction. "Where's your horse today?" he asked. "How come you aren't riding?"

"I rode earlier and turned him out to pasture for a bit. I just came back to put him away."

He nodded and dragged the brush over the horse's broad rump.

"My name is Dani, by the way."

"Uh-huh, I know. I'm Ray Crowley."

"I know," she teased.

Ray threw her a quick sideways glance; gave the horse one last stroke before tossing the brush in the box. Turning toward her, he returned her impish smile and unhooked the crosstie. "Want to grab that saddle pad for me and bring it out in the sun to dry?"

"Sure thing." Dani reached for the dusty blanket.

Outside, Ray motioned for her to throw it over the fence.

"There're some Cokes in my truck. Why don't you get us a couple cans while I graze this ungrateful plug?"

Dani laughed and caught the keys he tossed her way. In the cab of his GMC pickup, she dug two icy cans from a Playmate cooler resting on the floor of the passenger side. Folded papers, notebook and pen, a map, two screwdrivers and a pair of vice grips were arranged in the elastic-edged compartment on the door. A small folded towel with glass case and whiskbroom on top lay on the front seat. The cab was neat and orderly, no dust on the dash, no dirt on the floor.

"Is he always so nasty?" Dani tugged at the tabs on both cans, handed one to him and sat on a tree stump near the grazing horse.

"Yep. I got him as a three-year-old and he's been nothin' but trouble ever since." He glanced at her. "You're new here. How long have you had your horse?"

"Just bought him two months ago." Dani's eyes softened.

"I've been waiting my whole life for this horse."

"He's a great-lookin' horse. I've seen you ride a few times. You need some work."

Dani held a hand to her chest as she choked on the pop in her throat, then smiled at the twinkle in his eyes. "Very funny. But actually, you're right. It's been a long time since I've ridden and I never had any formal training." She wiped her mouth against her hand. "I've been taking lessons for about a month now."

"What's his breeding?" Ray asked. "Looks like a Dee Bar horse."

"Very good. Yes, he's a grandson of Sonny Dee Bar," she answered proudly.

He raised his eyebrows. "I'm impressed. So, where are all those chatty women you ride with? I haven't seen them in a few days. Been kind of nice around here for a change."

"I don't think it's so nice. It's really pretty lonely. Several of them moved their horses to another barn. They had some kind of a disagreement with the owner here and they all left." Dani lifted the can for a drink. "I don't have anyone to ride with now, and I was just getting to the point where I wanted to try going on trails."

"There's bound to be someone else around who would like to go on trails with you," he assured her.

"Do you ever go? I've only seen you working in the arena and the round pen."

"No, I don't go on trails. I do take him to horse shows, though I don't really know why. He always bucks and acts up at the show anyway." Ray smacked his horse affectionately on the rump. "But I have to do something with him to keep him in shape."

Dani gazed over the buckskin. "Is that what you bought him for—shows?"

Ray looked away, and his voice softened. "Yes. For my daughter."

"Doesn't she ride anymore?"

"You sure do ask a lot of questions, Missy." He bristled, yanked on the buckskin's lead line and started back to the barn.

Dani flinched at his outburst and snapped in return, "Sorry. I won't bother you again." She slammed the empty pop can in the trash and stalked toward her horse grazing in the pasture. She untied the jacket from around her shoulders and jammed her arms into the sleeves, shivering in the sudden afternoon chill.

Looking for a treat, Chance poked his nose toward Dani's pocket as she led him back to the stall. She dug a carrot from the plastic bag she'd tied to his gate, broke it in three pieces, and dropped them into his feed bucket.

"Bye, sweetie. See you tomorrow," Dani whispered, rubbed a hand against Chance's muzzle, and locked his stall door.

She hurried to her car, gunned the engine and raced from the lot, wheels spitting gravel against Ray's truck on the way.

"Little spitfire, isn't she?" Ray grumbled to his horse as they walked back to the stalls. He passed an arena where the ranch's owner worked a young horse through a barrel pattern.

Bud Morgan laughed. "Sure do have a way with the ladies, Ray," he called.

Ray waved. "Yeah, horses and women are my real strong suits."

He locked the buckskin in his stall and gave him an apple. "Sure handled that well, didn't I? Getting about as disagreeable as you are. I don't know why I bother with you." He rubbed the horse's neck. "Think she'll ever talk to me again?" he asked.

The visions of Dani's coppery hair brushing against her shoulders and her jaunty walk as she'd gone to his truck for

15

Cokes flickered through Ray's mind. It was difficult to ignore her trim figure in the snug black denims and Chicago Bulls T-shirt under the red windbreaker she'd tied around her shoulders.

He'd managed to keep his distance from most of the other boarders, ignoring the chatty exchanges among many of the women he found silly and irritating. Since Dani began boarding her horse at the Rockin' Horse Ranch, he found himself watching her ride, listening to her visit with the other riders, enjoying her tentative questions as she learned to ride and care for her horse. Lately the sound of her voice and her laughter chipped away at the protective shell he'd built around himself.

He shook his head. *Damned woman can't be over thirty-five. What's wrong with me thinking about her so much? Must be getting senile.* He rechecked the stall latch and headed for his truck. *Sure didn't leave any good impression snapping at her the way I did. Crabby old goat with a crabby old horse, that's me.* Ray opened his door, started the engine, and remembered how cute Dani had looked as she'd bent to open the cooler. *God, Crowley, you ought to be locked up.*

Dani turned up the radio and eased off on the gas pedal. Shivering slightly, she reached for the heat dial. *Sure ask a lot of questions, Missy.* Ray's words competed with the talk-radio station. *What got into him? Can't have a little friendly conversation? Never seemed very sociable to anyone at the barn. Must be a reason he kept to himself so much. No wonder his horse is so ornery, must be contagious.* She glanced at the clock on the dash. *Not today, I'm not in the mood. I'll go tomorrow after I ride.*

Dani picked up the entrance ramp to I-394 and headed for home. She'd been packing things at her mother's house for the last three days. If her sister, Lynn, was in such a big hurry to get the house sold, she could just give Dani a hand with the work. Dani frowned as she thought of her younger sister. Never around to help, Lynn only called or showed up when she needed or wanted something. *You're going to have to grow up now, Lynn. I'm not taking over where Mom left off.* A twinge of guilt gnawed at Dani. In her last few days, Mom had reminded Dani, "Now you take care of Lynn. She's not as strong as you are, Dani. She needs a push every so often."

I *need a push lately too, Mom. Just to get out of bed in the morning. Wish I could just let someone else handle everything for a while. Just for a while.* Dani flexed her shoulders and sighed. *Wish you were still here.*

# Chapter Two

Dani brought Chance to a stop near the fence where Bud Morgan worked repairing the faded white railing.

" 'Morning, Dani. Nice day for a ride." He nodded toward her horse. "Chance seems to be working out pretty well for you. You're riding much better too."

"Thanks, Bud." Dani ran a hand over Chance's shoulder. "He's really a nice horse and I'm feeling more confident every day. Now I'm looking for someone to go on trails with me."

"You could put up a note in the tack room," Bud suggested. "And we have several new boarders due in next week." He tossed the hammer in his toolbox and moved to the next loose fence board. He stopped, looked back over his shoulder at her, and chuckled. "Of course you could see if your admiring cowboy would like to go with you."

Dani looked puzzled. "And just who would that be?" she asked.

"Ah, come on. You know who."

"No, I really don't know what you're talking about, Bud."

"Ray Crowley," he replied.

"Oh, right." Dani laughed.

"He's been asking about you for the last couple weeks, and he's coming out a lot more than he used to," Bud teased.

Dani shifted in the saddle and frowned. "He's not very pleasant. He told me he got that rotten-tempered buckskin for his daughter. When I asked if she rode anymore, he snapped at me and said I asked too many questions."

Bud's tone turned somber. "His daughter's a very sad subject." He tapped the nail once more and sighed. "Kathy gave him a lot of trouble before she moved to Texas with her no-good boyfriend. He got her mixed up with drugs, and they both died of an overdose a few years back."

Dani winced. "Oh! I'm so sorry. I wish I'd known."

"Honey, there's no way you could have known. Don't worry about it." Bud hesitated and continued. "She was an only child, and they'd been married quite a while before they had her. The marriage broke up and Kathy was his whole world. A nice kid too, until she took up with that no-good punk. 'Bout broke Ray's heart."

"That's very sad and sure explains his behavior."

Bud gathered his tools and inspected the fence. "I have to get back to work and take advantage of this nice weather. You have a good ride. Don't be going out on trails alone. Never know when a deer or something will spook your horse and you'd get hurt."

"Okay, see you later," she said.

Dani turned Chance to the middle of the arena. She worked him in circles around the barrel, but her mind drifted back to her conversation with Bud. *I guess that explains why Ray's so remote. How does anyone survive losing a child? I can't imagine my life if anything happened to Trace.* A miscarriage when Trace was six years old had left an emptiness and sadness that haunted her still. Although Trace would soon be off to college, Dani was very protective of her only child.

Chance sensed her lack of attention and took advantage of it by breaking his stride and balking at her commands. Dani cantered to the fence line, rode him around the large circle several times, and brought him to a walk.

"Okay, big boy. I'm not concentrating, so let's call it a day."

After putting away her saddle and tack, Dani brushed Chance and led him to the nearest pasture to graze. She watched her horse nibble at the tender new shoots of grass. Occasionally his ear would twitch or he'd swish his tail, but nothing deterred him from his serious job of grazing. He'd been a little out of shape when she bought him, but she could see a definite improvement in his muscle tone. *The exercise has been good for me too. I'm in better shape.*

It'd been a long, dreary winter. Buying Chance brought a new focus to her days, a sense of freedom. Her son, Trace, going into his senior year and planning for college, needed her less these days. And Brian . . . well, Dani pushed away thoughts of her husband for now.

The sun warmed her face, easing away a bit of the tension of the last few months she'd spent sitting in the hospital with her mother. Even in the fresh country air she could remember the antiseptic smell that failed to fully mask the lingering scent of illness and death. It had taken Dani some time before she accepted the fact that her mother wasn't going to get better. As conversations shifted from the present and future to the past, Dani held her mother's hand for hours and listened as she reminisced about her life. For the first time, Dani saw her mother as a little girl, a young woman, and mother of two young daughters as she struggled to survive an alcoholic/abusive marriage. Relief was all Dani'd felt when her father finally did them a favor and walked out. Although her mother now expressed the same relief, she also recalled the fear she'd had of raising two children alone.

The first years were rough, but her mother worked hard at the large department store and moved up quickly. She managed money well and their lives became easier. Dani listened as her mother rambled, often feeling that she didn't always realize Dani was in the room. As the days lingered on, her mother weakened and their conversations waned. She smiled when Dani came into the room, attempted to talk, but tired easily and dozed off. Dani sat quietly next to the bed, watching her mother sleep. She tried to read; her back hurt as she squirmed repeatedly to get comfortable in the blue vinyl chair. Was it really too much to ask to have a decent chair for visitors who were going through enough without furniture designed by the Marquis de Sade? Wasn't likely someone would get so comfortable they'd want to hang around longer than necessary just soaking up the atmosphere of the oncology floor.

Dani stared out the window at the cars circling the parking lot in search of an empty space. She watched people enter and leave the hospital entrance, searched their faces, and wondered at their situations. A young woman holding a new baby sat in a wheelchair chatting with a hospital volunteer beside her as an excited-looking young man pulled to the curb. He jumped from the car, settled the infant carefully in the baby carrier and the new mom lovingly in the front seat. It was nice to see a happy event.

Dani shuddered. She closed her eyes and lifted her face to the sun. *Buying the horse was a good idea. I needed something just for me.*

Lost in her reverie, she didn't hear the approaching footsteps.

"Have a nice ride?" Ray asked.

Dani jumped at the sound of his voice. Chance crow-hopped a few feet before going back to his grazing.

"Sorry." Ray leaned against the fence. "I shouldn't have startled you like that."

"Guess he's too interested in grazing to go very far."

"Glad I caught up with you today." Ray adjusted his hat, fingered the brim. "Wanted to apologize for snapping at you. Sometimes I can be as ornery as that damned horse of mine.

Guess I spend too much time with him—makes me a crabby old man."

Dani raised a hand to shield her face against the bright sunlight and for the first time looked him square in the eyes. She flashed a lopsided grin. "You might be crabby sometimes, but you don't look like an old man to me."

A broad smile pulled at his face. He burst into a hearty laugh. "Honey, I'm sure old enough to be *your* daddy."

*Nice smile, great laugh.* "Really?" Dani regarded him thoughtfully. "How old are you?"

"Let's see now." He grinned at her. "I remember a time when George Washington and I used to play under this old cherry tree." He waved a hand in the air. "And . . . oh, hell, you probably read all about it in your history books. Except I chopped down the damned tree but he got all the credit."

Dani laughed. "You're a lot better preserved than George is then." She snapped the lead line onto the halter ring. "Come on, Chance—enough grass for today."

"Seriously, though." Ray fell in step beside her. "I am sorry about being such a crab-ass."

Dani stopped in her tracks. "You know, we've only had two conversations and it seems as if both of us have spent a whole lot of time saying I'm sorry about something. How about a fresh start?" She held out her hand. "Hi, I'm Dani Monroe. Nice to meet you."

He took her hand in his. "Nice to meet you, Dani Monroe. I'm Ray Crowley." Their eyes held for another instant before she pulled her hand away. His hand felt nice holding hers. *Too nice.*

"Okay, we got that squared away. I've got to put him up and get going," she said.

"How about having some lunch with me?" Ray asked.

A flicker of sadness clouded her chocolate brown eyes as she turned toward her horse.

"Sorry, I have something to do today." A tentative note crept into her voice. "Maybe . . . maybe some other time?"

Ray nodded as he touched a hand to his hat. "Sure thing. Have a good day, Dani Monroe."

Dani tucked Chance in his stall, secured the bolt, and headed for her car. As she started the engine and rummaged for her sunglasses, she saw Ray's truck stop at the gate. He sat for a few seconds looking in his rearview mirror, waved at her, and pulled into traffic.

Dani nudged up the volume on a George Strait tape and headed toward her mother's house to pack. She'd listed the house with a real-estate agent, promising to have it emptied out and cleaned soon. She replayed Ray's apology as she drove. Gentleness lurked behind his gruff manner, and the sweetness in his smile touched her. He'd made her laugh and lately that was quite an accomplishment.

# CHAPTER THREE

Dani packed the last of the canned goods into a box, and using a dolly she'd borrowed from Bud Morgan at the ranch, wheeled the box out to her car. Most of the kitchen cabinets were emptied and wiped clean, and she was ready to break for lunch.

Today she decided to alter her routine by working at the house first to enable her to anticipate riding Chance afterward. Also, Bud's words about Ray being an admiring cowboy worried her a bit. He seemed fragile enough with the loss of his daughter; best not to give any mixed messages here. Resigned to the fact that it was better not to establish a friendship with him, she'd vary her visits to the barn to avoid crossing paths more than necessary.

Maybe she'd think about moving her horse to another barn. So far the new boarders hadn't shown promise of someone to trail ride with. Two young men with well-worn and tired-looking horses were proving to be a troublesome addition to the ranch. Bud Morgan ran a tight place, and Dani didn't think the rowdy men would last long. A flashy-looking woman about ten years younger than Dani seemed more interested in meeting men— eligible or not—than in horses.

Dani sighed. Soon she'd be riding well enough that she just might try the trails alone. Certainly wasn't going to ride around the arena in circles forever. She turned her car onto the gravel drive under the Rockin' Horse Ranch sign. On his way out, Ray slid to a sudden stop beside her.

"Hi, there." He smiled and tipped the black Stetson in a greeting. "Haven't seen you around in a while." His smile softened his craggy features and showed slight crinkles at the corners of his eyes.

"Uh, been busy, that's all." Dani opened and closed her hand around the steering wheel. "I don't always come out at the same time."

Ray nodded, said, "Have a nice ride," and pulled away.

From the corner of his eye Bud Morgan glimpsed the exchange between Ray and Dani as he turned a young colt into the pasture. He'd owned the Rockin' Horse Ranch for twenty-five years; ran across all kinds of people. Saw a lot of romances start around the place. A few flourished, a lot fizzled; and some he knew from experience, wrecked marriages and caused a lot of pain.

Ray had boarded there for a long time. He'd moved in first with a little paint mare that he'd bought for his daughter. She'd been about eight at the time, sweet and excited as most little girls are about horses. Ray saw to it she had lessons from the best trainer around. Kathy learned fast and soon outgrew her little mare. Ray bought the flashy three-year-old buckskin, and Kathy was on her way to collecting a lot of ribbons and trophies at local horse shows. Bud watched as she grew into an over-indulged teenager and more trouble than Ray knew how to handle alone. Kathy's mother didn't care for horses, didn't understand her daughter, and chose to abdicate parental responsibility to Ray when they divorced.

Used to having her own way, Kathy rebelled when Ray tried to end a budding romance with a wild motorcycle-riding young man who had *trouble* stamped all over him. He was four years older than Kathy, and Ray struggled with how to keep them apart.

When the boy got into trouble and ran off to Texas, Kathy went with him. She'd just turned eighteen and there was little Ray could do to stop her. Within two years, they were both dead of a drug overdose and Bud watched friendly and easy-going Ray Crowley withdraw into himself and close off the world around him.

Dani Monroe had only been at the ranch about two weeks when Bud noticed Ray trying not to be too obvious about watching her ride. He usually came out once or twice a week during the winter months, more in summer when he took the buckskin to horse shows. Suddenly he was coming out three, sometimes four times a week, usually when Dani was around.

Bud could certainly understand Ray's attraction to her. She had a vibrant femininity about her, was friendly and pleasant to be around, even with the sadness he noticed in her eyes when her guard was down. He didn't know too much about her; she'd mentioned her son a few times, and that her mother had died recently. Probably accounted for the sadness. She wore a wedding band but never mentioned a husband. Maybe widowed or divorced—wore the ring because of her son. She'd made several friends right away but when the gals bristled at some of Bud's rules, they decided to board their horses elsewhere. Bud wondered why Dani hadn't gone along with them. Glad she hadn't; he hated to lose nice boarders. She took good care of her horse and he liked having her around.

He noticed that since he'd teased Dani about Ray being an admirer, she'd changed her routine. Whereas she'd usually come out in the mornings, she now came in the afternoons, several times arriving just after Ray had left. Seemed like Ray had an awful lot to do around the ranch lately. His horse was groomed and trimmed like he was ready for a parade. Ray spent a lot of time cleaning and polishing his saddle and tack, already in im-maculate condition. Spent a lot of time glancing toward the parking lot while he was around.

Bud sure hoped Ray wasn't setting himself up for more hurt. Dani had mentioned her son getting his driver's license, and even though Bud suspected Dani was older than she looked, there was still quite an age difference between her and Ray.

Dani had been at her mother's house every morning that week. With the day already warmed by the sun in a clear blue sky, restlessness stirred within her. She changed her plans at the last minute and decided to take the day off and spend it at the ranch. She might just take Chance for a ride down one of the quiet little roads near the stables.

It surprised her that when she pulled into the parking lot and noticed Ray's truck, she suddenly felt glad that he was there. Couldn't hurt to be friendly, have someone to talk to around here once in a while, could it?

"Doesn't that horse of yours have a name?" Dani called out as she rode by.

The buckskin chewed at the rope holding him to the hitching post beneath an old oak tree. Ray looked up from brushing his horse and smiled at her. "Sure, I call him lots of things."

"So I've noticed." Dani came to a stop at the fence. "That could be your problem. Maybe if you talk a little nicer to him he won't be so ornery. Cause and effect, you know?"

"Nah. I talk to him like that because he is ornery. Action and reaction, you know," Ray countered.

Dani shook her head and rode back to the arena. Ray saddled his horse and caught up with her. "You're riding much better. He isn't taking advantage of you as much. You could try some spurs for a little attitude adjustment from time to time."

"I'll keep that in mind," Dani said.

"Find someone to go on trails with you?"

"No, not yet. Bud suggested I put up a note in the tack room," Dani answered.

"Be careful about that. There are a few guys around here who just might take you up on it, but you wouldn't want to go riding with them."

Ray turned his horse to the center of the track, worked him through several figure eights, and cantered him in a small circle as Dani worked Chance along the outside rail.

He slowed up and joined her when she passed by. They rode side by side in silence around the arena for several minutes. "I was thinking." Ray cleared his throat and adjusted his hat. "Maybe I could go out on a trail ride with you."

Dani turned slightly in the saddle. "I thought you didn't go on trails?"

"I haven't wanted to go with anyone before now," he replied, looking straight ahead.

She tossed him a surprised look and pondered her reply.

Ray stretched his legs in his stirrups. "Just thought I'd offer . . . since you wanted to go and didn't have someone to ride with." He glanced sideways at her. "Wouldn't want you to go off with someone here you don't know well and . . ." His words trailed off.

"I don't really know *you* very well." Dani's words took on a teasing tone, hoping to keep the conversation light.

Ray nodded.

Dani gave in to the urge to tease. "I wouldn't want to end up with my picture on a missing poster."

He glanced around at her. "Are you always so cynical?"

"Just on good days," she said with a laugh.

"Do I look like a serial killer or something?" he questioned.

"Just what does a serial killer look like?"

"You have a point there. I hear you can't tell a serial killer by how they look."

"Guess I could check you out," she quipped.

"And how would you plan to do that?"

"I could start with the yellow pages. You know, see if you're listed under 'Serial Killers.' "

Ray nodded with a chuckle. "Okay, let me know what you find out." He spurred the buckskin and left her behind.

Dani cued Chance into a canter, urged him faster. She passed Ray with a wave. They played tag for several minutes until they were laughing too hard to ride and both horses were getting rowdy.

They cooled the horses and headed for the barn. "You surprise me. Very good riding," he complimented her.

"Thank you, kind sir." Dani beamed.

Bud Morgan stopped at the fence to watch the horseplay. He grinned, shook his head as he started to walk away.

"Hey Bud, hold on. Got my board money for next month," Ray called.

Dani and Ray rode to the fence. Ray pulled out his wallet, extracted several bills and tossed them to Bud.

"Crowley, when are you going to get a checking account like the rest of the world?"

"Hell, I wouldn't take a check from anyone, so why would I expect anyone to accept a check from me."

Bud stuffed the bills in his pocket, gave a wave of hopelessness in Ray's direction, and sauntered off.

"Why in the devil do you carry so much cash? That's dangerous," Dani scolded.

"I never know how much I'm going to need, that's why."

"Never known anyone without a checking account. How about a credit card?"

"Credit cards are dangerous." He shook his head. "Nope, I like cash."

Dani gave a little wave. "That explains one thing," she teased.

His eyes twinkled, "What would that be?"

"Carrying that fat wallet explains why you look so much taller sitting in the saddle."

Ray laughed hard. Dani rode beside him and continued. "Of course, it has its downside too. You kind of list to one side when you walk."

He grinned at her and said in a low, sexy drawl, "Spend a lot of time watching me walk, Monroe?" He kicked his horse and left her breathing dust.

As Ray rode back in her direction, Dani glanced at her watch. "I have to get moving; it's later than I thought," she said. Ray followed her back to the barn.

Dani unsaddled her horse, brushed him down and put away her tack. "Coming out tomorrow, could-be-serial-killer, or do you have a job?"

"No, no job. I retired to pursue my life of crime," he grinned. "Sure, I'll be out tomorrow unless I'm caught in the act tonight and get arrested."

"Be careful then. I'll probably see you tomorrow."

He watched her walk away—tan western shirt tucked into snug-fitting jeans, cocoa-brown Justin roper boots. "Hey!" he called after her. "Nice walk, Monroe."

With a little shake of her head and a slightly exaggerated swagger, Dani walked to her car with a spring in her step that had been missing for quite some time. As she reached her car, she turned to see him still watching her. She laughed, waved and shot back, "Glad to see you enjoying yourself, Crowley."

Something in her head whispered a warning to be careful, while deeper inside flickered the feeling of being rescued.

Ray turned, almost colliding with Bud Morgan leading a bay filly to the barn. "Hey, Ray, looks like you're improving your technique. Now if you can only get that mean-spirited buckskin to cooperate, you'll be batting a thousand."

"I should be so lucky," Ray said.

Bud continued on to the barn with the filly. Ray walked along beside him toward the tack room. Bud hesitated, and then called after him, "Ray, don't mean to stick my nose into anything, but during a conversation she mentioned her son getting his driver's license. I don't know if there's a husband or not. Take it easy, okay?"

"Yeah, nothin' to worry about. She's too young to bother with me anyway."

"Uh-huh," Bud whispered to the filly.

Ray straightened his tack box, locked up his saddle, and thought about Dani. *Spending a little too much time thinking about this young gal, you old fool. As if she'd ever be interested in me even if she were single.*

Deep in thought, he ambled back to his truck. She did seem a little friendlier today. *It's nice to have someone to ride with and joke around with . . . no harm in that, is there?*

# CHAPTER FOUR

Dani automatically pushed the vacuum cleaner around the living room. She smiled as she reminisced about the banter with Ray earlier in the week. She'd gone back to her former routine of riding each morning, and was surprised to see him at the barn every day. Not only did she look forward to being with Chance, but she also enjoyed Ray's company. He always seemed glad to see her, and their lighthearted teasing was a breath of fresh air to her spirits. Having someone to ride with and give her tips boosted her confidence and improved her performance. Her riding instructor had said Dani had the basics, and now all she needed was practice. She'd felt a little adrift when she stopped taking lessons, but Ray appeared happy to answer any questions and give suggestions.

Dani shut off the vacuum and shoved it toward the closet. Trace leaned against the doorway of the kitchen with a silly look on his face.

"What's so funny?" Dani inquired.

"You. I thought you were going to vacuum a hole in the carpet, you've been at it so long. And you look a million miles away while you're at it."

"I suppose I was." Dani chuckled. "Vacuuming doesn't take a lot of attention and I was thinking of being out with Chance instead."

"Ah. Good you have something happy to think about for a change."

"Yes, it is nice." She nodded. "Now, what are your plans for today?"

"Ryan and I are going over to apply for the jobs with the park district for the summer. You know, to help out with the day camp kids."

"Okay, good luck. I'm going out to the barn in a bit. See you later this afternoon."

Trace waved and hurried out the door.

Dani knocked and pushed open Brian's office door.

"Busy early today?"

"Trying to be. Thought you'd never get finished with that damned vac." He stared at his computer screen with a scrunched forehead.

"Sorry about that." Dani sighed. "I just wanted to get it done early. I'll go out to the barn and leave you in peace."

Brian doodled on a yellow legal pad before him. He waved a hand in her direction and mumbled, "Have a good time."

"Do you want anything special for dinner?"

Brian shot her an exasperated look. "No, Dani. Whatever you fix is fine, okay?"

Dani chewed against the inside of her cheek, decided against a response and closed the door.

*Suppose it's going to be one of his crabby days. Glad I have somewhere to go.* There were times when a whole week would go by without Brian leaving the house. He spoke to clients on the phone, worked at his computer, and watched television. *He spends too much time alone. You'd think he'd be glad to talk to Trace and me; instead he seems to resent the intrusion.*

More and more Dani wondered if Brian's working from home was a good idea. After his accident, it had seemed like a godsend, but over the years Dani thought he'd become too isolated. He should get out more. *We should get out more too.* Occasionally Brian would join her at school functions, or attend Trace's baseball games. But more often than not, Dani went alone. After a while, Trace stopped asking Brian to go to his games. He could always count on Dani being there, and if Brian came too, he was happy about it, but kept it to himself if it bothered him when his dad didn't see him play.

It hadn't always been that way—before the accident. Brian was a very attentive young father, eager to spend time with his pretty wife and rough-and-tumble little boy. The accident changed everything. Dani often felt that Brian's mental and emotional scars ran deeper than his obvious physical limitations. When his moods were particularly dark, they seemed to suck all the joy and life out of the house. *When Trace goes to school . . .* Dani found herself thinking about college and dreading the thought. Losing her mother and Trace going off to college . . . it like felt too much to handle at one time. She'd awaken at night, afraid of the loneliness ahead. *Don't think about it!*

Dani's mood brightened as she drove into the lot and saw Ray's truck parked in its usual spot. She checked her hair in the mirror, locked the door and hurried into the barn. *Don't think about anything but having a good ride.*

More and more she treasured her time spent at the ranch with Chance and tried not to worry about how much she enjoyed the lighthearted therapeutic banter with Ray. *It feels so good to laugh, to have someone to share common interests.*

To her surprise, Ray's buckskin had already been saddled. Standing in the crossties next to him was Chance, brushed and ready for tack. Ray smiled when he saw Dani. "Good morning, I have a surprise for you."

"So I see."

"I would have had him ready, but I don't have a key to your tack box. Hurry up. Get your saddle. We have places to go, things to see."

Ray followed her to the tack room. He carried her saddle while she collected the rest of her gear.

"You're in an awfully good mood this morning. Glad to see you still haven't been arrested for anything," Dani joked.

"I'm happy that since you didn't find me listed in the phone book under 'Serial Killers,' you're starting to trust me a little bit."

"It helped that I stopped at the post office on my way out and didn't see your picture posted anywhere."

"Ah, my luck's changing."

After Dani had positioned the thick pad, Ray tossed the barrel saddle in place. Dani tightened the cinch and attached the breast collar. "This barrel saddle is so much more comfortable than my new pleasure saddle. I never thought of buying a used one. Thanks for telling me about it."

"Come on. Get that bridle on. I have a surprise for you." His eyes sparkled like a kid's at Christmas.

As they led the horses from the barn, Dani motioned to the saddlebag tucked behind Ray's saddle. "What's that for?"

"That's the surprise. We're going on a trail ride," he announced.

"That's so sweet." Dani swallowed the lump in her throat, blinking behind her sunglasses. "You're really nice to me."

"You're easy to be nice to," Ray said softly, brushing his hand against her chin. He adjusted his hat against the bright morning sun and held her stirrup. "Okay, mount up, Annie Oakley."

Dani sprung easily into the saddle. She reached for the reins Ray held out to her. "*Annie Oakley* was one of my favorite TV shows when I was a little girl."

"Really? She was quite a firecracker, that one. I taught her how to ride."

"I'll just bet you did," she laughed.

"I'm surprised you're old enough to remember *Annie Oakley*," Ray said.

"I'm older than I look," she teased.

"Glad to hear it," Ray whispered to the buckskin as he mounted up.

Dani cast a worried look in his direction. "Do you know where we're going?"

"Sure do. I asked Bud, and he said the trails are easy to follow." Ray rode ahead to take the lead.

Bud Morgan pulled his truck to the gate and waved at the two riders. "Don't get her ambushed by Indians while you're out, General Custer," he joked.

Dani and Ray rode down the asphalt road that divided Illinois and Indiana. They crossed into the forest preserve trails on the Illinois side.

"Bud thinks he's so smart. He doesn't know I taught George to ride too," Ray snickered.

"George who?" Dani asked.

"Custer. General George Armstrong Custer, that's who."

"Here we go again." Dani laughed at him. "I feel a tall tale coming on."

Ray smiled. "Get with the program, Monroe."

"Okay. Let's hear it, cowboy."

Easily encouraged, Ray continued. "I tried to tell him, but he wouldn't listen. Several times he almost got us killed. I warned him—'George' I said, 'you keep pissin' off those Indians and your ass is grass.' Damned good thing I didn't ride with him that last time."

"You certainly do have a poetic way with words." Dani shook her head. "You're amazing. I hope you plan to leave your body to medical research. You're a real testimony to self-preservation."

He tipped his hat in her direction. "Thank you for the kind words, little lady. I plan to do just that."

After a moment, Dani said, "Bud's such a nice guy, so even-tempered."

"Yeah, he's great. Been a good friend to me for a lot of years."

"Does he have a family? I've never heard him mention anyone."

A heavy sigh preceded his words. "Yes, he had a family once." Dani glanced sideways at Ray, wondering if he was going to continue.

"Bud was pretty wild when he was young. He got married, probably too young, had a sweet wife, a son and a daughter. About two years after they bought the ranch, he had a fling with a wild little gal who boarded there. He knew it was stupid and regretted it. Anyway, his wife divorced him, took the kids and moved to . . . somewhere out East—Pennsylvania, I think. She had family there."

"Does Bud ever see the kids?"

"He tried for years. They're grown now and he sees them occasionally, but it's still pretty strained."

"He never remarried?"

"No. Had a gal who lived with him for a few years, but he was gun-shy about marrying again. After a while, she gave up and moved on."

Dani nodded and thought about the close relationship she had with her son.

At a point in the woods where the trail widened, they rode side-by-side in silence. Slivers of light sliced through a canopy of green. A squirrel darted across the trail and scampered up a tree. Several blue jays squawked at the intrusion.

The trees thinned out and the trail brightened. They rode through a clearing to the top of a hill. Sunlight bathed the meadow in a brilliant glow. Wildflowers floated in the gentle breeze like a pink-and-white sea. Dani held her breath. "Oh, how beautiful."

Ray made a shushing sound and touched her arm. He slowly pointed to the right. In the distance, at the edge of the woods, a doe and two fawns munched at the tender leaves on the low branches of a young sapling. The doe struck a rigid stance, sniffed the air, and fled into the woods with the fawns at her heels.

"This is what I dreamed about when I bought Chance. Thank you so much for bringing me here," Dani whispered.

Ray smiled at her pleasure.

They rode into the valley along a pristine narrow stream gurgling past a stand of towering oaks. Ray circled to face her. "Seems like a good spot for a picnic. Are you hungry?"

"Suddenly I'm starving," Dani exclaimed. "Is that what's in the saddlebags?"

"Sure is," he answered.

They led the horses to the stream for a drink then exchanged the bridles for halters. Dani tied the horses to graze.

Ray took a blanket from the saddlebag and spread it on the grass. He handed her sandwiches and chips while he carried cans of pop and sat beside her.

"Don't tell me you're a whiz in the kitchen too?" she questioned.

"Honey, I'm good at a lot of things, but not in the kitchen. Am a whiz at the deli however. Had these made up fresh for us on my way out to the barn."

Dani unwrapped the sandwiches and tore open the bag of chips. Ray pulled the tabs on the pop cans. He handed one to her while he took a drink from his. Dani bit into a thick turkey sandwich. "Um . . ." she swallowed. "Great sandwich; couldn't have done better myself."

They ate in silence while the horses grazed beside them.

"I was beginning to think I'd never get to go on trails. And this was sure worth the wait . . . even more relaxing and wonderful than I'd imagined."

"I rode around the fields and woods when I was a kid, but haven't ever gone trail riding like this. I have to admit it's pretty special."

When they were finished eating, Dani gathered up paper and cans for the trash. Ray stretched out on the blanket and closed his eyes. Dani studied his face, slightly shadowed by the Stetson he'd pulled onto his forehead. Although early in the season, he was already tanned—the kind of tan that comes easily to some people. She wondered about his age. His skin was firm and showed no wrinkles or damage from prolonged sun exposure. Slight laugh lines tugged at the corners of his eyes, but his jaw was taut. She noticed the beauty of his arms and hands crossed over his lean torso. Tiny shivers flickered across her shoulders; she turned away to watch the horses graze.

When she looked back at him, he was watching her. The tender look in his eyes turned inquisitive. "I find something strange," he said.

"And that would be?"

"Most women would have asked if I was married. You just wanted to know if I was a serial killer."

She smiled. "I already knew you weren't married."

He cocked his head and gave her a questioning look.

"Bud told me you were divorced." She hesitated and continued, "He told me the same time he told me about your daughter."

Pain deepened the shadows in his eyes. "I see," he replied softly. He rolled to his side, propped himself up on one elbow. "So when are you going to tell me all about you?"

"What do you want to know?" she asked.

"Bud told me you mentioned having a son."

"Yes, I do. My son, Trace, is sixteen."

His eyes searched hers. "And . . ."

Dani hugged her arms around her knees and pulled them close to her chest.

"And, yes. I am married." She rested her chin against her hands and met Ray's gaze.

He swallowed hard and glanced away. Dani looked down at the blanket. She followed the pattern with her fingertip.

"Can't be too happy or you wouldn't be here with me," he commented in a husky voice.

"There are unusual circumstances. We . . ." She rushed to her feet, tucked the empty pop cans and paper into the saddlebag. "Can we talk about it some other time? This has been such a special day. Do we have to ruin it?"

He rose and slipped the bridles from the saddle horn. "We can talk about it whenever you're ready."

"Can you . . . can we—can we still be friends?"

He dropped the bridles to the ground, reached out and touched her chin. "Of course we are still friends." He took her hand in his. "But we're already much more than that."

She struggled against the tears, seeing herself reflected in his eyes.

"Aren't we, Dani?"

"Yes, we are," she whispered.

He drew her close to him. Dani inhaled the crisp scents of spicy aftershave and horses that clung to him. His fingertips brushed aside her tears. He gently kissed her forehead and the tip of her nose. She met his gaze with eyes deep and dark through a pool of tears. He wrapped his arms around her and kissed her hard. She returned his kiss with an intensity that left them both too weak to stand. He sank to the blanket. Dani sat facing him with her head nestled on his chest. She felt his heart pounding as she struggled for a breath.

He reached for her again, but suddenly rose to his feet, pulling her with him. He grabbed the blanket, folded it, and stuffed it in the saddlebag. "Let's take a break, darlin', and ride."

They bridled the horses and rode toward home in silence.

Bud worked in the shadows repairing a stall door hinge at the far end of the barn. Conspicuously quiet, Ray and Dani unsaddled and groomed their horses and put away their tack. Bud whispered to the filly in the stall, "I think Indians would have been easier for them to deal with, little one."

Ray walked Dani to her car. "I didn't plan for that to happen, but I can't say I'm sorry."

"I know, and I can't say I am either. But—I'm scared."

Pain flickered in his eyes. "Don't be scared of me."

"I'm scared of *me*," she whispered.

"Don't be. Come on. Let me see a smile. I don't want you driving home upset. By the way, you always pull in from the west but turn east when you leave. Where do you go when you leave here that always makes you look sad?"

Dani drew in a deep breath. "My mother died six months ago. I've been trying to get her house packed up and ready to sell. It's so hard to be there alone. I have such good intentions of getting a lot done, but there are so many memories. Soon I'm daydreaming and it's time to go home." She dug her keys from her pocket and reached for the door.

"Don't you have anyone to help you do it?" Ray asked.

"No, not really. Trace came out a couple of times, but it's hard for him too. I don't want him to see me so upset." She dug a Kleenex from her purse. "It's really difficult to come out here, ride Chance, laugh and joke with you and then have to go there. It gets harder every day."

"Tell you what. Come out early in the morning. We'll ride,

41

have some lunch then I'll go with you. We'll get it done together. Okay?"

She stared at him. "You would really do that for me? You barely know me."

"That's what friends are for. And I do know you." He squeezed her hand and kissed her forehead. "I'll see you in the morning."

She touched his face and whispered, "I think it would be easier to deal with you if you *were* a serial killer."

"Such a smart mouth. Now go on, don't do any packing up today. Go home, and tomorrow we'll tackle the job together."

Ray unlocked his truck, started the engine, and headed for home. "Yes, Monroe. I already know you enough to know I love you," Ray whispered to the eyes staring back at him in the rearview mirror.

# CHAPTER FIVE

The packing tape curled, wrinkled and stuck to Dani's hands. *What in the devil is the matter with me?* She hadn't ridden well that morning, had pushed her salad around her plate at lunch, her stomach rumbling with anxiety at the thought of going to her mother's house with Ray.

She tossed a wad of tape into the garbage and started over. With the box finally secured, she slid it over the kitchen floor toward the door.

In the living room Ray stood looking at photographs on the shelving unit beside the television. A radiant bride and groom stared at him from the golden eight-by-ten frame he held in his hands. Dani sighed as she crossed the room and stood at his side.

"Still as pretty as you were in this picture," he said softly. "You make a nice-looking couple."

"Thank you." Dani took the photograph, folded it in bubble wrap, and placed it in the box. She gazed over the assortment of pictures that had been her mother's favorites. Placed together were several family shots taken of Dani, Brian and Trace—before the accident. All photos taken afterward were of Dani and Trace—alone, together, and with Dani's mother. The absence of any recent pictures of Brian was suddenly startling to Dani. *Why hadn't I noticed it before? Brian was always the one behind the camera, taking the shots; never wanting his picture taken after the accident.*

Ray pointed to a photo of Dani, her mother, and another young woman. "You look a lot like your mother. Who is the other gal?"

"My sister, Lynn."

"Ah. Cute." He grinned at Dani. "But not as pretty as you."

"Thanks, but maybe you're not objective."

"Where is she? Why isn't she helping you with this?"

"She lives in Iowa . . . for now, that is. She moves around a lot."

Ray waved his hand toward Brian's photo. "What about him? Why can't he help you?"

With an exasperated sigh, Dani turned toward him. "Now you're the one asking too many questions." She turned away. "You offered to help me, I didn't ask you."

"Oh, Dani." Ray put his arm around her shoulders. "I'm sorry. I wanted to make it easier for you, and here I am causing you to feel bad and making it harder. I'm angry that you've been doing this alone."

Dani shook her head. "I'm the one who should be apologizing. I really do appreciate your help. You're right. Lynn should be here. And Brian . . . well he's. . . . We'll talk about it some day, okay?"

"Right. No more questions. When you want to talk, I'll listen."

Dani nodded and sighed again. "I just never thought this would be so hard." As she reached for another frame, Ray took it from her.

"Why don't you pack something less emotional? I'll do this for you."

Brushing aside a tear, Dani gave his shoulder a pat and went back to the kitchen. The air felt stale and heavy. She pulled open the sliding doors in the kitchen, sat at the table and stared out into the yard. Two blue jays poked at the empty feeder. Tulips and daffodils bloomed in the flowerbed her mother had so lovingly tended. *Better fill that birdfeeder before I go. And the grass will need cutting soon. Maybe I can get that kid who used to do it for her—what was his name? Jack? Jim? Dammit, my brain feels like marshmallows lately.*

Dani jumped to her feet, pulled over an empty box, and opened the drawer where her mother kept cookbooks. *Don't think about everything you pack. Just do it!* She grabbed the books and shoved them into the box. Dani reached for the last book in the drawer and held it on her lap. She frowned at the old cookbook with the faded green cloth covering, frayed at the edges, its script lettering barely legible. She flipped through the pages, reading margin notations in an unrecognized neat, careful handwriting. Dani closed her eyes, searching for a nagging memory. *Cookies! Sugar cookies! I remember Mom making sugar cookies from this book. And telling me . . . oh, God. Telling me this was her mother's cookbook.* Dani rubbed a hand along the spine of the book. *My grandmother's cookbook.* Memories of Dani and Lynn, hands and noses dusted with flour, watching their mother and listening to stories of a grandmother they never knew flickered through Dani's mind.

"Hon?" Ray knelt beside Dani and brushed away the tears that had fallen on her hands.

"Everything brings back a memory." She raised the book slightly before placing it in the box. "My grandmother's cookbook. I never knew her. She died long before I was born. I remember my mom saying she would have been such a good grandmother. Whenever I watched how great my mom was with Trace, I realized what I missed."

Dani closed the box of books and smiled at Ray as she stretched her shoulders. "I'm glad I had my mom for as long as I did. I remember when I was in . . . sixth grade, yes, sixth. A boy in my class was absent a couple of weeks. Just before he came back to school, our teacher told us Butch's mother had died. I never knew any kid who had lost a parent. It seemed so unbelievable. Any time my mom got sick I was scared she'd die."

Ray laced his fingers through Dani's, and gave her hand a squeeze; but said nothing. Dani smiled. "Sorry, I'm rambling . . ."

"I'm listening. Ramble on. It'll help you."

"Yes, it feels good to talk to you. And . . . thanks for not asking questions."

"You'll tell me what you want me to know when you're ready to."

"Uh-huh."

"Let's get these boxes out to your car and quit for today."

As Dani reached for the door handle, Ray took her hand. "A little each day, and one day at a time."

"Thanks for helping. It makes a difference having you here." She gave him a quick hug and slid the key into the lock.

After three days of working at the house, Dani declared, "We've made a lot of progress at the house. Let's take a break today and just ride."

"Sounds good to me. Both horses could use a real workout. Show season starts soon and I'm not ready."

"I'm anxious to go to another horse show. I've only been twice."

"What did you like best?"

"That's easy," Dani smiled, "pole bending. I just loved it."

Ray nodded and smiled. "My favorite too, then barrel racing."

With Ray's help, they had accomplished more in a few days than Dani had in weeks alone. Working together had quickly become as natural and comfortable as if they had known each other for years. Dani found it easy to open up to Ray, telling him things about her life that she'd never shared with anyone else—not even Brian. Ray listened as she reminisced, held her when she cried, shared her laughter. Somewhere along the way, Dani wasn't sure just when, he asked a question, and she'd answered without hesitation, opening her heart to him and deepening the bond forming between them.

Dani and Ray warmed up the horses in the indoor arena, waiting for a light shower to end. Dani coughed and waved her hand in front of her face. "I don't like riding indoors; it gets so dusty."

Ray glanced outdoors. "It looks like it's about over. Let's check it out," he said as he dismounted to open the gate for her.

Dani trotted Chance once around the large sandy arena. "It's great. Just enough to settle the dust," she called.

"Good. I'm going to teach you something new today." He rode to her side, hopped off and handed her the reins. "Here, pony him around for a bit while I set up the poles."

"Are you serious? You're going to teach us to run poles?" Her eyes sparkled with excitement.

Ray raised a hand in warning, "Now, you aren't going for speed for quite some time yet. You and Chance need to learn the pattern slowly at first. Then work on speed." He gave Chance an affectionate pat on the neck. "Since we don't know his history, we don't know if he's ever run poles or done flying lead changes."

The buckskin side-passed toward Chance and nipped him in the shoulder. Ray smacked him on the rump. "Damned rotten horse." He reached up for the riding crop slung over the saddle horn and handed it to Dani. "Here, crack him one if he gets out of line again."

Dani kept a wary eye on the buckskin while Ray arranged six

poles in a line, twenty-one feet apart. Chance nickered and pranced as he watched the setup. Ray rechecked the line to be sure all poles were straight and motioned Dani to the center of the track.

"Here, you hold Mr. Personality. Let me ride Chance." Ray slipped on spurs, adjusted the stirrups, and eased into the saddle. He touched Chance lightly with the blunted tips and trotted him around the ring. The big sorrel was wired. He watched the poles, ears alert, nostrils flared. Ray slowed him, stroked his neck gently, and then proceeded at a walk down the right side of the pole line. He turned left at the end pole, walked through the line, weaving at each pole and back again. At the opposite end, he turned the last pole and trotted him back to the start. Chance pranced in excitement.

"Damn. He's done it before—or maybe he just likes precision work," Ray called out.

Dani shifted in the saddle. "Can I try it now, please?" she asked.

"He's pretty excited. Grab these spurs. Let me walk him a bit."

Chance switched gears as soon as Ray removed the spurs and kept him to a walk. Ray pulled to a stop in front of Dani and dismounted. "He's all yours, babe. Don't—I mean this now—*do not* go through the poles faster than a walk," he cautioned. Ray readjusted the stirrups for her and gave her a boost up before climbing back into his saddle.

Chance calmly walked through the poles for Dani. He snorted and shook his head at the finish.

"He's not too pleased. He wants to run them," Ray called out. He rode next to her, and nodded toward the far fence line. "Looks like we have an audience."

Following his gaze, Dani took a sharp breath, her eyes wide.

Ray frowned. "Problem, hon?" he asked.

"It's Trace—and Brian. Trace said he wanted to come out to see me ride, but I didn't know he meant today," she answered.

With blue eyes looking like storm clouds, Ray replied, "I suppose maybe I should get lost."

"No. No, of course not. I want you to meet them." In answer to his doubtful look, Dani slowly shook her head. "We haven't done anything wrong, Ray." She sat straight in the saddle and rode to greet Trace at the gate.

"I didn't know you meant you were going to come out today," Dani smiled at her son. "What a nice surprise. Did you see Chance with the poles?"

"Yeah, Mom, that's cool. Is it supposed to be that slow though?" Trace asked.

She laughed. "No, this is his first time. Well, we thought it was, but he seems to know what to do." Dani waved to Brian. "How's Dad?" she asked Trace.

"He's feeling fine and he wanted to see you ride too."

"I'm glad you both came." Dani smiled. "I want you to meet someone."

She motioned for Ray, reached down to open the gate and rode to the van. Trace held the gate while Ray circled his horse and rode toward them.

With a slight wave, Dani said, "Ray, I'd like you to meet my son, Trace, and my husband, Brian." Ray quickly dismounted. He shook hands with Trace and then shook the hand Brian extended through the opened window of the van.

Ray tugged at his hat. "I was just teaching her the pole pattern."

"It looks like she's doing pretty well. We saw the horse after she bought him but we've never seen her ride before," Brian remarked.

Trace rubbed his hand against Chance's muzzle. "Do the pole thing again, Mom. Faster this time."

"They aren't ready for faster yet," Ray interrupted. "She could get hurt." He motioned to Dani. "Why don't you just trot and canter him around the arena."

Trace's voice was edgy. "It's my Mom's horse. She can do what she wants to do."

"Easy now," Brian called out to him. "I'm sure he's just watching out for her safety. After all, she is a beginner."

Dani rode Chance to the fence to demonstrate a show ring routine—walk, trot, reverse, walk, trot and canter. She moved him to the center, stopped, backed him up a few feet, and trotted back to the van where the three men waited.

"Looks great, Dani." Brian waved. "Keep working with him."

"Nice job, Mom." Trace gave a thumbs-up.

Brian glanced at his watch and called out, "I promised you lunch at Burger King, son. Are you ready?"

"Sure, Dad." Trace climbed behind the wheel of the van.

Brian turned to Ray. "Trace recently got his license. He's anxious to drive every chance he gets. It was nice meeting you. Don't let her get too rambunctious with that horse, now."

Ray shook Brian's hand again and for the first time noticed the folded wheelchair tucked in the space behind him.

Ray moved to the driver's side. He reached out his hand. "Nice meeting you too, Trace. Drive carefully."

Trace shook hands. "Sorry if I was rude a minute ago. Nice meeting you." He turned toward his mother. "Mom, how about going for pizza tonight? I'll drive."

"Sure," Dani nodded to her son, "if Dad wants to go. I'll see you both back at the house."

Ray waved, turned his horse and rode back to the pole line. Dani watched Trace drive through the gate before joining Ray in the arena.

Without a word, Ray jumped from the saddle and handed Dani the reins to his horse. Dani ponied his horse and watched

Ray drag the poles to the corner of the arena, eyes squinted and his lips pursed in a scowl. *I wish I could have prepared him for meeting Brian. Dammit! Why do things always have to get so complicated?*

Ray climbed back into the saddle and headed toward the barn. He raised an eyebrow in her direction and gave a little nod. "Okay, whether you're ready or not, we need to talk."

Ray led Dani to his truck, opened the door for her and slid behind the wheel. With a tense set of his jaw, he pulled from the lot. In the forest preserve a half-mile away, he chose a secluded spot, killed the engine, and turned to Dani. Putting a hand on her shoulder, he urged, "Okay darlin', talk to me."

Dani took a deep breath. She stared at her hands folded in her lap. "It happened ten years ago. We were at a party. He wasn't drunk, but he'd been drinking. I usually drove home when we went out because I rarely drink, but I was so tired and hadn't been feeling well. I didn't even really want to go out that evening. Anyway—he insisted he was okay to drive and we were only a couple miles from home. It happened so fast . . ." Her voice broke; she bit against her lower lip.

"Take your time, honey." He reached for her hand.

"This driver crossed the center line and hit us hard on the left side." Dani stared out the window. "Brian suffered a spinal cord injury. I had some broken ribs, cuts and bruises. And—and in the hospital I learned why I had been so tired. I was pregnant." Dani struggled to continue. "I lost the baby."

"I'm so sorry." He caressed her hand.

"We learned the guy who hit us was stoned. Fortunately, Brian's blood alcohol was under the limit."

"What happened to the other driver?"

"He was ticketed and lost his license because he had a prior DUI. We collected from the insurance company and learned he left the area." She sighed. "He was young, and it seemed point-less to pursue a search and lawsuit, since he didn't have any property or even a decent job."

Dani gazed through the window a moment before she continued. "We spent so much time being angry and blaming him, ourselves and each other. Meanwhile our son was losing both his parents in the fallout. We finally went for counseling and tried to put our life back together."

Ray nodded and asked, "And how are things now?"

She ruffled her hand through her hair and sighed. Her voice edged with resignation, she said, "We've learned to accept it and have made adjustments. We are . . . kinder to each other." She managed a slight smile. "Trace is doing very well, although he's closer to me. It's difficult to get Brian interested in doing much. He's . . . distant, I suppose is the best way to put it. We converted a bedroom into an office for Brian, and he handles his graphic design business from home. I do the bookkeeping. Sometimes I think that was a mistake. Maybe he'd do better if he got out with people more." She picked at her nail polish and continued. "And this last year has been awful with my mother's illness. We were close, and she was very supportive. I also had a part-time job, but it was too much to handle when she got sick." She brushed away a tear. "I felt so . . . so disconnected from everything when she died. It was then I knew I had to have something just for me and I bought Chance."

For the first time, she looked him in the eyes. "And then I met you." She leaned against his shoulder. He tightened his arm around her.

He turned toward her and took her chin in his hand. "No matter what, you're not disconnected any longer. I'll always be here for you. Just as we are—or more—it's your call. We'll get through whatever we have to. Okay?"

Dani nodded and smiled at him. "I feel as if I've known you

forever—like I've waited my whole life for you."

"I feel the same way." He brushed a kiss softly against her cheek. "And I've had longer to wait," he teased. "Okay, you had better get home. You have a son waiting for pizza."

Ray waved to Dani and watched her drive away. *Well, you got yourself into a hell of a situation here. I can't help that I love her but I sure don't want to break up a marriage. And this sure wouldn't be a fair fight.*

He turned the key, sighed and eased into traffic. Fate's a real bitch sometimes.

# CHAPTER SIX

A horn sounded in the driveway. Trace grabbed his backpack, kissed Dani good-bye, and rushed out the door. "Bye Mom, love ya."

"I love you too. Have a good day." Dani watched Trace and his best friend Ryan pull away. The boys seemed to enjoy being counselors at the park district day camp. She glanced at the sky and hurried to the kitchen to wash up the breakfast dishes. Another rainy day. No trail ride for today. *If it keeps raining like this, we'll have the house packed up in no time.*

Brian glanced through the paper over his second cup of coffee. He looked up when Dani laughed at something on the radio. "It's nice to hear you laugh. There hasn't been much to laugh about for quite some time now," he said.

"It feels nice to laugh again, too." Dani dried her hands, bent to kiss his forehead. She cleared away his empty coffee cup. "I won't be too late today; I'm not going to ride. Looks like rain again so I'm just going to the house."

"How's it going?"

She gave a slight shrug. "Oh . . . fine. Almost finished up. I'm taking some things to the church rummage sale today."

"Good." He brushed away some crumbs from the table. "Uh . . . I . . . I'm glad you bought the horse. And—and it's good you're making some new friends. I know you need more than . . . well, you know what I mean."

"Thank you. I love you." Dani knelt beside his chair and

kissed him. "I'm glad you came out to the ranch with Trace. It's nice to share it with both of you."

"I'm glad I went too, but . . . well . . . it's not something I can really share with you, now is it?" His words stung with resentment. "I'd better get to work. Have a good day." He pushed away from the table.

Dani bit against her lower lip with a sudden deflated feeling. *You sure can ruin a moment, Brian.*

Ray looked over Dani's shoulder at the photo album on her lap.

"I've always liked this picture of Lynn and me." Dani pointed to a faded photo of two little girls playing in a sandbox.

"I wouldn't have guessed she was younger by your adult photos, but it's obvious in that picture. How much younger is she?"

"Three years." Dani frowned. "Actual years that is, emotionally, about twenty."

"How come she isn't around to help you out with this?"

"Because," Dani imitated her sister's melodramatic voice, "she *just had* to get back to her job."

"Must be some important job. Dare I ask?" Ray chuckled.

"Burger King and Mary Kay would fold without her." Dani shook her head. "Sorry, I'm just being bitchy. I don't really know what she's doing lately. Lynn doesn't stay at any job for very long—by her choice or theirs, I'm not sure."

"I can't say I'm sorry she's not here. If she were, you wouldn't need my help." He squeezed her shoulder.

Dani turned the page. The sisters stood with their arms around each other next to a Christmas tree.

"I suppose I'm partially responsible for the way she is. I covered for her a lot when we were kids, kept her from getting in trouble. Cleaned up after her bad judgments, probably too many times. She never learned to take responsibility for her actions." Dani sighed and tucked the album away.

Ray closed up the box and piled it by the door with the others while Dani packed up pots and pans. She ran her fingers through her hair. "People certainly do accumulate a lot of stuff over the years, don't they?" She waved her hand toward another closet. "Look at this. Why in the devil did Mom buy so many boxes of Kleenex? And there must be six rolls of paper towels. I took enough canned goods home to last us for months. Only *one* person lived in this house, yet she shopped like she was housing an army." Dani tossed the paper supplies in a large plastic bag and attached a twist-tie to the end. She sat cross-legged on the floor to take a break.

She laughed, "Reminds me of that old George Carlin routine about 'stuff.' He jokes about accumulating 'stuff' and needing more and more space to accommodate all our 'stuff.' Have you ever heard it?"

Ray nodded. "Yes, I have. It's funny—and so true."

"I'm going to think twice before buying things I don't really need. How about you?"

Mischief twinkled in his eyes. He sat on the floor beside her. "Honey, at my age I never buy in bulk."

Dani gave him a playful shove. They both said at the same time, "Or buy green bananas." Dani rolled to the floor, clutching her side, her laughter fueled by his comical look.

"Dammit, you're so cute." Ray smiled at her. "I love to hear you laugh." He stretched out beside her, took her face in both his hands and kissed her. Dani responded with a raw emotion that made her dizzy. He shook his head slowly at her. "We'd better get out of here before I decide to keep you prisoner and never let you leave." He pulled her to her feet. They finished packing and loaded the boxes in her car.

★　★　★　★　★

Dani slid into the gravel parking lot of the run-down hamburger place near her mother's house. She parked beneath the faded blue and white sign that read Jake's Fine Food. They entered through a squeaky screen door.

"A few more rainy days and we'll have the house all packed and ready to sell," she said.

They eased into a booth with a red and white checked tablecloth and glanced over the plastic-covered menu tucked behind the napkin holder.

A waitress waddled up to the table for their order, her salt-and-pepper hair tucked none-too-neatly into a bun at the nape of her neck. The rosy-red blush of her cheeks reached almost to the bright blue shadow encircling her eyes. She chucked her gum into the corner of her mouth and asked, "Wha'cha folks gonna have?"

She wrote out their order with a stubby pencil on a stained order pad, her eyes darting back and forth between them. She paused a moment to stare suspiciously at Ray. Chewing her gum again, she shuffled off to the kitchen.

"Did you see those looks she gave us?" Dani stifled a giggle.

"Yeah." Ray chuckled. "She's probably trying to figure out if I'm a dirty old man or if you're my daughter. Then again," he dropped his voice to a sinister pitch, "maybe she thinks I've abducted you and is filing all this in behind those beautiful eyes to tell the police when they come to inquire about the body they found hidden in the forest preserves."

Dani shook her head. "With your imagination, you should write a book."

Wide-eyed, Ray whispered, "I'll call it *Confessions of a Serial Killer.*"

"Uh-huh," Dani smirked. "I'll bet lots of criminals are caught by bragging about their crimes."

The Tammy Faye Bakker look-alike placed steaming burgers and fries on the table with a glance that said she'd overhead Dani's comment. She plopped the catsup bottle down and hurried off.

"Now you've got her worried for sure. I think she looked a little pale," Ray murmured.

Dani giggled, "How can you tell with all that make-up?"

"Better eat in a hurry and hope there isn't a squad car waiting for us outside."

The food was surprisingly good. "I tell you, I'm going to get fat as a pig. All this work and being on trails in the fresh air makes me ravenous," Dani complained.

He looked at her with that look she was growing used to—with his head slightly tilted, eyes twinkling behind partially lowered lashes and an impish grin curled on one side of his mouth. "Yeah, I know what you mean. Being out in the fresh air on trails with you makes me ravenous too."

Dani choked on a French fry and reached for her iced tea.

"Should watch what you eat, honey." He laughed. "You could track a rabbit in all that salt."

"Everything okay with you folks?" questioned their cartoon-character waitress.

"Sure," Ray replied, "the lady just swallowed a little too much salt. You can bring us the check, gorgeous."

Rosy-red cheeks grinned ear-to-ear as she fumbled in her apron for their check. She batted black mascara-coated lashes at Ray and drawled, "Ya'll come back now. Anytime at all."

As the waitress toddled off, Dani said, "You sure got her back on your good side, smooth talker."

Ray left a generous tip and they tried hard not to laugh as they paid the bill at the register by the door. Ray waved away Dani's attempt to pay half the check.

Back in the car, she again commented on his wad of cash.

"It really does bother me to see you carrying around all that cash. You could get mugged one of these days. That's why people carry credit cards and checks."

A hardness settled around his mouth. "Dani, I had a checking account, savings account, credit cards—the whole ball of wax—once. My ex was always taking off—'in search of herself'— she said. After a while I told her to take her time when she left. The last time she took off, she cleaned out the checking and savings accounts. It took me months to pay off the credit cards and get them cancelled. Now do you understand?"

"Sorry," she raised her hand in surrender and nodded. "I didn't mean to pry. Yes, I understand."

Dani darted from the lot, squealing tires and spraying gravel. She tromped the gas and headed back to the barn so Ray could pick up his truck.

Ray shook his head and grinned at her. "Notice you drive kind of fast, hon. Guess that's another reason I should carry cash. I'm probably going to have to bail your ass out of jail any day now."

# CHAPTER SEVEN

Dani lingered in the doorway of Brian's office. "You aren't going to work again tonight, are you? Brian? Didn't you hear me talking to you?" She walked in and stood beside him.

"Sorry." He barely glanced at her. "I just have a lot to do."

"You rarely work in the evening." Dani slid into the chair next to his desk. "We haven't spent much time together all week. Why don't we watch a movie or listen to some music?"

"Not now, Dani." He gave her an exasperated sigh. "I have a new client. I have to get this work done tonight."

"I thought you weren't taking on any new clients."

Brian tapped his fingers on the keys before he turned to her. "It's a good account. It'll mean I can put more into our investments. With Trace going off to college soon, I want to make sure you're both secure."

"Oh, we're fine. There's enough money for Trace's education." She brushed his shoulder. "I want us to spend some time together. You need to take a break too."

Brian tuned her out and went back to work. Dani kissed him on the cheek and closed the door. The ticking of the grandfather clock echoed through the house. Restless, Dani wandered to the family room, the empty evening stretching before her. She refolded the afghan on the sofa, straightened a stack of magazines, surfed through a few channels on the TV, and then switched it off. She selected a country music station on the radio, and curled up in the recliner with the latest issue of

*Quarter Horse Journal.*

Dani flipped through the pages, the glossy photographs blurring with memories of the past year. Her mother's death following a prolonged battle with cancer had left her exhausted and depressed.

Her sister, Lynn, arrived home just in time for the funeral, leaving all the arrangements for Dani. Lynn stayed three days and was more trouble than she was help. When all the bustle of having people around came to an end, and all Dani wanted was to rest and deal with her loss, she had bills, legal matters to go over with the lawyer, thank-you notes to write. Lynn could have helped with something. *It's not like she has any permanent job or ties anywhere. She's so irresponsible. Never hear from her unless she's in trouble or needs help.* Last week Lynn had called to ask when the house would be sold. Said she hated to ask, but she was a little short of money. *Tough! You're always short of money.*

"Mom, are you okay?" Trace called from the doorway.

Startled, Dani turned toward her son. "Sure, why?"

"You've been staring at that page for five minutes."

"Oh, I can't seem to concentrate." Dani tossed the magazine on the table. "Are you going out?"

"Yeah. Ryan and I are going to the mall. I won't be late."

"See you later," she called after him, "drive carefully."

The car door slammed. And again Dani was alone with her thoughts.

Trace was wrapped up with school, his friends and plans for college. Brian seemed to work more each day, tuning out both of them.

*I'm tired of being the strong one; the one who takes care of everyone else. I hate feeling so alone. Can't imagine what it will be like when*

*Trace goes away to school. Best times are at the stable with Chance—and Ray.* She smiled, thinking of their first conversation when she had gone back to the barn to put Chance in his stall and saw Ray riding alone. He always seemed to keep to himself. There'd been a sadness about him that touched her. She'd been in no hurry to get home, wasn't looking for any more complications in her life—only wanted someone to talk to. *We've become so close in such a short time. Where's it going to go? I'm afraid to let him become so important in my life, but . . .*

Dani drifted to the kitchen. On impulse she dug the phone book from the drawer, paged through it until she found the listing. She held the phone in her lap, tracing her finger over his name on the page. *Should I call him?* She slowly dialed Ray's number but hung up as it began to ring.

She dialed again.

He answered on the first ring.

"Hello."

Her pulse quickened at the sound of his voice. "Hi. It's me, Dani."

There was a short pause before he answered. "This sure is a surprise. Something wrong?"

"No, no. I was just sitting here and . . . and thought I'd give you a call. Is that okay?"

"Of course it's okay. You've just never called before, and it kind of surprised me. Hold on a second." She heard him turn down the volume on the television. Ray continued, "I just heard the weather forecast for tomorrow. Would you like to trailer the horses somewhere? Try out some different scenery? Kind of celebrate getting the house all packed up."

"That sounds nice." She sighed. "It's a relief to have that job finished, but kind of sad too. Soon it will be sold and then I won't have any excuses to go there."

Ray paused briefly. "I was just thinking of going out for some ice cream. Why don't you join me?"

"Oh, I . . ." Dani twisted the phone cord around her hand. "Well, I don't know why not. I'm not doing anything else."

"Great. I'll meet you at the new ice cream shop—you know the one next to the bookstore—in fifteen minutes."

After the connection had been broken, Dani cradled the phone next to her chest, pondering her decision. *Maybe I should cool this off while I still can—before someone gets hurt.* She redialed Ray's number. It rang several times with no answer.

Dani pushed away her nagging apprehension. She tucked her blue-and-white-checked shirt into her jeans, slipped on her Reeboks, and grabbed her purse. She peeked into Brian's office. "I'm going out for some ice cream. Want anything?"

Brian gave her a little wave and continued to work. "Okay, have a good time."

Parking her car in the last available spot in the strip mall, Dani spotted Ray getting out of his truck. Dressed in jeans, a denim shirt and his cream colored Charlie 1 Horse hat, she felt a flutter in her stomach as he walked toward her.

"You sounded so down on the phone." He put his arm around her shoulders. "Sure there's nothing wrong?"

"No." She shook her head and gave a little shrug. "Trace and Ryan went to the mall, and Brian's working again. He never used to work in the evening. I asked him to watch a movie, but he said he was too busy."

Ray stared ahead. "So as a last resort you called me."

"Dammit." Dani flashed him an angry glance. "That's not true."

"I had no right to say that. I have no claim on you." He gave her shoulder a little squeeze. "Let's get that ice cream."

In silence they nibbled at their cones at an outdoor table under twinkling lights and watched shoppers across the parking lot. Moments later Ray tossed his half-eaten cone in the trash, and waited for Dani to finish hers.

"I really don't need this," she replied, tossing hers in too.

He pulled her to her feet. "Let's go for a walk. Honey, I'm sorry for what I said." Ray held her hand. "I miss you so much when I'm home alone."

Dani nodded. "Even when I'm busy at home, I miss you and think about you. I can't stand this. I feel like I'm living in two worlds . . . like I'm being pulled apart."

"I don't want to complicate your life. Maybe . . ." He struggled with the words. "Maybe it would be better for us not to see each other so much."

Shoulders slumped; she stared ahead. "If that's what you want."

"Of course it isn't." He whirled around to face her. "What I want, I can't have. I want to have you with me all the time for the rest of my life."

He held her face in his hands as if she were fragile china. He kissed her lips that still tasted of peach ice cream.

"Dani, I love you with all my heart. I'd do anything for you, even if it meant never seeing you again if that would make your life easier."

She placed her hands on his shoulders, met the tormented look in his eyes. "You're the only thing making my life bearable right now—you and Trace, that is. I—I love you too."

He raised an eyebrow. "That's the first time you've said that."

Dani smiled. "I've been too afraid to say it until now." She wrapped her arms around his neck. "I haven't felt so alive in such a long time. I feel like a silly kid in high school—more Trace's age than my own."

"Yeah, me too, and that's a bigger stretch for me." He tugged at her hand and sat down on a bench. "Which reminds me, you've never told me how old you are either."

She tilted her head and gave him a teasing look. "As a matter of a fact, I have a birthday—two weeks from tomorrow. It's a big zero birthday too."

"Well, since Trace is sixteen I know you're over thirty," he stared at her, "but I can't believe you're going to be forty."

"That's it." She groaned, "The big four-oh."

He hugged her. "Well, that makes me feel a little less like a cradle robber. And may I say you sure don't look it, sweetheart."

"Guess we're both well preserved, huh?" She raised an eyebrow at him. "So now are you going to tell me how old you are?"

"Let's see, it's so hard to remember." He laughed. "How old was I when Abe and I worked on that Gettysburg speech?"

Dani gave him a playful punch on the arm. "Come on now, confess."

Ray squinted his eyes at her. "I'm still old enough to be your daddy. I just turned sixty-two." He tilted his head toward her. "Does it make a difference?"

"Not a bit." She smiled. "But I'm really surprised. I never would have guessed."

He shrugged. "Must be all this clean living."

Hand in hand they walked back toward her car. He gave her a light kiss as he opened the door for her.

"Let's have a great ride tomorrow. Meet you at the stable at nine. Okay?"

"Sure thing. Goodnight, sweet dreams," she whispered.

"I always have sweet dreams—lately." He winked at her.

# CHAPTER EIGHT

Dani slipped into a navy western shirt with white trim and pulled on some comfortable faded blue jeans fresh from the dryer. She brushed her hair until the copper highlights shimmered. With flushed skin and eyes sparkling from excitement at the prospect of exploring new trails with Ray, she rushed through folding laundry and preparing Brian's lunch.

Most afternoons were spent working on bookkeeping, billing for Brian and routine housework. Lately Brian worked almost every evening like a man possessed, and she'd given up trying to change it. She found the long evenings alone harder and harder to endure.

Earlier in the week she'd gone over college brochures with Trace, trying to match his enthusiasm and excitement. She dreaded the thought of the empty house when he finally left for school. The crack between her two worlds grew wider and deeper. In one world she merely functioned: wife, mother and homemaker. In the other, she blossomed, felt exhilarated and alive.

Dani tossed several cans of pop into the cooler and stashed it in the trunk then hurried in to say good-bye to Brian.

"I'm going. Your lunch's in the fridge. Need anything else before I leave?"

"No, I'm perfectly capable of taking care of myself. You have a nice ride." He brushed a kiss against her cheek when she bent to kiss him good-bye.

She opened her mouth to respond to his comment but changed her mind. *The hell with it. I'm not going to let anything ruin my day.*

With a wave to the neighbor walking his dog, Dani hurried from the driveway. *Time to use my Get Out of Jail Free card.*

Both horses had been brushed prior to Dani's arrival. Ray had the truck hooked up to his horse trailer; saddles, tack, and brush boxes were all secured in place.

Dani parked her car, tossed the cooler in the truck, and then hurried to help Ray load the horses. He spun her around, gave her a big hug, and kissed her cheek. "How's my girl today?"

"I'm great. We're going to have a super day."

"That's a girl." Ray hugged her again. "Let's get going."

Ray checked the trailer hitch one last time. After a wary glance at Dani, Chance jumped into the trailer. The buckskin pulled against the lead rope and balked as Ray led him forward.

"Nothing's ever easy with this one." Ray cocked his head toward Dani and suggested, "Here, why don't you see how he handles for you."

Without hesitation, Dani marched up, rubbed her hand across the horse's forehead, and grabbed the lead. She gave a tug, talked softly to the buckskin as she walked him in a circle, and led him up to the trailer. He bobbed his head once and jumped right in beside Chance. Dani stifled a smirk as she slid the back bar into place and slammed the door shut.

Ray shook his head and sighed. "Think you're pretty damned smart now, don't you?"

"Nope. As I said before, you just have to talk nicely to him."

"Uh-huh. I'll remember. Now get in the truck, Miss Horse Whisperer."

★ ★ ★ ★ ★

The drive took about forty-five minutes. They chattered and laughed as they cruised along narrow, winding roads through sleepy country towns dotted with neat frame homes and lush cornfields. Dani had no idea where they were going, but she didn't care. She was with her horse and someone who loved her. That was enough.

"Looks like we might have the trails to ourselves today," Ray said as he picked a shady spot in the empty lot.

They wasted little time saddling the horses and heading out. The sun simmered overhead with only the slightest breeze stirring the trees. The horses danced with anticipation of their new surroundings.

"Never thought I'd enjoy trails so much." Ray smiled at Dani riding beside him. "But then, I never had you to ride with before." He reached out to give her hand a squeeze. "Even this ornery horse seems happier with you around."

"Hard to tell when he's happy," Dani muttered.

Making a sharp bend, the trail continued behind a white two-story frame house separated from the forest preserve by wire fencing. Colorful plastic toys spattered the yard like globs of paint on an artist's palette. Within a smaller enclosure a black-and-white paint pony whinnied at the approaching horses. He ran toward the fence, poked his nose through a wire square and nickered. Chance bobbed his head up and down in a return greeting.

"Hi there, little guy." Dani reached down to pet the pony. "I'd sure like to take you home with me."

The buckskin pushed against the fence and pawed the ground. The pony regarded him with nostrils flared. He snorted and reared in defiance.

"Damned antisocial nag." Ray yanked hard on the reins.

The pony followed along the fence, watching until they were out of sight. The musty smell of damp earth and wet leaves hung in the air as the trail narrowed and wound deeper through the woods. Chance picked his way along the path, avoiding rocks, downed tree limbs and puddles. In contrast, the sounds of the buckskin's shoes as he kicked each rock, stumbled over branches and slopped in the water, made them laugh.

Ray ran an affectionate hand along the buckskin's neck. "He's sure a study in grace, isn't he?"

"Maybe if they spend enough time together some of Chance's good points will rub off on him."

"Don't hold your breath."

Suddenly both horses jumped. With a swoosh of air, a buck with a three-point rack darted across their path.

Ears pitched forward, Chance jumped sideways, and backed up. Dani pressed her boots against the stirrups and held tightly to the reins.

The buckskin spun and stared after the buck. Ray reached a hand forward to the horse's shoulder and glanced at Dani.

"Good recovery, honey."

As she felt Chance relax beneath the saddle, Dani pushed a hand to her chest and took a deep sigh. "Whew!" she grinned, "That's was . . . exhilarating."

"Exhilarating." Ray laughed.

A sharp twist of the trail brought them into a clearing. They squinted against the sudden brightness. From across a field a farmer on a dusty John Deere tractor waved. After they returned the greeting, Ray reached out to her and they rode hand-in-hand.

"I can't remember ever being as contented as I am on a trail ride with you," Dani murmured.

His only reply was a loving look that rippled through her heart.

The trail circled, leading them back to the parking lot. They unsaddled the horses, brushed them down, and tied them to graze. Ray secured the saddles in the trailer then carried the water bucket to an old-fashioned pump near several wooden picnic tables protected under a pavilion. Together they pumped water, washed their hands and carried the bucket to the horses.

Dani and Ray drank icy-cold Cokes and basked in the sun as they watched the horses graze.

"This has been a perfect day, about the best ride we've ever had," Ray said.

Dani nodded in agreement. "I hate to see it end."

As Ray pulled from the parking lot, he switched off the radio.

"What, sports nut like you and you don't want to listen to a Cubs game?"

"Sports fan yes, masochist no. The Cubs having a good team comes once in a century, and I saw the last one. Making it to the World Series will probably coincide with the end of the world."

Dani laughed and let her attention drift to the countryside sliding by.

The drive back was like going home after vacation, back to reality. Ray broke the silence. "Hon, I think I'm going to buy another horse. I've been watching Bud work that great-looking three-year-old bay in the arena. I'd really like to have that horse."

Dani twisted on the seat to look at him. "I've noticed him too. He's gorgeous. I like his disposition. Do you think Bud would want to sell him?"

"Sure, for the right price."

"Are you going to sell—what should I call your damned horse?"

Ray laughed. "Buck."

"You've got to be kidding." Dani slapped her thigh. "With your imagination, all you can call him is *Buck!*"

"It fits, doesn't it?"

"Yes, of course it does. It's just so . . . so boring."

His voice softened. "He was Kathy's horse. She named him Champ. Well, he's *not*. Every time I called him that I heard her voice—so I started calling him Buck."

It was the first time he had talked about his daughter. "Why did you keep him after . . . after she died?" Dani asked softly.

With a slight shake of his head, he sighed. "I tried to sell him, but then it seemed like he was a connection to her, so we just stayed together. Now, I think I'm ready to let him go. I don't need two horses, and I think Bud will make a trade for Buck and enough cash. What do you think?"

After a moment of silence, she replied, "I think there's another solution. You could keep Buck and we could buy the bay together."

"Well, now . . ." He hesitated. "Why don't we think about that a while?"

Dani stared out the window. "Okay. It was just a thought."

After a moment's silence, Ray glanced at her. "It's a good idea. You just surprised me, that's all. Let's talk to Bud next week."

They tucked the horses in their stalls, unloaded the truck and trailer. "Are you in a hurry to get home?"

"No. Trace and Ryan are going to a ballgame and Brian is going to a meeting with a friend of his. Want to get a sandwich and catch a movie with me?"

He smiled at her. "I think I died and went to heaven today, if there is such a place. How about if I drive, give your lead foot a rest?"

Dani frowned. "Hey, I'm a very good driver."

"I know, Babe. I just love to tease you."

Ray drove about a mile before slamming on the brakes. He pulled the truck to a stop near an empty schoolyard. He jumped from the truck, rummaged around in the back and returned, bouncing a basketball.

"Come on, Dani Monroe. You can be my ball girl." He sprinted through the gate of the playground and shot from center court.

"Just what does a ball girl have to do, may I ask?" Dani slid from the truck and followed him.

"You stand up there near the basket and when I shoot, you throw the ball back to me."

"And when you miss I have to chase the ball all over the court?" She stood with her hands on her hips in mock indignation.

"Honey," he grinned, "I don't miss too often."

And he didn't. To Dani's amazement, he sank nine out of ten shots. "I'm impressed. I didn't know you played. Five-eleven's kind of short for basketball, isn't it?" she teased.

"Hey, no short comments from you. Besides, what I lack in height, I make up with speed." He dribbled the ball and faked a shot at her. "What are you—about five foot even?"

Dani stood up straight. "I'll have you know I'm five-two."

He nodded, "All of that, huh?" He sank a shot from half court.

"So where did you play?"

"In school and in the service. Then I had my own little traveling team. It was basketball for short white kids."

Dani laughed, grabbed the ball and shot. And missed. "How come it was *your* team?" she asked.

Ray grinned. "We were all poor and it was *my* ball."

# CHAPTER NINE

Trace gathered his books as he gulped the last of his orange juice. He whispered to Dani, "Mom, do you think you could get Dad away from that computer long enough to talk about colleges with us?"

"I'll try." Dani straightened his jacket collar.

"Thanks." He gave her a peck on the cheek. "Hey—is today the day you get the new horse?"

"It sure is." She nodded, eyes sparkling.

Trace dropped his backpack to give her a hug. "What does he look like?"

"Well . . . he's built differently than Chance, more stocky. He's a bay—that's kind of coffee colored with black mane and tail—very flashy looking. And the bottoms of his legs are black."

"I'm glad to see you so happy, Mom." Trace smiled at his mother. "Have fun."

"Thanks, hon. Maybe on Saturday you can come out to see him?"

"Sounds good . . . have to go. Bye, Dad," he called from the door.

"Uh—Bye, Trace," Brian mumbled, still reading his paper.

*The news sure must be fascinating.* Dani cleared the table and loaded the dishwasher.

Brian glanced over the top of his newspaper at the sound of clattering dishes. "You seem to be in a real hurry this morning."

"Yes, I am." She struggled to sound pleasant. "Today's the big day."

With a blank look, he lowered the paper onto his lap. "What big day?"

"I told you—we finally reached an agreement with Bud on buying the bay." Dani turned to the counter to hide her irritation. "So today I own one and a half horses."

"Right." Brian nodded. "That's nice. Going to need your own ranch pretty soon." Once again engrossed in his paper, he missed the withering glance from his wife.

*What I need is a husband who cares what I do.* Giving the counter a final swipe, she grabbed her purse, and hurried from the house.

Bud Morgan watched Ray working the bay horse on a lunge line in the large sandy outdoor arena.

"Hi, Dani. You're out bright and early this morning." Bud's voice was slightly teasing.

"Couldn't wait to see him." Dani leaned against the fence. "He's so beautiful, he takes my breath away," she said.

"He's sure one good-looking horse. I hope you'll enjoy him." Bud raised a hand in caution. "Take it easy for a while. He's pretty feisty."

"I will. Thanks again." Dani dug into her jeans pocket. "Here's my check. Did Ray pay you yet?"

Bud nodded his head and raised his eyes in good-natured exasperation. "Oh, sure, and all in cash, of course."

"He's sure serious about not having a checking account, isn't he?" Dani gave a hopeless expression in Ray's direction.

Bud nodded and tucked her check in his pocket. "I have the transfer of registration papers ready. You can pick them up at the house before you leave," he said. She merely nodded before turning her attention back to the spirited bay in the arena.

"Come here, hon." Ray motioned for Dani. "Work him for a bit. I'm getting dizzy. Always did hate working with a lunge line."

Dani took the line from him, turning slowly while the horse trotted in a circle around her. Ray watched from the fence. Cracking the lunge whip against the ground, Dani called for a trot from the young horse. The bay bobbed his head and moved into an easy jog trot.

"He's smooth, isn't he?" Dani called out to Ray.

"Sure is, babe. We made a smart decision buying this little guy. Canter him a bit then we'll saddle up and work him in the round pen a while."

Ray rode the bay in the training pen while Dani watched from the gate. "We have to come up with a good name for him. Any ideas?" she asked.

He thought a minute. "Yeah, he sure cost us enough, we should call him Cash."

"Cash—Cash." Dani considered it a moment. "I kind of like it."

"Okay, Cash it is." He spun the bay around and slid him to a stop.

*I've waited a long time for a horse of my own. Now I have two— well, one and a half.* Dani daydreamed as she cleaned vegetables for dinner. *Chance is so dependable and I feel safe riding him . . . but he seems to be taking care of me. Guess he remembers me as a beginner. He's so different and ready to run for Ray.* She smiled to herself. *Cash is full of spirit and energy—I feel it and I ride him more aggressively.*

Trace dropped his backpack on the chair. "Hey, earth to Mom."

"How was your day?" Dani smiled at her son. "I didn't hear

you come in."

"So I see. Dreaming about the new horse . . . what's his name?"

"Oh, Trace." Dani sighed. "He's just gorgeous and such a dream to ride." She dried her hands on a towel. "We decided to call him Cash."

"Cool name."

"Do you think you can come out to see him this weekend?"

"Sure, how about Saturday afternoon? Ryan and I are going to work on his car in the morning. Maybe we could get Dad to come along."

"Sounds fine to me."

The ringing telephone interrupted their conversation. Dani answered and listened for a moment.

"Uh-huh . . . that's terrific. I'm happy to hear it. Sure, I'll be home all evening. I'll see you later. Thanks for calling."

She held the phone a moment longer, and finally replaced the receiver on the wall.

"Mom?"

"Uh . . . oh, that was the Realtor. They have a contract on Mom's house—full price."

"Hey, that's great."

"Yeah." Her voice was distant.

"Isn't it?"

"Sure, it's just sad that's all. Now I'll never be able to go back there . . . the house where she lived . . . where I grew up."

Trace hugged his mother. "I miss Grandma, Mom."

Dani ruffled his hair. "I know, so do I."

Trace searched for a snack, his brow knitted in a frown. "Mom . . . have you talked to Dad yet?"

Dani's eyes clouded slightly and she shrugged. "I tried this morning, but you know he's pretty busy lately."

"Yeah, I know." Trace scowled. "He seems to work all the

time. He never has any time to talk to me."

She gave his shoulder a squeeze. "Let's plan on all of us going to the stable Saturday morning. Then in the evening, we'll talk about colleges. How's that sound?"

"Sounds good . . . if he'll go." Grabbing a cookie, Trace hurried off to his room.

Dani gazed through the window. *Right, if he'll go.*

Trace brought up the subject at dinner. "Hey, Dad, why don't we go out to the stable with Mom on Saturday to see Cash?"

"Who's Cash?"

The boy groaned in annoyance. "Mom's new horse. His name is Cash."

"How about it, Brian?" Dani pushed the food around her plate. "Maybe we could go out to eat afterwards and discuss colleges. Trace wants to narrow down his choices of where he'd like to apply."

Brian rubbed his forehead and poured another cup of coffee. Dreading the thought of his son leaving home, he wanted to delay the talk about colleges. And the few times he'd been to the barn made him feel old and useless compared to the capable riders astride their powerful horses.

"Oh, I don't know. You two can go; I'll see him some other time." He gave a dismissive wave. "And we have lots of time on the college thing."

"No, Dad, I don't have lots of time." Trace glared at his father. He pushed his plate away and shoved his chair against the wall. "What's the matter with you lately? You act like you're not even part of this family." He stalked from the kitchen.

Brian threw his napkin on his plate and yelled after his son. "Trace, get back here." Loud music echoed moments after the bedroom door slammed. He cast a frustrated look in Dani's direction. "What's gotten into him?"

"He's right, you act like you don't care what we do." Her eyes flashed. She threw her fork on the table and shoved her plate away. "You're so wrapped up in your work that you don't have time for anything else. I'm fed up with it!" Dani pushed away from the table, scraped her plate into the garbage and slammed it into the dishwasher.

"Dammit! I don't know how to handle either one of you," Brian snapped.

"You don't know how to *handle* us? You could show some interest in what's important to us."

Brian waved his hand in a gesture of hopelessness, turned abruptly and wheeled to the family room. He grabbed the remote and jabbed it toward the television, turning up the volume on the news to drown out Trace's radio.

Dani chewed her lower lip and stared after Brian. Dishes clanked together as she shoved them precariously into the dishwasher. After a quick wipe of the table and countertop, she flipped off the light switch and headed toward Trace's room.

The door vibrated against her hand as she knocked at her son's room.

"Trace?"

Moments later the volume fell to slightly below glass-shattering range and Trace opened the door.

"May I come in?"

He waved a hand in the air and flopped on his bed.

"I'll talk to him in the morning. If nothing else, you and I can talk over the choices this weekend."

"Doesn't he care about either one of us?"

Dani sat on the bed next to her son. "I think he hates the thought of you being grown-up and going away to college. It's difficult for him because there is so much he can't share with us."

"He doesn't even try," Trace pouted.

*What can I say to him when I feel the same way?* "I'm sorry." Dani gave him a hug. "We'll get to it this weekend, I promise."

As Dani closed Trace's door, the doorbell rang. *I hope that's for Trace. I'm sure not in the mood to see anyone.* She sighed. *Oh, I'll bet it's the real estate people.*

Dani chatted with the agent and signed the papers that would confirm the sale of the house. When he left, Dani leaned against the door a while. *Another chapter closed. Seems strange that someone else will be living there now. After all the years Mom owned that house . . .*

Without comment, Dani passed the family room where Brian sulked and stared at the blaring television. She closed herself behind her bedroom door. *I wonder if moms run away from home? Maybe I'll go away to college too.*

With the exception of one day when they went trail riding with Buck and Chance, Ray and Dani worked Cash in the round pen most of the week.

"When can we take Cash out?" Dani asked.

"Not for a while. He's feeling frisky in this cooler weather. It probably isn't a good idea to take him on trails yet."

Dani's eyes narrowed in a look of disappointment.

"We'll work him indoors all winter, start him on trails in the spring," Ray said.

Dani trotted Chance in small circles and figure eights.

"Okay, let me ride Chance. I want to speed him up a bit through the poles," Ray called to her.

From the fence Dani observed Ray signal the sorrel for more speed. Chance executed a clean run without knocking down any poles. Ray waved. "We're going to have us a contest horse here, sweetheart."

She gave him a thumbs-up sign. "Maybe he'll give you a

twenty-second pole run by spring."

Ray laughed at her optimism. "I'll settle for a clean run in twenty-three by then."

Dani saddled Cash and worked a while in the training pen before she opened the gate and rode to the arena. "Ray, could we just ride a little way out in the pasture? Please?"

"Well . . ." Ray considered a moment. Three other riders had entered the arena and brought an end to his training session.

"Okay. But not too far."

He rode beside her across the arena into the pasture. Dani hugged close to the tree line while Ray rode protectively along the outside. The air was crisp with the scent of an early autumn. Trembling beneath the saddle pad, the sorrel gelding pranced, ears pitched forward. Ray reached down to stroke the horse's neck just as a hawk flew low above their heads. Chance hopped sideways and spun in a circle.

Cash jumped backwards and rocked to his hind legs. Dani leaned forward in the saddle as Cash reared, his front feet pawing as if to chase away attacking forces. Dani and Cash seemed to hang in the air, suspended in the crisp September breeze.

As the bay reached for the sky, Ray called out, "Dani, take your feet out of the stirrups—just slide off before . . ."

The hawk screeched overhead. Cash snorted and pawed the air one last time before hitting the ground hard. Dani's body shuddered with shock waves at the sudden jolt. Fighting to control her horse, she planted her feet in the stirrups and pulled on the reins. Cash shook his head against the bit, flattened his ears, and bolted for the field. Dani grabbed the reins tighter and tried to pull him to a stop.

Chance rocked in a series of small bucks, but Ray held him in check. As Dani fought for control, Ray groaned when the bay charged toward the open pasture. "Start to pull him in a circle," he yelled after her. "*Circle,* Dani." Ray nudged his spurs against Chance's sides and rode after her.

The thundering hoofbeats frightened the runaway horse even more. He spun toward the woods. Dani shifted her weight in the saddle and hugged her legs close to Cash's heaving sides. His muscles pushed hard against her thighs. It was like sitting astride a charge of dynamite, and Dani trembled with the power beneath her. Cash's heart pounded. Lungs worked frantically for air.

As Cash twisted suddenly away from a ditch, Dani's foot lost contact with the stirrup. She reached to the saddle horn for balance. The reins slid through her hands. In the seconds between leaving the saddle and connecting with the earth, Dani's mind flashed with images of the car accident she and Brian had been in many years before. The image of trees flying past collided with long-ago memories of crunching metal, breaking glass. Her son's face was the last thing she saw before meeting the ground with a jarring thud. The air exploded from her lungs. Panic and a flash of pain shot through her head before the darkness closed in.

"Dani—are you okay, honey?" As Chance slid to a stop, Ray jumped from the saddle and sank to the ground beside her. His shaking hand picked at a small twig tangled in a strand of hair partially covering her face. He tucked her hair behind her ear. Blood trickled from a cut near her scalp. Dirt smudged her pale face around closed eyes and an already swelling lower lip. A jagged tear in her shirt exposed the unnatural angle of her shoulder. Panic forced an acid taste into Ray's throat. His heartbeat echoed in his ears. He pressed his hand on the ground to steady himself against the dizziness sweeping his body.

The commotion brought Bud Morgan on a run toward the

pasture. Bud stopped in his tracks. "For God's sake, don't move her." He turned, yelled for someone to call nine-one-one, and joined Ray at Dani's side. She lay pale and motionless. Bud knelt beside her; covering her with his light jacket, he placed two fingers against her wrist. "Ray, don't move her. Help's on the way."

The wail of the siren split the air as the ambulance sped into the pasture and slid to a stop. Ray moved back to let the paramedics work.

Chance stood, head down, alone in the pasture. Bud spoke quietly to calm the horse and led him toward the barn where a group of riders and ranch hands had gathered.

"Unsaddle this horse and put him in his stall." He handed the reins to one of Dani's friends. "Jack," he called out to one of his most experienced riders. "Go after that goddamned bay for me, will you?" Jack gave a tug on the hitch, sprang into the saddle, and nodded to Bud.

By the time Bud reached Dani again, the paramedics had started an IV, had her immobilized in a cervical collar and were securing her to a backboard. Pale and shaken, Ray stood silently beside her.

"Are you hurt, Ray?" Bud asked.

Ray shook his head, his brow scrunched above anxious eyes.

"Come on, she's going to be okay." Bud gave Ray's jacket sleeve a tug. "You go with her. We'll tend to the horses. I'll meet you at the hospital."

As the paramedic reached for the door, Ray climbed in beside Dani. "Call her family, okay?" he called out to Bud.

Bud nodded and headed toward the house. The ambulance inched over the rough pasture terrain, increased speed and hit the siren as they reached the blacktop.

# CHAPTER TEN

Ray tagged along as the paramedics rushed Dani into the Emergency Room. He gave what little information he could to the admitting personnel, then wandered into the waiting room. He hesitated in the center of the empty room, walked to the window, stared at the parking lot, and sighed as he slumped into a chair. He tossed his hat on the chair beside him, rested both elbows on his knees, and cradled his head in his hands.

Bud burst through the sliding doors. At the admitting desk, the clerk motioned toward the waiting room.

"Any news yet?" Bud asked as he slid into the chair beside Ray.

"No, nothing." Ray stood, his hands jammed into his pockets, gazing out the window. He turned to Bud. "She's on her way to X-ray. Did you call her house?"

"Yes, but no one answered. I left a message." Bud frowned at Ray's pallor, crossed the room to a vending machine and got some coffee. "I'm going to call the ranch to check on the horses. I'll try Dani's house again too." He patted Ray's shoulder.

Trace tossed his backpack on the kitchen chair and grabbed a handful of potato chips. On his way through the family room, he hit the play button on the blinking answering machine, and listened to the message. Ashen-faced and shaken, he rushed into his father's office.

"Dad, there's a message on the machine. Mom's been hurt at

the stable. She's on the way to the hospital." Trace hit his fist against the door. "Why didn't you answer the damned phone?"

"Watch your mouth, young man," Brian snapped. "I rarely answer that phone." He shut down his computer and wheeled toward the door. "What happened to her?"

"I don't know." Trace's voice rose with irritation. "Guy just said she'd been hurt, was on the way to the hospital."

"Let's go." Brian brushed his damp palms against the arms of his chair and rolled toward the garage. Brian reached for the keys. "I'll drive, Trace." The no-nonsense tone in his voice guaranteed no argument from his son.

Trace hit the switch for the garage door and followed his father to the van.

With his arms crossed tightly across his chest, Trace gazed straight ahead with a stony stare.

Brian reached a hand toward his son. "She'll be okay, son."

Trace grunted but made no further comment to his father.

At the ER entrance, a guard hurried to escort them to the admitting office.

Brian answered the routine questions at the desk. "Is she going to be all right?" he asked. "When can I see her?"

"We'll let you know as soon as we hear something." The admitting clerk pointed to the room across the hall. "You can both have a seat in the waiting room."

Slumped in a standard emergency-room blue vinyl chair, Ray sat with his head resting in his hands. He jerked to attention as Brian wheeled his chair to a stop.

Annoyance furrowed the lines around Brian's mouth. "What happened to her, Ray?"

"I shouldn't have let her . . . I knew better." Ray squeezed his eyes shut and shook his head. "I'm so sorry."

"Shouldn't have let her do what?" The irritation was evident in Brian's voice.

"She wanted to ride out in the pasture." Ray ran his hand through his hair. "A hawk spooked Cash. He reared and took off. She couldn't hold him." He gazed out the window. His voice scratchy and dazed, Ray continued, "I called to her to pull him in a circle. I don't think she heard. Didn't have time . . . She lost her balance."

Brian scowled, "Was she conscious?"

"Not when I reached her. She kept fading in and out in the ambulance."

Ray slumped back into the chair; brooding eyes stared at the wall.

Bud Morgan returned from making his phone calls. Ray automatically made introductions. "Bud, this is Dani's husband, Brian. And her son, Trace."

Bud shook hands, and sat next to Ray. "Jack finally caught the bay and brought him back. He's pretty scratched up and has a nasty puncture wound. I called the vet for you."

Ray raised his hand and sighed, "Fine. Damned horse."

Bud shuffled his feet against the floor. "Uh, since there isn't much I can do here, I'm going back to wait for Doc. Said he'd be right out." He rose and shook hands with Brian again. "I'll check back later. I'm sure she's going to be all right." Brian merely nodded his head. Trace stared through the window, his hands jammed in his pockets and a scowl on his face.

Trace stalked the hall. Brian and Ray waited in tense silence, glancing repeatedly at the crawl of the hands on the large black-and-white clock. A game show hummed on the TV above them, interrupted by the fading wail of a siren. An ambulance pulled to the doorway; the ER buzzed with activity. Paramedics rushed through the entrance, an IV pole swung over the blood-splattered gurney. Rushed instructions were given as the double doors swallowed the patient into the caverns of the hospital.

The routine beeping and humming machines, the disembodied voice over the sound system and antiseptic smells of a hospital triggered Brian's memories of his accident. He stretched his arms in front of him. The tension in his shoulders radiated toward the knot forming on the right side of his neck. His mind raced through the possibilities of Dani's injuries. Perspiration trickled along his spine.

The sounds and smells familiar to Brian were frighteningly foreign to Ray. "I need some air. Be back soon." He rushed outdoors. He leaned against the wall; the coldness of the bricks penetrated his shirt, sending chills fluttering through his shoulders. His chest was tight with fear, a wave of nausea rolled through his gut. *I have no right to love you, but I do. Please be okay, Dani.*

Through the window Ray saw Brian and Trace being led past the forbidden double doors. An adrenaline rush propelled him back into the hospital. The woman behind the admitting desk was arguing with someone on the phone. A nurse hurrying by told Ray only family was allowed to go in with Dani. He shuffled back to the waiting room where fifteen minutes seemed an eternity before Brian and Trace returned. Ray searched Brian's face. "Is she okay?" he whispered.

His eyes glistening with tears, Trace rushed outside. Brian worked his fingers nervously at the back of his neck. "The doctor said she has a concussion and a dislocated shoulder—they've fixed that. Tests and X-rays show nothing else wrong, but they're admitting her for observation. He's pretty optimistic that she'll be okay." His voice cracked and he turned away.

After Dani was admitted to ICU, Brian and Trace were allowed a five-minute visit. Ray sagged in the waiting room chair.

A thick fog of loneliness settled over him. He closed his eyes and waited.

Brian returned with a faint look of encouragement. "She's conscious now and her color's better." He sighed hard. "I think . . . I think she's going to be okay."

His eyes filled with pain, Ray stared at Brian.

Brian hesitated a moment before wheeling back toward the desk. "Hold on, Ray, I'll be right back." He spoke briefly with the nurse. She picked up the phone and after a short conversation, nodded to Brian.

Brian returned to the waiting room, put his hand on Ray's shoulder. "They said only family could visit with her, but I asked the doctor's permission for you to see her. You can go in for just a few minutes."

Ray opened his mouth to speak, then merely nodded, and followed the nurse to Dani's room.

Ray walked slowly to the bed where Dani lay, her eyes closed, the sheet pulled up to her chest, looking fragile with her copper hair, still dulled with dust, spilling over the stark whiteness beneath her. He watched the leisurely drip of fluid through the IV tube taped to her hand and listened to the steady beeps of the monitors at her side. Her eyelids fluttered. A small smile tugged at her mouth. "Sorry," she managed to whisper.

"Oh, it wasn't your fault, honey." Ray curled his fingers through hers. "I should never have let you go out." He bent down to kiss her hand. "The doctor said you're going to be okay. I can only stay a minute . . . I just want you to know how much I love you."

"Love you too," Dani murmured and dozed off.

He brushed a kiss on her forehead and squeezed her hand.

Before heading back to the waiting room, Ray stopped in the men's room to splash cold water on his face. In the hall, a guard stopped Ray and informed him that Bud had had someone bring the truck over. He handed Ray the keys.

Trace stood beside his father's chair. The ordeal registered in the dark circles around Brian's eyes. "Ray, they said she'll probably sleep all night and we should go home," he said, his voice reflecting his fatigue.

Ray walked beside them to the parking lot. He ran his hand along the edge of his hat. "Thanks for letting me see her."

Brian nodded. "We'll talk in the morning."

After the lift had raised Brian into the van, Ray closed the door. For a few minutes after they pulled away, Ray sat in his truck before he reluctantly started the engine and eased into traffic.

# CHAPTER ELEVEN

Brian watched the dawn creep into his room. His heart beat in rhythm with the grandfather clock in the hall, and from time to time, he heard Trace tossing in his sleep. He thought of Dani lying in the hospital room. He shuddered at the thought that she could have been seriously injured or even killed. At the same time, he dug his fist into the bed, angered at her for being reckless with the new horse.

A new emotion edged in among the other feelings rumbling within him—jealousy. *Face it, you're jealous.* Brian wrestled with the feeling. Jealous of her energy. Her freedom. Her passion for her horses. *Dani's so full of life; she has more in common with Trace than with me.* Brian pounded his fist against his side. *Makes me so tired just to be around them both. And I'm jealous of this guy who is obviously in love with her.*

Brian recalled the months after the accident: the anger, guilt, fear and depression. Enraged at being paralyzed, he'd lashed out at everyone. Mostly he'd berated himself. If he hadn't been drinking, he might have been able to avoid the oncoming car. He knew it wasn't fair, but he was angry with Dani for not telling him she didn't feel well before they went out and for not driving home. He hated the stoned driver who hit them. He'd been so filled with self-pity, he couldn't see Dani's pain as she dealt with his paralysis and her miscarriage. They had wanted another baby, and it was gone before they even knew it existed. And poor Trace. Only six years old, old enough to know his parents were angry, but too young to understand it.

He thought of the months and years of counseling they went through to cope and put their lives back together, and then how the tenuous grasp started to erode as Dani's mother lost her battle with cancer. Dani'd quit the part-time job she so enjoyed, spending more time with her mother in the hospital. Brian hired someone else to do the bookkeeping. Trace helped with housework, meals and laundry. At night after a rough day at the hospital, Brian heard Dani crying as she tried to get to sleep. Brian rubbed his palms against his face. *Dammit! I didn't know what to do for her . . . how to comfort her. I know I let her down. I didn't know what in the hell to do!* She lost weight and he could barely remember when she didn't have those dark circles under her eyes.

It angered him that her sister wasn't more help getting the house ready for sale. He offered to hire someone to help but Dani turned him down, saying she didn't want strangers going through her mother's belongings.

Brian recalled the afternoon not so long ago when she came home with a flicker of life in her eyes. She announced she wanted to buy a horse, said she needed something just for herself. She began her search, and he warmed to the idea because she seemed happier just thinking about it. He had hoped she would find her horse and it would give her the peace and happiness she so much deserved.

"I should have remembered the saying about 'be careful what you pray for, you just might get it,' " he muttered aloud. *So, now she has her horses, and it's evident she's happier. She looks positively radiant after a day of trail riding. Of course, I never counted on having someone else come along to share that pleasure with her.* Brian punched the pillow with his fist. *I never planned on Ray.*

From the little time Brian had spent with Ray and from comments that slipped into Dani's conversation of things he'd said or done for her, it was difficult for Brian not to like him too. Even with the age difference between them, Brian felt older than Ray. It seemed everyone around Brian was filled with a passion for living he couldn't seem to grasp and hold on to. In spite of what he told Dani and his therapist, he never really got over his guilt or absolved himself for the accident, for robbing Dani of having a whole husband, for all the things he couldn't do with Trace and for the loss of their baby. He loved Dani but had stopped being a husband to her long ago. His impotence reached deeper than his body; it penetrated his soul. All he could do to make it up to them was to be successful in his business. He grew obsessed with his goal to make Dani and Trace financially secure.

Brian heard his son roll out of bed, turn on his radio, and head down the hall. Trace called to Brian from the doorway. "Hey, Dad, have you called the hospital yet? Are we going there this morning? I need to call Ryan if I'm not going to school."

Feeling relieved that his son's anger of the day before seemed to have faded, Brian motioned for him to slow down. "I just finished checking with the hospital. The doctor wants to keep her until tomorrow as a precaution. She should be able to come home in the morning. I'll probably visit her for a while today. Why don't you go to school and we'll both go see her when you get home," Brian suggested.

"Are you sure? I can stay home and drive you."

"Trace." Brian smiled. "I've been driving that van since long before you got your license. I think I can still manage."

"Yeah, I know." Trace frowned. "I suppose I should go to school anyway. I have two tests today. I'll come straight home." He started back to the kitchen. "Do you want some breakfast before I go?"

"No, I'll fix something later. You could bring me a cup of coffee though." He grabbed the trapeze bar overhead and eased himself into his chair.


Brian twisted the coffee mug in circles on the kitchen table after Trace left for school. The walls of the too-quiet, too-empty house pressed in around him. He dreaded the thought of Trace going off to college. How had he grown up this fast? He had enjoyed him as a little boy, loved to wrestle around with him, play ball, take him fishing. Before the accident. There were still things they could do together, but Brian couldn't seem to muster up the enthusiasm for anything, and Trace asked less and less often. Brian noticed when Trace had a problem he more often than not turned to Dani. And somewhere along the way Dani had stopped asking Brian's advice and confiding in him. *Because I never really listen to either of them. I'm too busy working.* But he couldn't find the energy to change what his life had become.

The ringing telephone interrupted his thoughts. He grabbed the phone, fearing it was the hospital.

"Hello."

"Uh, Brian? It's Ray . . . I . . . uh, I was just wondering if you had heard anything from the hospital."

Brian struggled with his jealousy. He stretched the coiled phone cord and let it snap.

"Yes, I called them this morning. The doctor wants to keep her to repeat some tests. She had a good night."

"Ah, that's good." Ray hesitated, "Is it all right . . . I mean, can I visit her today?"

Brian paused. "Sure. She's been removed from ICU and is in a regular room. I was going over there later this morning and then I'll go again with Trace when he gets home from school."

"Do you need any help? Do you want me to pick you up or anything?"

Brian stifled his irritation. "No." He cleared his throat. "No, that's okay. Thanks. The van is equipped for me to drive."

"Okay, maybe I'll see you at the hospital then."

"Sure. Good-bye, Ray." He hung up the phone. The strong, healthy timbre of Ray's voice echoed in Brian's mind.

The sound of voices coming from Dani's room stopped Brian in the hall. He tapped against the door, wheeled into her room and pretended not to notice how quickly Ray let go of Dani's hand.

"This is quite an improvement," he commented in a voice that sounded more cheerful than he felt.

Dani's eyes narrowed above the embarrassed flush of her cheeks. "My head still hurts a little and I'm pretty achy and sore." She managed a faint smile. "I guess I was pretty lucky, huh?"

Brian nodded and wheeled closer to her bed. "You sure were."

Ray twisted the brim of his hat balanced over his knee. He slid his chair back and stood up. "I'll go so you can visit." He glanced from Dani to Brian. "Uh, let me know if I can help with anything, okay?"

"Sure thing." The brief feeling of satisfaction Brian felt at Ray's discomfort stung somewhere in the part of him that wanted to be a better person. "Uh, I can't stay long and I'm coming back with Trace this afternoon. So, if you want to hang around and visit after I leave . . ."

Ray's eyes flickered with surprise. He nodded. "Ok, I'll go for a walk and come back in a bit." He gave a slight wave to them both, and at the door flashed a smile to Dani.

Ray chatted with the nurses and browsed through the most current of the old magazines in the waiting room. Brian found him there on his way out.

"She sure looks better this morning, doesn't she?" Ray commented.

"She does." Brian wheeled closer. "I was pretty worried about her. I guess I never thought about how dangerous horses can be."

Ray attempted to ease the tension. "That's why cowboys walk the way they do—always hurting somewhere." He groaned inwardly. *Good job, Crowley. Great thing to say to a guy in a wheelchair.*

Brian's chuckle died quickly. "I don't want her hurt again, but I guess I can't protect her from it." He slid his hands along the rubber-coated wheels of his chair. "She's pretty wrapped up with these horses, and I have to admit they do make her happy." He chewed against his lower lip and looked Ray squarely in the eyes. "I also have to admit it isn't just the horses making her happy."

Ray pulled in a deep breath, met Brian's gaze but said nothing.

"I love her." Brian closed his eyes for a moment then continued. "And I want her to be happy," he said softly.

Ray nodded, "I'm sure you do." He fingered the rim of the hat in his lap and mirrored the challenge in Brian's eyes. "So do I."

"I already figured that one out." Brian managed a faint smile. "And the fact that Dani returns the feeling."

A brief flash of surprise showed on the older man's face.

When Ray failed to comment, Brian continued. "She's very vulnerable. I don't want any horse or anyone to take advantage of her."

Ray's eyes sparked with sudden anger. He slapped his hat against his knee. "I'd never hurt her or take advantage of her." He stood up to leave. "And just for the record, I am *not* out to break up a family."

"Steady, Ray." Brian raised both hands, palms up. "I'm not making any accusations. Just trying to clear the air and see where we all stand. I know Dani is not about to leave me or break up our family." His voice cracked slightly; he paused and took a deep breath. "But I also realize . . . I know she needs more than I give her."

Ray stopped in his tracks and raised an eyebrow at Brian. Their gazes locked. Brian broke the connection first. He turned and rolled toward the elevator without further comment.

Wide-eyed, Ray stared after him. He shook his head. *Well I'll be damned.* He watched until the elevator door closed and slowly walked back to Dani's room.

# CHAPTER TWELVE

Dani ambled through the house, wiping away imaginary dust, straightening pictures and adjusting pillows. She'd been home from the hospital for three days. Brian was busy in his office and Trace was at school. She tossed the dust cloth in the closet and headed to Brian's office.

"I need to get out of here." She lingered in the doorway. "Why don't we go for a drive and see the horses, or go out for lunch?"

Brian raised a hand to indicate he needed a moment to finish what he was working on. He punched in a last key on his computer and hit print before turning toward Dani. "I can't just take off in the middle of the day. And you need to rest."

"I'm okay, and I've been resting for three days." Dani flopped into a chair near his desk. "I'm going crazy just sitting around. And why can't you take a few hours off?" She attempted a smile. "You're the boss. Give yourself a break."

Brian sighed, his look of reproach more appropriate for an errant child. "Dammit, Dani. I have a deadline on this project." When he returned to his computer, she stalked from the office and slammed the door.

Trace had been so solicitous when Dani came home from the hospital, obviously glad she was all right and home again. Brian's concern and worry appeared to have been replaced by irritation and anger. Any mention of the horses brought a scowl or negative comment. The first time she mentioned Cash, Brian's comment had been "Just remember your primary responsibilities. You have a home and a son. You're not a stunt girl for a western movie." Dani had been so stunned by the remark, she refused to give him a reply. *I can't live my life in a security bubble because he's afraid of me getting hurt. His mind is more confined to that chair than his body. He wants to drag both of us in there with him and shut us off from living. I won't let him do it. Trace will soon be off to college, then on his own. Free. Will I ever be?* Dani cringed at her thoughts. She felt herself pulling away from Brian, careful of her words, unwilling to share her thoughts or feelings with him.

Brian tapped his fingers against his desk. He pushed out a heavy sigh and wheeled from his office. He found Dani slumped on the sofa with her face buried in a pillow, crying. He wheeled next to her. "We need to have a talk."

She reached for a tissue, sat up, and stared defiantly at him.

"Dani," he began, "your accident really scared me. These horses . . . I didn't think about how dangerous they could be. I don't want you to get hurt again."

"I can't just sit around this house doing nothing." Dani pulled the flowered throw pillow to her chest. "I'm tired of cleaning house, washing clothes, cooking, doing the books. I need more. I love being outdoors and on trails with the horses. Can't you understand that?"

He nodded to her, creases etching his forehead. "Yes, I understand a lot of things." He met the defiance in her eyes. "And I know I can't be all you need. I want you to . . . to follow your heart. Do what you need to do to be happy." He touched her hand. "Just be discreet about it." He managed a lopsided smile and wheeled from the room.

Dani stared after him in stunned silence. His words stung

like a slap in the face. She felt like she'd been thrown away. She stared out the window and replayed his words over and over again.

*How the devil did we get to this point? That damned car accident didn't just happen to* him. *We lost a baby. It happened to me too. And to Trace.*

Dani punched her fist into the pillow on her lap. *Apparently he's willing to throw me away because he can't cope. Be discreet? Dammit! Do what I need to do to be happy, huh? He doesn't care as long as I'm discreet about it?*

The ringing phone jarred Dani from her thoughts. She picked up the extension in the kitchen.

"Hi, hon. I was just wondering how you're feeling," Ray said. "I sure miss seeing you at the stable."

Dani's heart fluttered at the sound of his voice. "I'm feeling great, just bored to death. I need to get out of this house. I'm going nuts."

"I know you aren't supposed to ride for a while yet, but why don't you come out to the barn and help me brush and graze the horses? Then we can get some lunch."

"That sounds wonderful. I'll be out in about half an hour. Is that okay?"

"That's fine. See you then."

Dani changed into a black AQHA sweatshirt with horses on the front, jeans and boots. She started for Brian's office. "The hell with it," she muttered. She scribbled a hasty note for him, tucked it under the saltshaker on the kitchen table, and hurried to the garage.

With the volume turned up on the country station, she put the window down and inhaled the crisp September air as Alan Jackson sang about the Chattahoochie River. Dani slapped her hand against the window frame in time to the music. *It feels so good to be out. Hope Chance and Cash remember me.*

She slid into the parking lot at the stable with her usual cloud of dust, and pulled next to Ray's blue-and-white truck.

Both horses stood in the crossties. Engrossed in combing tangles from Chance's tail, Ray didn't hear her creep up behind him until she tapped him on the shoulder. He spun around, hugged her, and whispered, "I've sure missed you."

"I've missed you, too. You have no idea how much."

Chance nickered. Dani grinned as she turned to her horse. "I guess he didn't forget me, after all." She slid her arms around his neck, closed her eyes and inhaled his sweet horsy smell.

"Oh, I forgot to bring them some treats."

Ray handed her a bag of apples. "I remembered for you."

Dani smiled at him. "What would I do without you?"

He squeezed her shoulder. "Please don't ever try." He selected two brushes from the tack box, tossed one to Dani, and began grooming Cash.

As Dani moved between the two horses, Cash pushed his nose toward her, nuzzled her shoulder.

"Are you glad to see me too?" She ran her hand along his neck. "We didn't part on the best of terms last time, did we, buddy?" He bobbed his head, and looked around at her again.

Slipping him a chunk of apple, Dani crooned, "I know you're sorry. I forgive you."

Ray snorted. "Maybe you forgive him, but I don't. One more stunt like that and I'll take a two-by-four to his butt."

"He's half mine, remember. I don't want you smacking him with anything."

"Hah." Ray chuckled, "I'll whack my half if I think he needs it."

Dani playfully jabbed the brush at Ray's side. "We'd better get our parenting skills in synch or we're going to have one screwed-up horse here."

"We shouldn't have any more trouble with him. I've been

teaching him who's boss all week. He's almost spook-proof now."

Dani snuggled against Cash's shoulder. "No wonder you're glad to see me."

"When you're able to ride him again, you're going to work in the round pen and show him you're also the boss."

"Aye, aye." Dani gave a mock salute and returned to brushing Chance.

They brushed the horses until their coats glistened, spoiled them with extra apples, then led them out to the pasture. Leaning against the fence to watch the horses graze, Ray slipped his arm around Dani's shoulders, and hugged her closer. "I hate to have you very far from me."

She shivered at his touch. "Seems like I've been on auto pilot for a week now. It feels so good to be here with you and the horses." *Where I belong, with someone who loves me. Loves me enough to listen to me, and share things with me.*

With a determined set to her jaw, she pushed away thoughts of Brian and listened to Ray fill her in on some bits of news around the barn.

Dani went directly from her doctor's appointment to the barn.

"Guess what?" Dani danced around the tack room. "I saw the doctor this morning. Got a clean bill of health and the okay to ride again."

"That's great, darlin'." Ray grabbed her hand. "I'm sure Chance will enjoy having you back because I've been working him hard all week. I can barely wait for spring so we can take him to some shows."

"Where can we ride tomorrow?" Dani asked.

"We aren't going anywhere. Remember, the shoer is coming tomorrow." He clicked the padlock on his tack box. "Afterwards you can ride in the arena and training pen. You need to take it easy," he cautioned. "And you will ride Chance while I work on Cash's manners."

Dani started to protest but caught the no-nonsense look in his eyes. "Okay, if you insist." She positioned her saddle on the rack. "Look how great my saddle looks. I took it home and cleaned it." She locked the tack box and followed Ray to collect the horses in the pasture.

"Hey, I keep forgetting to ask you." Dani came to a sudden stop facing him. "What in the devil is everyone talking about here—about Congress? What do horses have to do with Congress, anyway?"

Ray laughed at her confusion. "It's not like congress in Washington. It's Quarter Horse Congress—it's a huge horse show in Columbus, Ohio. It's always held a couple of weeks in late October—horses and riders from all over the country. Really quite a big deal."

She glanced at him. "Have you ever been there?"

"No, I haven't." His eyes clouded. "Kathy and I planned to go one year, but we had a big fight over her taking that damned boyfriend, so we didn't go."

"What kind of events do they have?"

With a wave of his hand, he answered, "Oh, just about everything—English and western pleasure classes, barrel races, pole bending, team penning, roping."

"Sounds so exciting. I'd love to go."

Ray raised an eyebrow and smiled. "Well, why don't we, then?"

Dani's enthusiasm faltered when she contemplated the ramifications of such a trip together. She gazed out over the pasture as if answers could be found in the swaying grasses on the horizon.

"Are you serious?" She glanced at him. "Could we really?"

He looked doubtful. "The question is: can you go with *me?*"

Brian's words burned in her mind. Defiance flashed in her eyes. "I can do anything I damned well please."

Ray stared, his eyes wide with surprise. He smiled and nodded. "Okay, then." He slid his hat back a bit and rubbed his chin. "If you're sure, I'll check with Bud, see where they usually stay and try to get some rooms reserved. Hope it isn't too late." He grabbed her hand. "I'm one of the few people left around here during Congress. Most everyone goes for part of it—a week or a few days at least." His eyes sparkled. "I've always wanted to go but never more than I do with you."

Dani rummaged through her purse and handed him her Visa card. "You need a credit card to reserve rooms. Use this, but you'll have to make them in my name."

Ray waved away her card. "I have a card, got it after I cleared up all the trouble with the ex. Just never use it much."

Dani squinted and shook her head. "So you're not such a nonconformist after all."


Brian and Trace shot glances at each other as Dani scurried around the kitchen putting dinner on the table. Just as she pulled out her chair to sit down, the phone rang. She answered it and seconds later let out a yell. "Whoa! Okay! Talk to you later." She hung up the phone and slid into her place at the table.

"Mom," Trace stared at his mother, "what in the devil has gotten into you?"

"I'm going to Congress," she announced.

Brian and Trace glanced at each other and then at her. "You're going where?" Brian asked.

Trying to calm down, she closed her eyes and took a deep breath. "Quarter Horse Congress. It's in October—Ohio. Everyone from the barn goes—practically everyone, that is.

Horses from all over the country—the cream of the crop to compete in all kinds of events." She babbled, her dinner getting cold on her plate. Brian and Trace nibbled at their food in astonishment at her excitement. Dani rambled on and on about how some of the people at her barn had horses good enough to go to Congress but most just went to watch and enjoy.

"So, you'll be going with all the people from your barn, Mom?" Trace asked.

"Yes, I'll know lots of people there. And since I've gone to a few horse shows I'll know other riders there with their horses too."

"It's nice to see you so happy. I hope you have a great time." He kissed her on the cheek and carried his plate to the sink. "I'm going over to Ryan's to study for a test. I'll see you later. Okay?"

"Sure. Say hi to Ryan and his parents for me."

Trace called out his good-bye from the door.

Dani carried her untouched plate to the sink and began scraping dishes and clearing the table. Brian pushed aside his plate and watched her flutter around the kitchen. He remained at the table toying with his coffee cup. "You didn't really answer Trace's question, did you?"

"What question is that?" She took Brian's plate and wiped the table.

He reached for her hand. "The one about if you were going with the people from your barn," he whispered.

"I will be with the people from my barn."

"Are you driving or flying?"

"Driving."

"And anyone in particular you're driving with?"

"Yes, there is." Dani tilted her chin. "Ray and I are driving out together, and I'll be gone for five days."

Brian let go of her hand. "I see." He turned toward the family room, "Hope you have a good time."

Dani's defiance faded as she watched her husband's retreat. She caught up with him at the doorway.

"In spite of what you said the other day, Brian, that's not my intention." He rolled down the hall without a reply.

Dani returned to the kitchen. *What am I thinking of? I can't go on a trip with Ray. No matter what Brian says. Can I?*

The battle line had been drawn. Somewhere between her head and her heart. The problem seemed to be that her heart had been split in two. The faint noise from the family room where Brian had turned on the news, and the jabber in the kitchen of Dani's talk-radio station competed with the war being fought in Dani's mind.

*If he's not willing to share my life, he can't complain if I find someone else to share my interests.* Dani shoved the last of the silverware into the dishwasher and set the dial.

*He gave you permission to do as you pleased, didn't he?*

*Sure he did.*

*Did he really mean it?*

*How could he? If he loves me, how could he say such a thing?*

And so the battle raged until she was exhausted with the effort. Dani finished up in the kitchen, tossed a load of clothes in the washer, and retired to her room with a book.

Brian called to Dani as she headed toward the laundry room to put the clothes in the dryer. "Dani, stop in here on your way back, please."

"Yes, what is it, Brian?" Dani's voice was weary and said she wasn't in the mood for an argument.

"About your trip . . ."

"Forget about it. I'm not going," she interrupted.

"I'm sorry I was so abrupt. You just surprised me, that's all. I want you to go. Have a good time. You need a vacation. It's been a rough year."

Dani's face was as blank and empty as she felt. With a slight nod to her husband, she turned and left the room.

*Thanks for making it easy, Brian. I'll go and have a damned good time.*

# CHAPTER THIRTEEN

Dani punched her pillow one last time, gave up, and rolled out of bed. She'd tossed all night, too nervous to sleep. As she dressed and stood before her mirror, putting the finishing touches on her make-up, she avoided the eyes in the mirror. *Am I doing the right thing going with Ray? This trip may change my life . . . am I ready for that? Dammit! Stop analyzing everything. Have some fun for a change.*

She waved good-bye to Trace, then hurried to her room to finish packing. As she flung last-minute items into her make-up case, she ran through a mental checklist before zipping her luggage. After tucking the tail of her gray-and-white shirt into her jeans, she secured the oval silver buckle on her belt.

Brian sat in the doorway watching her, his eyes anxious, hands rubbing against the cold metal wheels. "You're really excited about this trip, aren't you?" he asked.

She slid the closet door closed and hefted her suitcase to the floor. "Yes, I am. I've been talking to people at the barn all week. I can't imagine what it will be like to see so many horses in one place. Two of the guys are taking their horses to run poles and barrels."

Brian rolled back as Dani wheeled her suitcase to the garage door. She picked up the map, checked her purse for money and credit card and slipped into her jacket.

After packing the car, she hurried in to say good-bye to Brian. She knelt beside his chair. "Remember, I have meals in the freezer. Everything is marked with cooking instructions . . ."

"I'm sure we can survive for a few days." He gave her hand a squeeze. "Do you have the route all mapped out? Enough money . . . ?"

"Yes, I have everything." Her smile quivered as she gave him a hug.

He struggled with a smile. "I hope you have a good time and—you are coming back?"

Dani looked at him in surprise. "Of course, I'm coming back. What a thing to say." She kissed him lightly. "I'll call you as soon as I get there."

Ray paced near his door watching for Dani. As she drove up, he carried his suitcase to the porch, locked his door and hurried to her car. He tossed his bag into the trunk and slid in the car beside her.

"Do I sense you're anxious to get on the road?" she asked.

"I've been awake most of the night, almost called you half a dozen times to see if you were on time."

She laughed, "I couldn't sleep either. I almost called you to see if you wanted to leave earlier, but I wanted to see Trace off."

Dani eyed the jeans with matching denim jacket over a red western shirt and his favorite black Stetson. "You sure do look sharp."

He looked her up and down with exaggerated slowness. "Um . . . so do you. You'll have to beat the guys off with a stick."

Dani blushed. "Nice to know I'll have you to protect me." She tucked the map in her visor. "Do you want to drive first or should I?"

He motioned with his hand for her to drive. "I'm in a hurry to get there, so you better drive."

"Very funny. Keep making cracks about my driving and you'll

be coming home on a bus." She pulled into traffic with a squeal.

"You keep driving the way you do and we'll both be sitting in some little country jail."

Dani took the east ramp to I-94. Falling in with the flow of traffic, she pushed the accelerator to sixty-five and hit the cruise control. With a little sideways glance, she said, "Happy now?"

He raised his hands in surrender. "Improving. You're only ten miles over, but since I hate buses I'll keep my mouth shut."

The weather was clear and cool; the light traffic made it an easy trip. They took turns driving. Laughed and talked, mostly about their lives before they met each other.

As Dani picked up I-65 and headed south, Ray gazed out over harvested cornfields. "It's been a long time since I've been on this stretch of highway." His voice softened as he spoke of growing up in rural southern Indiana.

"My brother couldn't wait to get off the farm, but I loved the country. If Dad hadn't died when I was only seventeen, I probably would have stayed."

The silence stretched into minutes. Dani glanced at him but left him alone with his thoughts until he continued.

"Mom sold the farm after Dad died. I got stupid one night and ran off with a girl I was seeing." He tossed his hat in the back seat and brushed his hand through his hair. "Didn't take us both long to realize our mistake, and she went home to her folks. I was restless and getting rowdy so I joined the Air Force."

"You have no family left at all?"

"No. Mom died a few years after my brother was killed in Korea. My sister passed away about ten years ago." His sigh sounded with a heavy sadness. "Then . . . then when I lost Kathy . . . Well, something inside me died too and I've felt like I've just been marking time."

He turned to look at Dani. "And then you came into my life."

She smiled at him before she glanced in her mirror and signaled to pass a slow-moving pickup truck full of lumber.

"Your turn now. You've told me quite a bit about your mother and sister but you've never talked about your father."

"Not much to talk about." A hard edge crept into her voice. "He was an abusive alcoholic. He left when I was about eight. My mom worked hard and money was tight, but we were happier without him. Mom and I slept better for not being afraid all the time. Of course, it was hard to figure out my sister Lynn. She was always kind of scatterbrained. She doesn't remember too much of him. It's probably just as well."

Dani stole a sideways glance at him. "Did you ever wonder what it is about traveling in a car with someone that makes it so easy to talk, open up about things?"

He thought a minute. "I suppose it's because a person can talk without having to make eye contact so there's a little comfort zone there." He chuckled, "And the driver can't react too strongly because she has to pay attention to the road first, being the good driver that she is."

She reached over to pat his shoulder. "You're learning, cowboy."


They arrived in Columbus late in the afternoon. After checking into their hotel they met at the Congress Annex with Bud Morgan and a group from the ranch. Bud suggested a cozy restaurant nearby and the evening flew by with talk, laughter and plans for the week.

Back at the hotel, the group dispersed in the lobby, each heading off toward their own rooms. Dani's fingers fumbled with the key in the lock. Avoiding Ray's eyes, her hand gripped the edge of the door. Hesitation hugged her words as she asked,

"What time are we going to get started in the morning?"

Dani's rigid hold on the door and the tension in her face spoke more than words. Ray brushed his hand against her shoulder. "How about eight o'clock?" he said gently.

She nodded. "Sounds good to me."

He circled his arm around her waist and brushed a kiss against her cheek. "Make sure you lock up good. I'll unlock my inner door—if there's anything you need, knock or call me, okay?"

The anxiety in her eyes eased a bit. "Sure, uh . . . goodnight then." She closed her door, locking the security latch inside. A damp trickle between her shoulder blades sent a chill along her spine. She leaned against the inside of the door letting her heartbeat return to normal.

Forcing all thoughts from her mind, Dani washed her face, brushed her teeth, and slid into bed. The long drive and chatty evening had tired her out enough for her to fall asleep at once.

She woke with a start, heart pounding. Glancing around the strange room, Dani sucked in a deep breath. Ohio. Columbus, Ohio. Quarter Horse Congress. She peeked at the green numbers of the clock beside her bed. Seven o'clock.

Dani rolled to her back; let her mind wake up and her heartbeat slow down. *First night alone in a motel room. Survived it, didn't I? No Norman Bates in the shower. No serial killer hidden under the bed.* Dani laughed. *No—the serial killer's in his own room, next door. She raked her fingers through her tousled hair. Girl, you do need a vacation. Up and at 'em. Life awaits.*

Dani put the finishing touches on her make-up. At the soft knock on her door, she slipped into a yellow silk robe. She checked the peephole to make sure it was Ray.

"Sorry, I'm running . . . late. Whoa, look at you. Who's going to be beating them off with a stick?" She eyed his charcoal denims, soft gray shirt with pearl snaps and monogrammed pocket set off with a dark gray leather belt and silver western buckle.

Ray beamed at her approval, letting his gaze drift slowly over the silky robe that ended just above her knees. Head cocked, he raised an eyebrow. "Nice legs, Monroe."

Suddenly feeling embarrassed, Dani fumbled with the tie at her waist, rubbing one bare foot against the back of her heel. Ray took a step forward with a teasing smile. "Maybe we should stay here for a while."

Her sharp gasp and frightened look stopped him cold. He raised his hand and backed up. "Sorry. I'll meet you downstairs for breakfast when you're ready." With a squared set of his jaw, he turned and left the room, pulling the door closed after him.

Dani shuddered, took a deep breath. She pulled on dark blue jeans, a white shirt with blue-and-red trim and slipped on her boots. As she fastened her silver loop earrings, she met troubled eyes in the mirror. *Are you sure you know what you're doing here?* Eyes flashed defiantly. *No, I don't. I just know I want to be here.*

Alone in the elevator, Dani pushed the incident into the dark little corner of her mind where she banished the things she would deal with later. Through the opening doors a sign pointed the way to the breakfast buffet.

Enticed by the tantalizing aroma of bacon, sausage and coffee, Dani entered the room, scanning the tables for Ray. Only about a third of the twenty small tables were occupied. It was evident that Ray wasn't there. Across the room several hands waved to her. Dani headed toward the table where three women from her boarding barn were just finishing their breakfast. Laurie, a short bubbly woman with lively blue eyes and curly blond hair, pulled up another chair motioning for Dani to sit down. "Hey, come on and join us. What are your plans for today?"

Dani stole a tentative glance around the room before sliding into the seat beside Laurie. "Well, I . . . I was supposed to meet Ray here for breakfast but . . ."

Jill, a tall, plain dark-haired woman interrupted, "Oh, he was just here. He left with Bud Morgan, said to tell you they were going to check out some stallions and he would catch up with you later."

Dani nodded, trying to hide her disappointment. She accepted the cup automatically placed before her, sipping the strong black coffee as she listened to the chatter at the table. Not really a coffee drinker, she clasped her hands around the cup, comforted more by the warmth than the brew inside.

While the others finished their breakfast and paid their bills, Dani debated returning to the room to wait for Ray.

A busty blond named Peggy who tended to chatter incessantly about nothing brushed Dani's shoulder. "Why don't you come along with us today? We can all ride over together."

Dani hesitated. "Tell you what, I'll go with you, but I may need my car later so I'll drive, too. I'm not sure what Ray's plans are."

Dani sank against the seat of her car, closing her eyes. The day had been long and exhausting. She usually enjoyed the company of the other women, but today their exuberance and bubbly banter grated on her nerves. She had tagged along wherever they went trying to join in the conversations, but her heart simply wasn't in it. Finally unable to contend with the chatter, Dani excused herself, pleading a headache. When Peggy urged her to join them later that evening to line dance, she'd mumbled that she would try. She drove back to the hotel for a nap.

With a dejected slump of her shoulders, Dani wandered through the long, maze-like hallway of the hotel. She knocked softly at Ray's room. Receiving no response, she walked on and inserted the key in her door.

Tossing her purse on the table, she turned on the small corner lamp. She wiggled out of her jeans and shirt, flinging them on the chair. She rummaged through her cosmetic case, found some aspirin, swallowed two with a gulp of water from the tap and crawled into bed.

The jangling phone next to her head jarred Dani from a troubled sleep. She squeezed her eyes tighter, pulled a pillow over her head, willing the incessant racket to stop. After several rings, the beige monster was silent. Beside the phone an illuminated clock read six-thirty. Dani sighed, flung the pillow to the floor and rolled onto her back, staring at the shadows cast against the ceiling by the fluted lampshade.

A growling emptiness in her stomach had replaced her earlier headache. She'd skipped breakfast and eaten only half of an overpriced greasy hamburger for lunch. She ran her tongue over her teeth wincing at the skuzzy feeling. Struggling from under the twisted blankets, she shuffled to the bathroom, scrubbed her teeth and splashed cold water on her face.

Dani slipped into her robe and peeked through the drapes. Two floors below bright neon lights danced in the darkening sky, beckoning travelers into the surrounding restaurants. In the well-lit parking lot, she watched a couple walking hand-in-hand as they strolled toward a steak house flashing a giant steer's head over the door. She moved away from the window. Using the remote to turn on the TV, she slumped into a chair and stared at a Tom Brokaw wannabe on the local newscast.

Startled by the ringing phone, she reached for the receiver.

"Hello?"

"It's Ray. I called a little earlier but there was no answer. Did you just get in?"

Her knuckles grew white around the phone. Dani snapped

through clenched teeth, "What do you care?"

There was a conciliatory tone in his words. "Oh, I do care. I'm sorry about today. What are you doing?"

She fought to keep her voice cool and controlled. "I just woke up. I had a headache, so I took a nap."

"Well, I'll be right over. Get into something pretty and I'll take you out to dinner," he said and hung up the phone.

Dani slammed the receiver down. *Who in the hell does he think he is? Thinks he can just snap his fingers and I'll jump.*

Tightening the belt on her robe, she flopped into a chair. Within ten minutes a snappy knock sounded on her door. She remained seated, waiting for him to knock again before she sauntered across the room to open the door. She turned off the security lock, partially opened the door and walked back to her chair. Bare feet tucked under her, she feigned an interest in the TV program.

Ray hesitated briefly before closing the door. "Uh . . . I see you aren't quite ready yet."

Dani bit against her lower lip. "I think you owe me an explanation for today. I didn't do a damned thing to deserve it."

He raked his fingers through his hair, sighed and sat on the edge of the bed. "You're right, you didn't. I'm sorry."

With her hand resting against her chin, she stared at him in brooding silence.

"Honey, I don't ever want to be responsible for that look on your face again."

Her brow creased in bewilderment. "What are you talking about? What look?"

He grimaced as if in pain, "That damned frightened deer-in-the-headlights look this morning, that's what. Like I was going to attack you or something."

Dani folded her arms across her chest; her eyes flashed with anger. "I didn't think any such thing."

He watched, waiting for her to continue.

With a slight sag of her shoulders, Dani said, "Ray, I'm overwhelmed by our feelings for each other. Everything has happened so fast—I don't want either of us to get hurt." She looked away. ". . . Or to hurt anyone else," she added softly, thinking of Brian's words for her to follow her heart and be happy.

He nodded. "I never want to hurt you—or your family, honey."

Ray sat on the edge of the bed, leaned forward with his hands resting on his knees. Her heart flip-flopped at the tenderness in his eyes. She pulled her feet from under her and stood next to the chair a moment before sitting on the floor, leaning her head against his knee. He massaged her shoulder, easing away the tension but igniting feelings she fought hard against.

*I've never felt so loved and treasured. Being with Ray seems so right . . . the most natural and best place to be.*

The tightness in her shoulders eased. She shivered beneath his touch. Dani glanced up at him, the passion in his eyes mirroring her own. She sat up, slid her arms around his neck, kissing him with an intimacy long held in check. He stretched out on the bed and hugged her closer. Dani shuddered as his strong hands slid over her body. She fumbled with the top snap on his shirt.

Ray pushed her up, grabbing both her hands in his. "Darlin', are you sure this is what you want?"

Dani looked deep into his eyes, gave him a shy smile, and said, "I love you and I'm positively sure. I'm just . . . nervous. It's been a long time."

He smiled at her with a look that she felt all the way to her toes. "I hear it's like riding a bike—you don't ever forget how." He pulled off his boots and belt, tossing them to the floor. With one quick tug, he loosened all the snaps on his shirt. He grinned at her. "Darlin', now you know why western shirts have snaps."

Dani's laugh was cut short by his kiss and his hands moving against the silky robe. He loosened the tie and slipped the robe from her shoulders. He nuzzled her neck, running his fingers along the back of her bra. She eased his hand toward the front. She grinned at him. "Now you know why some bras fasten in the front."

He laughed, and made quick work of the hooks, tossing the scrap of powder blue silk and lace to the floor with his shirt. He teased at her bottom lip with his tongue, kissed her breasts and slipped off her panties. His breath caught in his throat as the soft light played against her skin. "My God," Ray whispered, "you're beautiful." He touched her face and ran his finger slowly down to her toes as he raised off the bed. He kicked off his jeans and pulled her tightly against him.

Dani stretched and opened her eyes. Ray lay on his side watching her with a loving look that made her tingle. She snuggled her head against his chest. He slid his arms around her, kissing her forehead.

"How long have you been awake?" she asked.

"Just a few minutes."

He tilted her chin upwards. "Any regrets?"

With a shy smile, she shook her head. "None at all. You?"

His eyes twinkled. "Just one."

Dani propped herself up on one elbow. "What's that?"

"We were in too much of a hurry. Next time we'll take it slower."

His look made her blush. An angry growl prevented a reply.

Ray rubbed a hand against his stomach and laughed. "That's what woke me—I'm starving. How 'bout you?"

She nodded her head. "I haven't eaten much all day. I skipped breakfast and had half of an awful hamburger around noon."

She glanced at the clock—nine-thirty.

Ray sat up. "How about going out for something to eat?"

"Sounds great to me."

They walked hand-in-hand to a cozy-looking café boasting "best food in town." The dinner crowd had thinned and the café was only about half filled. In a small corner booth they glanced through the menus.

A tired-looking waitress brought them fresh hot rolls, and took their order. Ray reached for Dani's hand over the pristine white tablecloth. "Dani, I'm truly sorry about today. Forgive me?"

Dani tilted her head, pretending to give the matter some thought. "I suppose so," she replied. "Let's just forget about it and enjoy the rest of the trip. Okay?"

"Deal." He patted her hand just as the waitress brought their salads.

The food lived up to the boasting sign in the front window. They ate, talking only with their eyes and an occasional smile.

The lights of the few bars still open looked fuzzy around the edges in the foggy mist that had rolled in. They pulled their light jackets closer against the night chill. Ray reached for Dani's hand.

Halfway back to their hotel they were drenched in a torrent of cold rain. Ray clutched her hand tighter and they ran the last of the distance.

They hurried down the hall, laughing at each other's soggy appearance. Fumbling in her purse, Dani dropped her key. Ray retrieved it and opened her door. "You look like a drowned cat," he said.

Dani shook her wet hair, spraying him with water. "You don't look much better. It's a good thing you didn't wear your hat. It would have gotten ruined. Come to think about it, why didn't you? I never see you without it."

"You're right about that. I just forgot it, that's all. You've addled my brain, I think."

Ray helped Dani struggle out of her wet jacket and hung it to dry. "You'd better get into a hot shower fast. Don't want you to catch your death," he said.

She turned on the shower. Ray flung his jacket over his shoulder watching her as she began to peel off her wet clothes.

Dani dangled her belt in her hand as she glanced over her shoulder. "I think you need a hot shower too."

With deliberate slowness, he unbuckled his belt. "Thought you'd never ask."

Dani and Ray woke at the same time, snuggled together just as they had fallen asleep, warmed by the hot shower and exhausted by Ray's promised slow, luxurious lovemaking.

Dani shook her head in an attempt to clear the cobwebs. "I can't seem to wake up, I feel drugged. I don't remember ever sleeping so soundly."

Ray ruffled her hair. "Me neither. And I'm usually a light sleeper." He nuzzled her neck and cuddled closer.

Dani struggled to sit up. "Don't start or we'll never get out of this room."

Glancing at the clock, he groaned. "You're right. We have a lot of things to see today. Let's get moving."

Dani slipped on her robe and headed for her shower. She turned as Ray got up, pointed to him and then to his room. He rushed toward her, laughing as she slammed the door shut. "Okay, you win—this time," he called in to her.

He gathered his clothes, enjoying her laughter as she turned on the shower.

★ ★ ★ ★ ★

At the sight of her reflection, Dani's laughter died in her throat. For a long moment she gazed at the woman in the mirror. Tousled hair framed a glowing face, relaxed, carefree, looking years younger than it had the day before. Eyes, deep, dark, wide and sparkling stared back in wonder. She gently touched a fingertip to her lips. They were fuller, slightly swollen from Ray's kisses. The features belonged to Dani Monroe, but she didn't feel like Dani Monroe. *I don't remember ever feeling so complete. So loved and . . . cherished. I should feel guilty, but I don't.*

*Dani Monroe, straight-arrow: honest, obeys the rules (okay, I do speed), makes complete stops at signs, doesn't park in handicapped spaces, and doesn't cheat on taxes. Good daughter, mother . . . wife? Haven't felt like a wife in a long time. Sure picked a big rule to break, didn't I? Where do I go from here?*

The steam crept around the mirror, distorting the reflection behind a drippy haze. Dani dropped her robe to the floor and stepped into the shower.

# CHAPTER FOURTEEN

Under breezy, pewter-tinged skies, Dani and Ray hurried toward the coliseum. The cavernous structure, arrayed with colorful sponsorship banners, echoed with the hoofbeats of an early morning warm-up session. Elevated above the large sandy arena, bleacher-type seating circled the oval building. The damp, chilly air was thick with the scent of horseflesh, leather, and rich earth.

"Glad I brought this along." Dani shivered as she zipped her denim jacket. "It's cold in here."

Ray led her to center seats in the second row to watch the riders. He put his arm around her shoulders. "I'll help keep you warm."

Contentment showed in her smile. *It's nice to feel so cared for.*

Across the arena several people from the ranch waved to them.

"I hope they don't join us," Ray whispered. "I don't want to share you with anyone today."

After the warm-up session ended, the two-year old snaffle bit class entered the gate. Pampered equines adorned with colorful saddle pads under lavishly silver-trimmed show saddles paraded into the arena. Riders, equally bedecked in flashy show attire, sat erect astride their mounts.

Ray sniffed the air. "Notice that smell?" he asked.

Dani chuckled. "Which one?"

He gave her knee a playful tap.

"The smell of money. What these saddles, tack and clothes cost would amaze you."

Under the watchful eye of the judge, the riders walked their horses around the arena.

"Trot your horses, please," called the announcer. The judge observed twenty-three horses obey their riders' commands. Moments later, at the judge's signal, came the request, "Reverse direction, riders and canter your horses, please." A young bay balked slightly and shook his head before moving into his clumsy stride.

A scowl crept over Ray's face. He gestured toward the arena. "Look at the headset on these horses. I can't stand the trend lately of the judges who insist on low headsets. Here—here, watch when they canter." He slapped his thigh. "Horses aren't supposed to canter with their damned noses on the ground."

"I see what you mean." Dani nodded. "They look awkward and uncomfortable."

Ray grunted and stood up. "Let's go look around, I can't watch this." He tugged at her hand. "We'll come back later for poles and barrels . . . see some real riders and horses."

"Kind of prejudiced, aren't you?" Dani teased.

Ray smiled. "Just a little bit."

Early morning browsers strolled through Congress Hall, enticed by a vast assortment of vendors. Dani gazed at displays of boots, belts and buckles, hats, animal art, pottery, Indian arts and crafts, custom sign makers and engravers. "I can't believe this. I feel like a kid in a candy shop," she exclaimed.

Ray held up a hand in caution. "Only problem is—this isn't penny candy."

They ambled through rows of silver-trimmed saddles, each more ornate than the last. One in particular caught Dani's eye.

She ran a hand over the soft suede seat and reached for the price tag.

"Whoa. Are we out of our league here." She dropped the tag as if it had burned her fingers.

Ray glanced at the price. "You've got that right, babe."

"We could go on a cruise for what one of these saddles cost."

"Who would want to go on a cruise?" Ray groaned. "A week surrounded by water and no place to ride a horse."

Dani laughed and raised her hands in surrender. "I'm going to have a tough time deciding what to buy. It sure won't be an easy choice."

"I'm sure you'll be up to the task," Ray teased.

They caught the last half of the reining class, and settled down to watch cutting horses.

"I enjoy reining horses for a little while, but it gets boring fast," Dani remarked. "I like watching cutting horses better . . . maybe because it looks so . . . so western." Her attention turned to the arena. The rider and his horse seemed to move as one. With little rein action, the muscled chestnut responded to the leg pressure of his rider, moving sharply—right, left, cutting off the calf and herding him toward the pen. The spectators cheered him on.

The speaker system crackled with the event results as Dani and Ray left the stands.

"I think I'm ready to shop," Dani announced as she stood and stretched her shoulders.

"Don't get carried away, now."

They made their way back through the crowd to Congress Hall.

Dani studied belt buckles in a display case.

"While you're busy here," Ray said, "there's something I

want to get. I'll meet you back here in about half an hour. Okay?"

"Sure, that's fine," she mumbled. As soon as he was out of sight, Dani hurried toward the booth where earlier in the day Ray had admired a pair of taupe Dan Post boots. He had even tried them on, so she knew what size to get.

She bought a mug with a colorful Southwestern design and a book of scenic photographs for Brian, a shirt for Trace, and a new belt and buckle for herself. Ray returned, no packages in hand, to find Dani tugging at a laden shopping bag. He shook his head, rubbing his forehead in mock horror. "That'll teach me to leave you alone. How could you buy so much so fast?"

"I'm a power shopper." She eyed him suspiciously. "Didn't you get anything?"

"Yes, I did. Right here." He patted his jacket pocket then peered toward the shopping bag. "So, are you going to show me what you bought?"

Dani slid her package away. "Later. Right now, I'm hungry. Let's go somewhere for dinner."

"You seem to have quite an appetite lately."

She flashed a lascivious grin. "Don't worry about it, I'm sure I'll work it off later."

His eyes twinkled. "I can hardly wait."

Dani pretended to look confused. "I'm not sure what you mean, cowboy. I meant we were going line dancing after dinner."

He nodded. "I guess a hearty dinner is in store then for *all* the physical activities to come."

Seated near a massive fireplace where a crackling fire had been lit against the continued chill, Dani and Ray lingered after dinner. Ray reached over to his jacket on the chair beside him, and handed Dani a small white box. He squeezed her hand.

"This is for your birthday. We seem to have missed celebrating it since you were busy being hooked up to an IV bottle."

Dani looked surprised. "I completely forgot about my birthday." And apparently so had Brian.

She gasped when she opened the box. Cradled in cotton on a gold chain of hearts was a small gold saddle with diamond chips around the edge.

"Oh, Ray. It's beautiful." Her voice cracked as she slipped the chain around her neck. "Thank you so much. I love it."

"I'm glad you do. Happy birthday." He beamed and kissed her cheek.


Ray opened the passenger-side door for Dani. "I'll drive. Are we going dancing or back to the hotel?" he asked.

"I'd really like to listen to music and compare notes with Bud and the gang. How about you?"

"Sure, but I want to dance, too."

"It's been such a long time since I've danced . . ." Dani looked wistful.

Ray grinned. "Oh, it's like . . ."

She waved her hand at him. ". . . Riding a bike. I know," she finished for him.


Echoing from the sound system, country music competed with the noisy crowd gathered to celebrate the wins of the day or drown their sorrows over losses. Laughter and rivalry surged through the room overflowing with western hats, fringe and leather.

On a crowded and stuffy dance floor scattered with sawdust, Dani floated in Ray's arms. "You're a very good dancer. Do you do everything well?"

He did a poor Bogart imitation. "Stick with me, sweetheart. I'll teach you everything I know."

As Randy Travis crooned "Forever and Ever, Amen," she smiled. "I can hardly wait."

Ray sang along with the CD. "This will be our song, darlin'." He leaned in closer and whispered, "Whenever you hear it, think of me."

As the evening wore on, the music grew louder, the crowd more raucous. Dani and Ray were jostled on the overcrowded dance floor. Nearby two liquored-up young hotshots appeared close to a fistfight over a shapely little blonde who seemed uninterested in either one of them.

"I've had enough of this, how about you?" Ray strained to be heard above the racket.

Dani nodded. "I'm anxious to show you what I bought this afternoon. Let's go."

Back in her room, Dani tossed the shopping bag on the bed to display her purchases. At last, she handed him the large box.

"This is to say thank you for helping me with Mom's house . . . and for just being there when I needed you most."

Dani beamed as she watched Ray's eyes widen when he opened the Dan Post box to find the boots he had admired.

"Oh, Dani. This's really too much. They were so expensive, honey."

She smiled and kissed him softly. "You liked them, and I wanted to get them for you. You deserve the best."

He touched his hand against her cheek. "I have the best . . . I have you."

Dani stretched, brushing her head against Ray's shoulder. He tousled her hair.

"Good morning, sleepyhead," Dani said.

"Not really. It's our last day,"

"How could it have gone so fast?" Dani rolled on to her stomach and lifted herself up on both elbows. "I've had such a good time. I don't want to leave." She felt a slight stubble as his cheek touched hers.

"I know. I could stay right here forever," he said.

"Let's make the most of it then." She grabbed his hand to pull him out of bed, and laughed at the wide-eyed look on Ray's face.

The light caught his shoulder and she noticed a small crescent-shaped scar. "Where did you get that scar?"

"Oh, I fell off a bike." He grinned. "Never did learn how to ride very well . . . got too busy learning to dance and . . ."

Dani smacked his bare butt. "Never mind."

Warm and still damp after a shower, Dani and Ray slid back into bed and made love.

They lay silent in each other's arms, closing out the world, willing time to stand still.

"I don't know how I'll ever be able to sleep without you now," Dani whispered.

Ray was silent. Propped up on one elbow, she searched his face. "Ray, are you awake?"

Eyes closed, he rubbed a hand over his chin.

"Yeah. I was just thinking of how you've changed my life. You know, I've been married twice and there have been other women in my life . . ."

Dani interrupted. "Lots of women?"

"Not important—don't worry about it." He kissed her hand. "I know now that I've never really loved anyone until you." He hesitated with a rueful laugh. "I've been told many times that I was remote, that I made love mechanically."

Eyes squinted, her face scrunched into a frown. "I find that impossible to believe," she said.

He laughed at her expression.

"It's true . . . and I never understood it until now. About five, six years ago, I just gave up on any relationship." He turned to her, his eyes filled with wonder. "It's like I've waited my whole life for you." He ran his hand along her shoulder, his voice filled with awe. "I've never cuddled like we do, or held anyone all night long in my sleep."

Dani's eyes were misty. "I might have gone my whole life without knowing what it was like to love and be loved like this. I finally know what it means to be soul mates. I always thought things like this only happen in books, now I know that's not so."

Ray kissed away a salty tear.

With maddening swiftness, the clock ticked away their remaining time alone. They reluctantly packed in silence and checked out of their rooms.

Dani drove the final stretch toward home. Ray glanced at the speedometer.

"Notice you haven't had a problem with your speed today," he commented.

"I'm in no hurry to leave what we have behind me," she whispered.

He reached for her hand. "What we have will always be with us, darlin', wherever we are."

# CHAPTER FIFTEEN

Ray slid his luggage into the hall while he held the door for Dani. She unloaded his purchases from Congress onto the sofa as he stood in the middle of the room looking as miserable as she felt. She walked toward him, dark eyes brooding with sadness, shoulders slumped.

"Ray, I . . ."

"Let's not say anything." He pressed his finger to her lips. "Just let me hold you for a while before you go."

Dani buried her face against Ray's shoulder as his arms circled tightly around her. Her heart beat in rhythm with his; she wished the world would go away and leave them alone.

Reluctantly, Dani forced herself from his arms. "I'll call you later." Her voice was low and pain hung on each word.

Ray merely nodded. He closed his eyes, listened as the door clicked shut, heard Dani start her car and toot the horn as she drove away.

"Damn! Dammit to hell anyway," he cursed against the lump constricting his throat. He dragged his luggage down the hall and threw it on the bed. He yanked hard against the zipper. In the silence, the grinding sound sliced through his heart like a saber saw. He clutched at the clothing, throwing it toward the hamper. *I need something to do—anything. Something to keep from punching a fist through this damned wall.*

After putting away his clothes, Ray tossed the empty suitcase into the closet. He gazed at the Dan Post box, lifted the lid, and caressed the soft leather of the boots nestled inside. *Now what do I do? When Dani leaves, it seems she takes the oxygen along with her. What if she has a change of heart after she gets home? Decides she's made a mistake.* He sucked in a deep breath. *And what if she doesn't? Where do we go from here?*

Ray flopped down on the bed, dragged his arm across his face, and closed his eyes.

Dani drove, dazed, through traffic blurred from sunlight and unshed tears. Rigid shoulders strained against the seat belt. *Oh my God, how can I go home? How can I face Brian and Trace? What am I going to do with the mess that I've made of my life?* Her hands gripped the wheel. *How can I be so happy and so miserable at the same time? I love Brian and Trace—but I love Ray too.*

Traffic snarled to a crawl. Dani made a quick right turn, navigated through two short blocks, and jerked to a stop by a park on a dead-end street. She slumped against her arms, folding them over the steering wheel. A flood of tears raged like whitewater rapids over boulders of conflicting emotions. Like angry thunder her heartbeat pounded in her ears. Breath came in jagged gasps, tightening the knot twisting in her stomach. Through the windshield the landscape began to spin. Her hands clenched against the wheel. *Oh, please. Help . . . me.* The words were whispers, but in her mind they screamed. Heart pounded, blood rushed, words echoed . . . in her head. *I can't breathe . . . I can't . . .*

As the trees in the park spun in a carousel of fuzzy green globs, her hands, clammy from fear, slid from the stirring wheel anchoring her to safety. *Please . . .*

A shaggy-haired young boy with huge blue eyes stood holding onto his bike with one hand and peering into her window.

"Are . . . are you all right, lady? Should I call nine-one-one?"

Dani strained to focus through gritty eyes as the boy repeated his suggestion to call for help.

Slowly she shook her head. "No, no. I'm okay. Thank . . . you."

Looking doubtful, the boy gave his bike a push. He circled in the street, glanced at her once more, and then rode away.

Dani sat still, hands resting in her lap. She stared at the trees standing motionless in the sun-drenched park. The pounding in her head had ceased. The dizziness had passed. Numb. *I just feel . . . numb.* Puffy, red-streaked eyes looked back at her from the rearview mirror. She raked her hands through her hair, slipped on sunglasses and dug through her purse for lipstick. *Little better. Deep breath. Start the car; pull into traffic. Be alert. Drive—home. Home.*

Mechanically, Dani put the car in gear and pulled away from the curb. She drove slowly, knowing each block took her farther from Ray and closer to the reality of her life.

Dani eased the car onto the drive just as Trace and Ryan drove up. Her heart pummeled against her ribcage. *My son. Reality.*

"Hi, Mrs. Monroe." Ryan poked his head through his opened window.

Behind the sunglasses, Dani winced. Mrs. Monroe. Dani Monroe. Mrs. Brian Monroe. "Hi, Ryan." She forced a smile.

Trace grabbed his backpack, closed the door, and waved as Ryan drove off. Dani hugged her son. He reached for the suitcase in the trunk.

"Have a good time, Mom?"

*Deep breath.* "Yes, I had a very good time. I've missed you. Is everything okay?" She collected her packages from the trunk. *Breathe; smile.*

Trace shrugged. "Yeah, I guess."

Suddenly alert, Dani glanced at him. "You *guess?*"

His voice snapped with tension. "I hated to leave Dad alone, but I . . . He works so much, and I couldn't get him to go out." He slammed the trunk down. "I had Ryan over a lot. It felt a little less . . . lonely having him here too."

*Welcome home.* With a grimace, Dani nodded and followed her son into the house.

"Hey, Dad. Mom's home." Trace carried Dani's luggage to her bedroom, calling to Brian in the family room.

Back in the kitchen, Trace hugged Dani. "Sure am glad you're home, Mom."

Dani held her son, awash in guilt of tsunami proportions.

Brian tossed his book aside and wheeled out to greet Dani.

"Hi . . . how was the trip?" He reached a hand toward her, his smile failing to conceal the anxiety lurking in his eyes. "Did you have a good time?"

Dani dumped her packages on the table and bent to give him a hug. She rubbed her hand against the back of her neck and shrugged. "Hectic—always something going on—but I had a nice time. Good . . . good to be—home."

A chill slithered down her spine. Even to her ears, her voice sounded flat.

"Mom, Ryan and I rented some movies. Is it okay if he stays over tonight?" Trace leaned against the doorframe, his hand wrapped around a Pepsi. "Can we get a pizza for dinner?"

Dani smiled in spite of herself; it would be nice to have the boys at home for the evening. "One question at a time. Yes, he may stay and yes, we can get a pizza."

Trace rushed off to his room to call his friend.

"Looks like you did some shopping." Brian eyed the packages on the table.

"You wouldn't believe the damage I could have done to my credit card." Dani rummaged through the shopping bag to find the mug and book she'd brought him.

Brian paged through the book of scenic photos Dani hoped might renew his old interest in photography.

"Terrific book. Thanks."

"It was incredible, the beautiful—and very expensive—saddles, tack, clothes. Truly amazing." She rattled on to fill up the space left by Trace's absence.

Brian watched her every move. "Dani, are you going to wear those sunglasses in the house all evening?"

She reached toward her face. "Oh . . . I forgot I had them on." She peeled off the sunglasses, tucking them into her purse. "I drove with the sun in my eyes all the way home. I have a headache."

He searched her face. "You look tired."

Dani nodded with a sigh. "Yes, well, I guess I am. Traffic was heavier coming home at this time of day."

"Why don't you relax in the family room? I'll bring you something cold to drink . . ." His eyes met her surprised look. "It's good to have you home."

Dani stared at him. Why *now!* Dammit, why so solicitous and caring *now*.

As if he could read her thoughts, Brian looked away. He tossed ice cubes in a glass as she left the room.


The house was soon alive with teenaged exuberance as Trace and Ryan clowned around, asked Dani questions about her trip, and decided on what to have on their pizza.

The boys ignored Brian's groan as they slid *Die Hard* into the VCR.

"You've seen this several times now, guys."

"But we like it," came their response in unison.

The doorbell rang, and Dani went to pay the delivery boy. Trace followed her and carried the two large pizzas into the family room.

Dani sat with the boys on the floor, feet tucked under the coffee table. She'd missed Trace, and it was good to be home with him. His spirits had improved once she'd returned home. Brian was strangely quiet as they all munched the gooey pizza and watched the movie.

After two slices of pizza, Brian yawned and said, "I can't sit through this movie again. I'm going to bed. See you all in the morning."

Dani watched as Brian wheeled from the room with no further comment. She pulled her attention back to the screen and tried to concentrate, seeing instead scenes from the Congress Horse Show. Memories to treasure—to last a lifetime. Would there be others to add to it, or was that all they'd have? Or was it the beginning of better things to come? She felt a sudden chill.

Dani stared past the empty pizza box and glasses littering the coffee table to her son and his friend engrossed in their video. The screen flashed with a frantic car chase, tires squealed, music thundered.

"That's okay, Mom." Trace motioned her away as she moved to clear the table. "We'll clean it up when the movie's over."

She smiled at him. "Thanks. I'm tired. Think I'll go to bed. See you in the morning."

" 'Night, Mom."

"Goodnight, Mrs. Monroe," Ryan echoed.

Dani checked the door locks, looked in on Brian, and went to her room. Alone in the darkness, she leaned against the closed door. A tension headache nagged behind her eyes as fatigue washed over her. She reached for the light switch. *Routine. Wash my face. Brush my teeth. Jeans folded, on the shelf. Shirt, underwear in the hamper. Night light.* She pulled back the comforter, and slid into bed. In the darkness she lay naked, staring at the phone beside her.

The illuminated dial of the clock read ten-twenty. She reached for the phone, dialed and waited to hear his voice.

"Hello."

He sounded tired.

"Hi, it's me," she whispered. "I didn't wake you, did I?"

"No, I was just watching TV and dozed off."

Dani heard the warmth in his voice and could almost picture him rubbing his hand across his face to wake up.

"Hate the thought of going . . ." He hesitated. "Guess I should watch what I say on the phone. You know what I was going to say."

"Yes, I know. I just called to say goodnight and I love you."

"I love you too, darlin'. Goodnight, sleep well."

Dani hung up the phone. She wiggled from beneath the comforter, rummaged in her dresser drawer. She pulled a flannel nightgown over her head and went back to bed. *This bed had never felt so big before.* She hugged the spare pillow to her chest and closed her eyes, eager to escape.

# CHAPTER SIXTEEN

Dani burrowed her head in her pillow. Each night her welcomed escape ended too soon as a new day stretched ahead. She heard Trace in the kitchen. From the next room drifted snatches of conversation between Brian and Greg, a physical therapist who came three times a week for exercises and massage.

Sitting up, Dani sighed, and reached for her robe. She paused at Brian's room.

"Good morning—Hi, Greg."

Brian waved a hand in her direction.

Continuing his massage, Greg smiled. "Morning, Dani. How're you doing with the horses?"

"Oh, fine . . . fine." She hesitated a moment before heading for the kitchen.

The two men had developed an easy friendship over the years. Greg frowned. "Dani seems a bit . . . distracted. Isn't she feeling well?"

"Her moods have been all over the place for quite some time now." Brian sighed. "This last year or so—you know, with her mom and everything—has been rough. The horses have perked her up a bit, but . . ."

Greg finished his massage and brought a chair next to the table. He faced Brian, and met the troubled look in his friend's eyes. "Maybe . . . maybe she should see someone—I can recommend a good psychologist if you need a referral."

"I suppose that might be a good idea." Brian rubbed a hand against his forehead. A weary sigh punctuated his words. "Leave the number, okay? Maybe I'll talk to her about it."

Greg searched through his case, found the business card he wanted, and placed it on the nightstand. He helped Brian get dressed and into his chair.

"I'll see you for our regular session on Monday. If you want to talk before that, call me." He hesitated at Brian's far-away gaze. "You need to get out of this house a little more. Why not come over and watch the Bulls game with me tomorrow?"

"I'll give you a call." Brian waved his hand in the air. "I usually don't stay up late and . . ." he trailed off.

Greg gave Brian's shoulder a slight shake. "Hang in there. I'll see you on Monday." He gathered his supplies, called good-bye to Dani and let himself out.

Brian found Dani staring out the window, her hands clutched around a flowered mug, the tag from a teabag draped over the edge. Trace had left for school. The kitchen was strangely quiet without the talk-radio station she usually listened to most mornings. She didn't seem to notice him in the doorway. He could tell by her stare that her thoughts went beyond the view through the large bay window.

She'd been home from Congress for over a week. Other than the first day, she hadn't mentioned it again unless he or Trace asked her a question. Her words, or lack of them, told him little. The sadness in her eyes told him more. Whatever happened—and he really thought he knew—would it have happened anyway, or had he pushed her toward it? *Dani, if I could give you more—if things were different . . .*

The clouds drifted, and with the bright sunlight spilling through the bay window, Brian heard her defeated sigh.

"Dani . . . ?"

She jumped at the sound of his voice. "Oh, my gosh . . . I didn't know you were there. You startled me."

"I'm sorry." He wheeled next to her. "Why so glum? You haven't been spending much time with . . . the horses all week."

"I've had a lot of housework and things I needed to get caught up with . . ." Dani added some honey and a squeeze of lemon to her tea. "Thought it would be a good time."

"Uh-huh . . . well you should take a break today. Why not go for a ride."

She nodded as she appeared to think it over. "Maybe. I'll see later."

Her fingers brushed over the phone as she resisted the urge to call Ray. She'd spent the day organizing closets and sorting magazines to throw out, and trying to push away memories of her trip to Congress. She floated through a purgatory of indecision about her life. In a search for a solution to her dilemma, she weighed the consequences of leaving Brian—his needs and feelings—the effects on Trace.

"I can't do this to them." Dani threw a stack of magazines in a box. She sat on the floor and rested her head against the wall. "What about what I need? Does everyone else always come first?"

Fatigue and defeat weighed heavily. Dani rubbed a hand across her churning stomach. With a deep sigh, she pulled herself up, closed the box of magazines and hauled it to the garage.

Water sloshed in the washing machine as Dani pulled a load of clothes from the dryer. She carried the laundry basket into the family room and glanced in at Brian reading the paper.

Trace had got a part-time job after school two evenings a week and weekends. His absence in the house seemed a harbinger of days to come when he left for college.

The laundry, still hot from the dryer, warmed her hands. As she folded and stacked towels in the basket, she felt Brian's eyes following her.

"Is there something wrong?" Dani snapped.

Brian flinched at her tone and took a sip of coffee. "Uh—no. Why?"

"You always seem to be . . . watching me lately." Dani cocked her head slightly. "Why all the attention all of a sudden?"

His voice was low and sad as he replied, "I just missed you while you were gone, that's all." He lowered the paper to his lap and traced the edge of his coffee cup with his finger. "Thought maybe I've been working too much lately and . . ."

The sadness in her eyes stopped him cold. Their eyes held for seconds before she whispered, "Great timing, Brian."

Tears trickled down her face as she carried the laundry down the hall.

Sleep was broken and fitful as Dani struggled with her feelings. There seemed no easy answer to her situation. She tossed and turned, exhausted from the internal struggle. She woke early in the morning with a nagging backache and the beginning of a migraine. *I need to get out of this house and get some exercise.*

Dani rushed out of bed and dressed in old faded jeans and a sweatshirt. She pulled her hair back and applied only a quick trace of lipstick. She scribbled a note for Brian and Trace and left it with a magnet on the refrigerator.

The horses banged their heads in the feed buckets for any remaining oats they could find. Dani gathered her gear and murmured a greeting to the stable hands mingling in the tack room for a break.

She saddled Chance and led him to the outdoor arena. He

nuzzled against her back, giving her a little push as she reached the fence. "I know—I've been neglecting you lately. I'm sorry. Let's have a good ride this morning. Okay?" She put her arms around his neck. He brought his head down hard against her shoulder in a gesture she had come to realize was his way of returning her hug.

After a good warm-up session, Dani pushed Chance into a canter. His smooth easy gait soothed her like a rocking chair. She relaxed, breathed in the chilly morning air, and felt the connection of spirit with her horse she so loved. *It's so true the saying: the best thing for the inside of a person is the outside of a horse.*

After their ride, Dani brushed Chance and put him back in his stall. Next she worked Cash on the lunge line. After a few bucks to show he was enjoying the cooler air, he settled down and obeyed like the little champ she knew he would be. She saddled him up and rode in the indoor arena. *I'm going to have to do this more often. It's nice being here alone with the horses.*

Dani had just slid into her car when Ray pulled in beside her. He hurried toward her car and tapped on the window. Hesitating briefly, Dani hit the button to unlock her doors. Ray eased into the passenger seat, turning toward her with a frown.

Dani braced her hands on the wheel. Tension crept in on the peace she felt after her ride. Happiness at seeing him fought against her guilt that the feeling brought.

"Are . . . are you avoiding me, Dani?" A nervous tension made his voice crack.

She stared ahead, reluctant to meet the hurt in Ray's eyes.

He snapped on his seatbelt. "Let's go for a drive."

"I need to get home."

"Honey, we need to talk."

★ ★ ★ ★ ★

The parking lot at the forest preserve was empty, and Dani pulled into the first spot and killed the engine. She stared at her hands folded in her lap.

"Come on, Dani. What's wrong?" Ray turned to face her. "I wanted to call you but I don't know if . . ."

"It's okay. Most of the time I'm the only one around to answer that phone anyway."

"Okay." He nodded. "Now, why haven't you called me? And why haven't you been out to the barn much all week?" His voice rose slightly. "And why so early today? Are you avoiding me?"

Her eyes squinted in annoyance, Dani looked up. "What is this, an inquisition?"

Ray pounded a fist against the dashboard. "Damned right, it is. Answer me." His voice was tight with frustration and anger.

"Don't tell me what to do." Dani glared at him.

"Then stop acting like a child." He raised his hands to his face.

With a shake of her head, Dani started the car, and headed back to the barn. "I just can't keep this up. I'm being torn in two and . . ."

"I'm sorry, honey." He rubbed a hand against his forehead and closed his eyes. "I love you so much."

Her voice trembled with her reply. "I know. I love you too, but there are other people involved besides us."

They sat silently in the parking lot at the ranch for a few minutes. With an angry set of his jaw, Ray slid out of the car and slammed the door.

Ray shook his head as Dani drove away. "Damned women . . . enough to drive a man nuts. Should just stick to horses. A lot less trouble."

★  ★  ★  ★  ★

"Have to run, Mom. I'm late." Trace aimed a kiss at Dani's cheek and rushed out the door. Trace had a date with a new girl in school. They were double dating with Ryan and his girlfriend.

"That boy is never home anymore," Brian grumbled as he threw his copy of *Newsweek* on the coffee table.

"That boy is almost a grown-up, and we had better get used to not having him around."

"Don't we sound philosophical tonight?" There was an edginess to his voice that Dani chose to ignore as she paged through the television listings.

"Bulls game starts at seven. Want to watch it with me? Or we could go to a movie . . ."

"No, I'm tired tonight. Think I'll just read a while." He wheeled down the hall to his room.

Dani lit a fire. She sat as close as she could to the warmth trying to ease the chill that went through to her soul. *I'm so tired of sitting around this house alone. I feel ancient, like I'm just marking time until I die.* She rubbed her face with the palms of her hands. *My life's running out and I'm denying a man who loves me for a husband who doesn't seem to care. Why? Dammit, why?*

It had been three days since she'd seen or spoken to Ray. Her conscience felt better, but her heart hurt with an unbearable emptiness.

She dragged the phone next to the fireplace, dialed, and lay on the floor as the phone rang on the other end. She was just about to hang up, when he answered.

His "Hello" was gruff and scratchy.

Dani shivered. "Uh, it's me."

The silence stretched.

"Well, talk," he said, his tone flat, "it's your nickel."

"Um . . . I just wanted to apologize for the other day. You

didn't do anything to deserve that."

Silence.

Dani sat up, fumbling with the phone cord. "Okay, then. That's all . . . I'll let you go. Probably getting ready to watch the game anyway."

The gruffness eased a bit. "What are you doing?"

"Nothing, sitting by the fire."

"Where's everyone?"

"Brian is asleep and Trace is spending the night at Ryan's."

"I miss you," he whispered. "Why don't you come over and watch the game with me?" The warmth in his voice melted the ice around her heart.

She gave in to the need to be with him. "Uh . . . I'll be over in a few minutes."

"Great, I'll make some popcorn."

She smiled at the happiness in his voice.


Ray opened the door before she could knock. As she tossed her jacket on the chair, he stepped closer, grabbed her shoulders and pressed her against the wall. His kiss was rough with leftover anger and frustration.

She wrapped her arms around his neck and pressed her head against his shoulder. He held her tightly, needing her to be part of him, to love him as he loved her.

He felt the fury of her heartbeat and the warmth of her body through his shirt. He took her hand and led her down the hall.


The third quarter was just under way when Ray finally turned on the TV in the bedroom. They snuggled in the center of the bed, munching popcorn from a bowl resting between them.

"Looks like a good game," Dani said.

He winked at her. "Never enjoyed a game so much in my life."

Michael Jordan sprang into the air, twisting as only Jordan could, and sank the shot. Ray bolted upright, sending popcorn flying in all directions. "Damn . . . is he absolutely the best or what?"

Dani searched for the scattered popcorn and laughed. "Almost as good as you are. Bet you taught him everything he knows."

Ray looked reverent. "Oh, no. He's the greatest. I couldn't teach him anything." He caught her teasing look and took the bait.

"But . . ." he continued, eyes twinkling, "I do try to help Phil Jackson out occasionally. Send him ideas, you know." He pointed to the screen. "See there, that one. That's one of my strategies."

Dani shook her head and played along. "I'm sure glad he listens to you. Doesn't it ever bother you not getting the credit you so richly deserve?"

Ray bowed his head slightly and held his hand over his heart. "Oh, I'm secure enough to be the brains behind the power."

"But, dammit." Dani's eyes flashed in mock indignation. "Phil could send you a ticket once in a while, maybe let you sit next to Michael on the bench or something."

He laughed at her. "I'm just glad my strategy helps them win some games. At least Phil listens—better than that stupid Ditka."

Dani groaned at the monster she had unleashed. She choked back her laughter.

"Ditka didn't listen to you, huh?"

"Nah, he was *da coach*—didn't need any help from me. Got so damned busy with his commercials and motivational speeches. Motivated himself right out of Chicago, he did."

"Serves him right, doesn't it?" she sputtered through tears of laughter.

"Hell yes." He reached for her. "Damn, I love to make you laugh."

Ray scooped up the rest of the popcorn and sat the bowl on the floor. At a safe distance from Ray's flailing arms, Dani settled against two pillows to watch him be captivated by the last minutes of the game.

The Bulls won by ten points. Ray took credit for three major plays.

Dani let herself into the quiet, dark house. Without turning on a light, she crept down the hallway toward her room. Soft snoring came from Brian's room as she passed.

Seated by her window, she stared into the darkness. Within her raged a war between happiness and guilt that was to plague her for months to come. Unable to deny the feelings she had for Ray, Dani could not find the strength to dissolve her marriage. How on earth could she leave a man confined to a wheelchair? Whether or not she left Brian, she was terrified of losing her son.

Just as Dani turned out the light beside her bed the telephone rang. She snatched up the receiver before another ring. Her smile faded as she realized the caller was not Ray, and listened to the official voice on the other end.

"Yes, I understand. I'll be right there. Thank you for calling."

Dani rubbed her eyes with an exasperated sigh and jumped to her feet. She pulled on her jeans and a T-shirt, looked in the mirror, changed her mind, and switched to a pair of gray wool slacks and a black turtleneck sweater. She ran a comb through her hair and splashed on a touch of lipstick. *Looks better, less like a saddle bum and more like a caring suburban mother of a teenager in trouble. Dammit!* Dani reached for her purse and switched off the lamp.

As she passed Brian's room, he called out to her.

*Dammit!* "Yes?"

"Is there something wrong? I heard the phone . . ."

She hesitated before entering his room. She turned on the lamp beside his bed. Brian reached his hand out to shelter his eyes from the sudden light.

"It was . . . it was the police. Trace is at the station with a group of other kids. Seems things got out of hand at a party. I need to go pick him up."

"I'll go with you . . ."

"That's okay. I think I should get there as soon as possible."

"Yes, of course, you're right. I'll be up when you get back."

Brian sat in his chair in the living room, hair disheveled, a scowl on his face, when Dani and Trace arrived home. His hands clenched against the sides of his chair as he waited for them to hang their jackets in the hall closet.

"Okay, let's hear what this's all about, son."

"It's no big deal . . ."

"Don't give me that. Any time we get a call in the middle of the night from the police, *it's a big deal.*"

Trace gave a heavy sigh. "Okay. Okay. We went to a party. One of the guys was watching a neighbor's house while they were on vacation. He decided to have a few kids over . . . it kind of got out of hand. There were a lot of kids there and someone called the police."

"You certainly know better than that, Trace . . ." Brian began.

"Dad, I didn't know all the details. Didn't know they were on vacation. Just one of those things that kind'a snowballs. You know . . ."

"Yeah, I know." Brian watched Trace fiddle with the edge of his earlobe, something he always did when he was upset.

"Have you been drinking, Trace?"

Trace's eyes widened and he glanced at his mother.

"Trace?" Brian's tone sharpened.

"I only had a few beers . . ."

Brian slammed his fist against the arm of his chair.

"Only had a few beers. You were driving, Trace."

"Dad . . ."

"What about the other kids with you?"

"Ryan's Dad picked him up, and the girls' parents came for them."

Brian's face was red with rage. "I'm in this dammed chair because of a stoned driver and because I had 'just a few beers' that might have caused me to be unable to avoid the accident. How much of a reminder do you need about drinking? And especially drinking and driving . . . or being in a car with someone who's been drinking?" He ran his hand through his hair in a gesture of frustration.

Tears pooled in Trace's eyes. He lowered his head into his hands. Dani rubbed a hand over his shoulders.

"Okay, we've had enough for tonight. Trace, go to bed. We'll talk about this more in the morning."

Trace brushed a kiss against his mother's cheek. "Thanks for coming to get me, Mom."

Without looking at his father, he muttered, " 'Night Dad."

Brian made no comment to his son as he left the room.

"You didn't have much to say to him," Brian snapped.

"We talked on the way home from the station."

"You don't seem too upset with him."

Dani groaned. "Of course, I'm upset with him. I don't think screaming at him is going to do any good. We'll talk about it in the morning." She checked the lock on the front door. "I'm going to bed."

"Whole damned family's falling apart." Brian muttered as he rolled down the hall toward his room.

*Takes a team effort to hold a family together, Brian. I've been do-*

*ing it alone for too damned long now and I'm so tired.*

Dani and Trace were in the kitchen having hot chocolate when Brian woke the next morning.

"I just plugged in the coffee, it'll be ready in a minute."

"Fine."

"Dad." Trace's expression was contrite. "I'm sorry about last night. It won't happen again."

"I'm glad to hear it. But you don't get off that easy. You're grounded for a week and no driving for a month."

"Oh, Dad . . ."

Brian raised his hand to end the discussion.

"It's final, Trace."

"How will I get to school . . . and to work?"

"You can ride the school bus with the rest of the kids. When you start acting like a grown-up, then you may drive again. As for work, your mother can drive you and pick you up."

Trace drained his cocoa with a scowl clouding his face, rinsed the cup, and went back to his room.

Dani glared at Brian.

"What?"

"Don't you think you and I should have discussed this first?"

"He needs to know there will be a consequence for his behavior."

"He knows that."

"So what was wrong with what I did?"

"You didn't discuss it with me, for one thing. I'm the one who'll be running all over town with him for a month, not you. Don't you think I should've had some say in the matter?" Dani poured coffee for Brian and pushed the mug on the table.

"You know, Brian, you've been very uninvolved in this family for quite some time. Now all of a sudden you're being heavy-handed and issuing orders. Maybe if you showed a little more interest in Trace's life . . ."

"Now it's my fault?"

"I didn't say it was your fault. Kids rebel. They test the boundaries. Things happen sometimes. I'm just saying you can't just ignore him and then all of a sudden start throwing out punishments. You didn't even give him a chance to explain anything. He was telling me how everything happened . . . and . . ."

"Oh, I've had enough, Dani." Brian pushed his coffee away and rolled toward the door. "You go ahead and handle it. Handle everything."

★ ★ ★ ★ ★

# PART TWO

★ ★ ★ ★ ★

# CHAPTER SEVENTEEN

*One year later*

Scenes from a sit-com, complete with laugh track, flashed across the television screen. Ray slouched on the sofa, stocking feet propped against the coffee table. He stared at the TV but saw instead the kaleidoscope in his head. It'd been over a year since Ray had met and fallen in love with Dani Monroe. Try as he might, it was difficult to remember the years before her, except for the realization that they had been empty. Pragmatic about his life, he had grown used to being alone. Since the death of his daughter, he had become cynical, protecting himself from hurt behind a wall of indifference. Bored and uninterested in the women he met, he stopped looking for companionship.

Not until his world and Dani's collided, did Ray grasp the emptiness of his solitary existence. Dani's smile and her laughter lit up his life, made him feel young and eager for each new day. Her voice still soothed his heart as her touch still ignited his senses. What was the phrase she often used? Soul mates. Yes, soul mates. Loving, and being loved by Dani made him believe in such things, in a lot of things he'd never thought much of before. They were two halves made whole by loving each other. He wasted little time with regrets; in reality, he had few. His only regret now was that they hadn't met years ago, that they didn't have a whole lifetime ahead together. They spent whatever time they could manage together, but his heart ached at the end of the day as he crawled into bed without her next to him.

He loved to make her happy and hear her laugh. But he also knew that their situation tore at her soul, bringing guilt and pain along with the happiness.

Recently while in the waiting room at his dentist's office, Ray noticed an open magazine on the table. The bold headline jumped at him: ANXIETY AND PANIC ATTACKS!

His hands trembled as he read the article. At last he knew that what Dani was experiencing lately had a name. *Panic attack.* He gripped the pages, his palms moist, his knuckles white. He thought of the times she'd called him in the evenings, just asking him to talk to her—about anything, just talk, needing to hear his voice. And after watching television together one evening last week, she struggled through her worse attack yet. As she reached for her jacket, she started to shake. Her face flushed and damp, she gasped for air. Pressing a hand tightly against her chest as the pain made it harder to breathe, her eyes registered a fear that had scared the hell out of him. He'd held her until she relaxed and her breathing returned to normal.

His gut twisted with the thought that the stress of their relationship caused her panic. It wasn't that she didn't love Brian; she did, and that made it worse. She could never leave him, but they shared little and there was nothing left of their relationship that resembled a marriage anymore.

Ray thought of last evening when he had snuggled with Dani while watching television. Her torment haunted him when she told him how guilty she felt at having so much while Brian had so little. He worked harder than ever, spent little time with Dani, and was pleasant but distant with Trace.

Struggling into her jacket as she left for home, her eyes filled with tears. "I don't think I can do this anymore," she'd said.

After riding Cash and Chance, Ray turned them out in the pasture with Buck. He cleaned tack, generally killing time.

Finally realizing Dani wasn't coming out to the stable, he hefted the saddle to his shoulder and headed for the tack room. Angry voices stopped him at the door. Damned gals having another squabble. The mention of Dani's name caught his attention.

"Dani's got enough problems. She doesn't need any more. Why can't he leave her alone?"

"What in the hell do you know about anything? I sure wouldn't want to have to cope with her life at home. Can't you see how happy she is here with her horses? And what fun she has with Ray. Why don't you mind your own business?"

A third voice entered the fray. "Don't mind her. She's just jealous. She's had the hots for Ray for ages and he ignores her."

"You bitch!" A door slammed and a padlock snapped on a tack box. Stalking from the room, a teary-eyed woman collided with Ray. He stepped back; eyes flashed with surprise then realization. "Uh, hi, Karen," Ray stammered. The blonde bit her lower lip, turned crimson, and ran from the barn.

Ray adjusted the saddle on his shoulder and stared after the distraught woman as she hurried to her car and sped from the lot. Eager to avoid the tack room, he locked his saddle in the back of his truck and left the stable.

Dani dragged the comforter up to her chin, still unable to get warm. Her body wracked with chills, pain seared through to the bone. Snuggling her face into the pillow brought knife-like jabs to her head. Her empty stomach burned from repeated assaults during the night.

Brian had brought her water, tea, juice—nothing stayed down. He left a pitcher of ice chips beside her bed.

"It's just the flu. You need to sleep. You'll feel better in a day or so. Yell if you need anything."

*Yell? If I had the strength to yell* . . . In the shade-darkened room, Dani rolled to her side, her eyes scrunched in irritation.

As her pain and nausea eased, she fell into an exhausted sleep.

For three days she lay in bed, plagued with fever and chills, achy and sore, bordering on delirium. She was vaguely aware of Brian bringing her soup and juice. Trace was spending spring break in Arizona with Ryan and his parents.

On the fourth day, Dani squirmed from beneath a mountain of blankets, suddenly much too warm. Sitting on the edge of the bed, she waited until the dizziness passed. She shuffled to the kitchen. Her stomach lurched at the heavy smell of bacon and eggs.

Brian turned his chair and glanced over his shoulder.

"Welcome back to the land of the living. Want some breakfast?"

Dani shook her head and slid into a chair at the table. "Maybe just some toast."

Brian placed two slices on a plate for her and switched on her favorite radio station.

Dani munched on her toast. Her brain cells kicked in as her body responded to nourishment. "What did he say?" her voice fuzzy with confusion. "What day is it?"

Brian poured her some tea. "It's Friday."

Dani stared at him; eyes squinted in disbelief above the sharpness of her cheekbones. "I've been sick for over three days?"

"Yes, you have. I was beginning to get worried." Brian finished his breakfast. "I was going to call the doctor today if you weren't better."

Dani glared. "You—were—beginning—to—get—worried? When would you really worry, Brian? Before or after rigor mortis set in?"

Brian stared at her as she left the room.

Dani left the mess in the kitchen. Back in her room, she crawled into bed dragging the phone next to her. She dialed Ray's number. After ten rings, she replaced the receiver. Must be at the stable. She pulled the blanket over her head and fell asleep.

The wind whipped torrents of rain against the window. Dani woke to the sound of a tree branch scraping against the side of the house. The clock beside her bed read five-thirty. No longer nauseated, she was ravenously hungry. She kicked the blankets to the floor, tugged on cotton slacks and a sweatshirt. Again the phone went unanswered at Ray's house. Should be back from the barn by now. Maybe he went out for something to eat.

Dani padded to the kitchen, noticing Brian engrossed in a movie in the family room as she passed. She slathered two slices of wheat bread with mayonnaise, piled lettuce and tomato over shaved ham, and poured herself a large glass of milk. The kitchen remained as she'd left it in the morning. Brian had fixed himself lunch and left the mess along with the breakfast dishes unwashed on the counter.

Glad for something to do, and with her renewed energy, Dani washed the dishes and cleaned the kitchen. The rain cascaded against the window pane. Trees bowed and swayed, casting ominous shadows in the murky luminescence of the streetlights.

Dani found Brian still in the family room. She sat in the chair beside him. He switched off the television and hit the remote button to rewind the movie in the VCR. "So, you're up again. Heard you in the kitchen. Feeling better?"

"Much better. I had a sandwich and cleaned up the kitchen. Are you hungry?"

"No, I had a big lunch."

"I don't remember much, but I do remember you bringing me soup and juice. Thank you."

Brian brushed away her thanks with a wave of his hand. "Sure. Glad you're okay."

"Has Trace called?"

"Yes, last night. He's having a good time. I didn't tell him you were sick, didn't want to worry him. I said you were at the store."

Dani nodded. She ran her hand through her hair, knowing she must look awful. Brian removed the tape from the VCR. "I have a few calls to make."

Dani watched him head for his room. She picked up some magazines, straightened pillows and settled with a novel she'd started over a week before. *How can two people be married for nearly twenty years and have almost nothing to say to each other?* What little life left in the house seemed to disappear without Trace around.

After realizing she'd been reading the same page over and over, Dani tossed the book aside. She watched television a while and finally went to bed still unable to reach Ray. *He's probably mad at me for not calling and he's not answering the phone.*

Dani woke just before six the next morning. Unable to stay in bed another minute, she jumped into a steaming shower, lathering up twice with her favorite shower gel. She washed her hair with a mountain of suds and stood in the soothing hot spray until she felt renewed and energized.

After feeling so miserable, the simplest routines felt delicious. She closed her eyes and savored the warmth of the hair dryer against her neck. She brushed her hair until it shimmered, applied make-up and a touch of perfume.

Dani stopped in the family room on her way to the kitchen. "Good morning. Do you want some breakfast?" Brian rummaged through the paper with the *Today* show babbling on the television in the background.

He glanced up from the page. "No, I'm not really too hungry. I'll have some cereal later. You can put the coffee on for me though." He smiled at her. "You look better today."

"Thanks. I feel much better."

Dani plugged in the coffeepot. She poured orange juice for herself, scrambled an egg with fresh mushrooms and cheddar cheese, and made wheat toast. The best thing about having the flu is when it's over it's so absolutely wonderful just to feel normal again.

She piled her dishes in the dishwasher. The clock chimed nine o'clock as she grabbed her jacket. She paused on the way to the garage to call Ray's house. A recorded message told her the number had been disconnected. *I must have dialed wrong. I'll just surprise him at the barn.*

Parked in front of the barn when she arrived was a shiny black Dodge Ram truck attached to a matching three-horse-slant trailer.

Bud Morgan stood beside the trailer as a tall, thin man dressed all in black—and looking as if he'd been plucked from Central Casting for a western movie—struggled to load the fractious buckskin.

Dani raced toward Bud. "What's going on here? Where's he taking Buck? Where's Ray?"

"Dammit, Dani, not now. Go on up to the house and I'll be up in a minute."

"Just tell me . . ."

Buck nipped at The Cowboy and kicked out, just missing Bud.

"I said not now." Bud's tone was brusque.

Dani stalked to the house. Bud's golden retriever greeted her as she pushed the door open. Dani watched through the window as the men secured the buckskin in the trailer. Buck stomped his foot and snapped at the man tying his lead rope in place.

The men exchanged a few words, shook hands, and the Marlboro Man pulled his rig from the lot. Squaring his shoulders, Bud raked a hand through his hair, and strode toward the house.

Bud nudged the door closed with his boot and headed straight to the coffeepot spewing Colombian-scented steam above the counter. He held a cup out for Dani.

"Want some coffee?"

Dani shook her head. Sitting with her arms folded over her chest, legs crossed, foot tapping in the air, she looked ready to explode.

He placed his cup on the table, reached in a drawer beside the stove and pulled out an envelope. He slid into the chair next to her. Bud squinted his eyes and sighed.

"Now, Dani." His words were firm and accentuated by his raised hand. "I don't want you yelling at me. Just listen until I finish." He took a deep drink of black coffee.

"First of all, honey, I don't know what 'n the hell is going on . . . he wouldn't tell me." Bud tapped the envelope on the table as he spoke. "He gave me this letter to give to you when you came out. Said he didn't want to hurt you, but things couldn't go on the way they were. He paid full board on the bay for six months—said you could decide if you wanted to keep him. He sold the buckskin to a guy who's wanted him for years." He rubbed a hand against his forehead. "And . . . and . . . dammit. This is the hardest part. He said he's going away—wouldn't tell me where—just that it was best for you." He pushed the envelope toward her.

Her trembling hand curled around the pale-blue square.

Bud poured himself another cup of coffee. Dani ran a finger along the edge of the envelope. She felt a chill trickle between her shoulder blades.

Her voice was raspy as she managed to ask, "That's all you

know? You have no idea where he went or how long he'll be gone?"

Bud sipped at his coffee. He shook his head. "No, I'm sorry, I don't."

Dani slid her feet on the floor, pushed back her chair and stood up. She picked up the envelope as if the edges were razors. Shoulders slumped, she paused at the door. "Bud, promise me something?"

He followed her to the door, slipping his arm around her waist. "What's that?"

"Promise me you'll let me know if you find out where he is? Or that you'll ask him to call me, please?"

"I promise you I'll do both."

Her newfound energy trickled away like water down a drain; Dani decided against riding. She brushed both horses, gently gliding the soft-bristled brush over rippling horseflesh and replaying Bud's words. She stroked Chance and leaned her head against his neck. Sensing her mood, the sorrel rubbed his muzzle against her arm.

She shuddered as she passed Buck's empty stall on the way to her car. Dani stood at the car door, staring at the envelope she had tucked into the visor. She started the engine, pulling from the lot without her usual flare.

Standing at the kitchen window, Bud reached down to pet the retriever at his side. "Max, that's the first time I've ever seen her leave my lot without seriously rearranging the gravel."

At the forest preserve where she and Ray had spent so much time, Dani parked the car. Winter wasn't giving in to spring easily this year. Angry gray clouds slid above the bare tree branches. Her fingers played around the edges of the envelope as she stared through the window, not really seeing the landscape before her. Minutes ticked by; her toes and fingers tingled in the cold. With a sigh of resignation, she tore open the envelope and gazed at Ray's shaky handwriting.

My Darling Dani,

This isn't easy for me to say—maybe the hardest thing I've ever had to do. When you told me you couldn't do this anymore, I hoped you'd change your mind. This last week I waited, hoping you'd call. I tried to call you a couple of times but got no answer. I love you so much—more than words can say but I know this is causing you a lot of pain and I can't continue knowing that I'm hurting you. Maybe with me out of the picture you can sort things out. I hope so. I only want what's best for you.

You'll always be the best part of my life and I'll treasure the memories of you.

Be well, be happy.

Love always, Ray

P.S. I paid full board on Cash for six months. You can decide what you want to do with him. Both our names are on the registration but only one signature is needed for a sale. Whatever you decide. . . .

His last words grew fuzzy in the pool of giant tears dripping onto the page. Dani reread the letter and stared into the woods, trying to imagine her life without Ray. The dreary, sunless day matched her mood.

*He'll be back. He can't walk out on what we have. Just can't. Has to come back.*

# CHAPTER EIGHTEEN

Dani flipped the page on the calendar beside the kitchen sink. It had been two months since Ray had left. No word. No call. Nothing. She'd run out of tears; her heart no longer jumped whenever the phone rang. Moving robot-like through her life, she buried all thoughts and memories of Ray. After a time the hurt sank deep enough for it to be manageable. *Almost.*

Other than saying he was sorry she was unhappy, Brian made no further comments when Dani told him Ray had left town. He did seem to be making an effort to spend more time with her, watched television, listened to music. He initiated conversations with Trace about his job and colleges; and Trace, wary at first, responded to the attention from his father. Other than grumbling when he was told to turn down the volume on his music, clean his room, or some arguments about curfew, there had been no major troubles with Trace.

Brian asked Dani about the horses and if she planned to keep Cash. She knew he still harbored fears of the young bay horse and would have been relieved had she chosen to sell him.

Though it was a job to exercise both horses regularly on her own, Dani decided to keep Cash. She'd grown fond of him, and she couldn't cope with another loss.

By riding early she had the arena to herself. Cleaning tack, polishing saddles, and grooming the horses filled in some crevices of time. Between workout sessions, she ventured out in the forest preserves with Chance. The trails offered her a peace she was reluctant to share with anyone other than Ray, so she declined all invitations to join the others. Bud Morgan tried to discourage her from riding alone, but the only concession she'd made was not taking Cash on trails.

Allowing herself little time for idle thoughts, Dani searched for projects at home to keep her occupied. She cleaned, polished, organized; cleaned, polished and reorganized as she got ready for Trace's graduation party. Martha Stewart would be proud, Dani thought, gazing over her neat, sterile, lemon-scented home.

Trace rushed in each day after school to check the mail, eagerly awaiting responses from the colleges he'd applied to. His SATs were good, he had a three-point-eight GPA, and had sent in three applications. He was accepted at U of I in Champaign, which was his second choice. He seemed ready to burst at the seams waiting for news.

Dani shuffled through the mail, found the envelope he had been waiting for and rushed into Brian's office. She waved the envelope over his keyboard.

His eyes lit up. "What does it say?"

"I can't open his mail. We'll have to wait until he gets home."

She held it to the light, couldn't read a word. *Please let it be the answer he wants to hear.* She glanced at the clock all afternoon, shivering when she heard the car door slam.

Brian wheeled toward the kitchen as the front door opened and Trace yelled something as Ryan pulled away.

Dani picked up the envelope and held it out to Trace as he entered the kitchen. He made a gulping sound, dropped his backpack and reached for the envelope.

"What does it say?"

"It's your mail. I wouldn't open it. We can find out together." She laughed. "Hurry up, we've been on pins and needles all afternoon."

Trace's hand shook slightly as he ripped open the envelope from Notre Dame. He scanned the page, a grin spread across his face and he let out a war whoop probably heard down the block.

Dani read the acceptance he thrust at her, handed it to Brian, and hugged her son.

"I'm so happy for you, honey."

Brian reached out to shake his son's hand. "Congratulations, son. I'm proud of you."

Trace beamed. "Damn, I thought it would never get here." He tossed the letter on the kitchen table. "Have to go call Ryan," he said, and rushed off to his room.

The getting-ready-for-college project soon replaced the graduation-party project. Dani read advice articles on how to survive your teen's first year at college, surviving the empty-nest syndrome. She made lists, shopped—and shopped even more. She tried to match Trace's enthusiasm and exuberance about attending Notre Dame. Did her best not to think past the immediate tasks, trying not to think of *the day* when he would actually leave for school. With a flurry of preparations to consume her thoughts, summer slipped through her grasp.

"Mom, stop shopping. I can't think of one more thing I need." Trace wedged towels into the empty spaces of a large cardboard box, tucked in the flaps, and slid it near the door. With a groan, he flopped on the bed as Dani added another carefully folded shirt to the stack on the dresser.

"Where am I going to put all this stuff?" Trace waved a hand in the air. "My room at school is the size of a closet—and I have to share it, besides."

Glancing around the room, Dani sighed and slid into the chair beside Trace's bed. "I suppose you're right. Maybe we'd better weed out some of these clothes. After all, it's not like you're so far away that . . ." She closed her eyes and rested her head against the back of the chair. When she stopped in mid-sentence, Trace glanced toward his mother. "Something wrong, Mom?"

A look of sadness flickered through her eyes as Dani rubbed her arm over her forehead and looked at her son.

"No, why?"

"You don't seem . . . happy," Trace stammered. "You don't talk about the horses as much or mention anyone at the ranch, even Ray. And you haven't gone to a horse show in months."

"Trace, Ray moved away." Dani cleared her throat. "I still enjoy the horses. It's just . . . just not as much fun alone."

"Gee, Mom, I'm sorry." Trace sat up on the bed. "Where did he go?"

"I don't really know." She avoided his eyes and shrugged. "It doesn't matter."

"What about the horse . . . Cash?"

"He said I could decide . . . if I want him, he's mine."

With a puzzled frown, Trace watched his mother. "Mom, are you going to be okay when . . . when I go to school?"

Dani shrugged and fought to sound cheerful. "I'll miss you, but I'll be okay."

Shifting to his side, Trace propped his head against a pillow. He waved a hand in the air and frowned.

"It's just . . . Dad's been a lot better at home lately. And I love him, but . . . but he doesn't get out a lot." An uncomfortable scowl stretched across his face. "You know, get involved . . ."

"We're working on it. Everything will be okay and I'll be fine," Dani repeated with a smile, hoping the smile reached her eyes.

"I'm excited for you to be going away to school, and happy you got the scholarship. I want you to get a good education and have fun too." She reached over to squeeze his hand. "South Bend isn't that far away, you know. It's close enough you can come home when you want to and I'll e-mail you to make sure you're on the straight and narrow." She rolled her eyes to make him laugh.

Trace groaned. "I'm sure you will." He suddenly grinned at her. "Just think of how much less laundry you'll have. And less groceries to buy."

"And less loud music . . . and the phone won't be ringing all the time . . ." Dani teased along with him.

"See, you're getting it. You won't miss me at all."

Dani brushed away a tear and attempted a grin. *My grown-up son—I'm so proud of the nice person you've become. You have no idea how much I'm going to miss you.*

# CHAPTER NINETEEN

Traffic swooshed by as Dani sat beside the road listening to the only radio station ever playing in her car: Chicago's WGN. It was the annual "going back to school" cry-a-thon. *I knew this was planned for today. Why am I in the car?* Giant tears puddled up and ran down Dani's face as Suzy Bogguss sang about a daughter going off to college in "Letting Go":

> Seems like all I do lately is let go. My mother.
> Ray. Now Trace.

As the song ended, the station took a call from a distraught mother who had just taken her only daughter to college. "I feel so stupid," the caller sputtered through her sobs. "I'm sitting in the parking lot at the grocery store bawling over this song." Dani grabbed a fistful of Kleenex and wondered how many other mothers were sitting in their cars—or at home—crying and coping with empty-nest syndrome. A band of tightness wrapped around her chest. Any movement she feared would tear apart whatever held a heart in place. The picture of a beating heart flopping out of control against other terrified organs brought a fit of teary laughter rumbling through her throat. *Get a grip!* She dried her face, put the car in gear and headed for home, feeling connected to the moms who laughed and cried together on the radio.

★ ★ ★ ★ ★

In an effort to keep busy, Dani tore into redecorating her house. A nagging voice asked what she was going to do when she ran out of projects. Life had become a treadmill. She ran to avoid confronting her feelings. Turn up the speed; outrun the pain.

She repainted several rooms, and to her surprise, Brian liked the changes and helped pick out new wallpaper for the kitchen.

Wiping away a smudge of paste from the last piece of border paper, Dani stood back to survey the finished product.

Brian watched from his chair in the doorway. "Looks very nice. You did a good job."

Dani nodded at his admiring look. "Thanks. It was fun." She dried her hands on a towel. "I'd better get things cleaned up here."

"You're probably too tired to cook. Why don't we go out for something?"

Her surprise must have shown on her face because Brian laughed. Dani smiled slightly. "It's nice to hear you laugh even if you're laughing at me."

"I'm not laughing at you—it's just your expression was so funny."

"You've surprised me lately. Last week suggesting we see a movie, now wanting to go out for dinner." She brushed a hand on his shoulder. "It's nice, that's all."

Brian cleared his throat. "Good. Then let's go out."

"Okay. Give me about a half an hour to put away this stuff and get cleaned up."

As Brian studied his menu, Dani gazed around the nearly empty restaurant. A young couple huddled in a darkened booth along the wall, oblivious to their surroundings. Two tables away, a middle-aged man and woman attempted civility with their clipped-sentence conversation, but their rigid body language exposed the facade.

Dani's eyes lingered on a chubby dark-haired toddler at the next table as he thrust his just-colored picture into his mother's lap.

"Seems like only yesterday . . ." Brian's words trailed off. He reached for Dani's hand resting beside her water glass.

Her voice husky with nostalgia, Dani replied, "Sure does." She hesitated briefly before pulling her hand from beneath Brian's to reach for the water glass.

Sounding a bit Bogart-ish, Brian said, "I guess it's just you and me, kid."

Dani sighed through a small chuckle. "I suppose it is."

"Is that so bad, Dani?" He searched her face. "We can make it, can't we?"

Unable to put words to feelings still too jumbled to sort out, Dani merely nodded.

Brian hesitated, his eyes holding her attention. He traced a finger around the edge of his coffee cup. "This has been a rough couple of years . . ." He cleared his throat and continued. "I know how much you miss your Mom—so do I." Looking down at the table, his voice was barely audible. "And . . . and I know you miss . . . miss Ray, too." He raked his hand through his hair. "And I haven't been much help." He looked up and smiled at her. "I'll try to do better."

"Me too," Dani whispered.

Dani pondered the workings of fate. For so long she had hoped her relationship with Brian would improve, that despite the tragedy that had altered their lives, they would find a way to overcome it and grow closer. After feeling so alone for such a long time, she now found Brian's renewed attention bittersweet.

Dani Johnston had been nineteen when she'd met Brian Monroe at a picnic given by the owners of the animal clinic where she worked. Working full-time and attending classes at night at the community college left her little free time.

After an extremely busy week at the clinic, and with a mountain of studying to do, she almost decided against going. She relented at the last minute, planning to go for a short time, relax a bit, and then get down to studying.

Brian, the best friend of the youngest vet at the clinic and five years older than Dani, had sandy blond hair, laughing blue eyes and a confident-older-man air about him that appealed to Dani.

They talked about music, books, and animals; people they knew in common, favorite movies. To their amazement they found themselves spending more time talking to each other than to anyone else at the picnic, and when the party broke up, were reluctant to end the day.

Brian suggested a ride in the country to a little bar and grill where a friend was playing in a band. A full moon glowed in a clear, starry night as Dani and Brian cruised along in his new pride and joy, a flashy red Mustang convertible. It was the kind of night songs declared were just right for falling in love, and by the end of the evening, Dani and Brian were well on their way.

Studying forgotten, Dani and Brian spent the next day cruising the countryside, stopping for fresh vegetables at a roadside stand, walking trails in the forest preserves, and going to a movie in the evening.

Brian called Dani every day, and when he picked her up for their date the following Friday, he made the same favorable impression on Dani's mother, who had expressed eagerness at meeting the young man who had put such a sparkle in her daughter's eyes.

The couple was inseparable all summer. Brian spent many hours at Dani's house, helping her mother with little repair jobs that never seemed to get done. Even Dani's sister Lynn, a rebellious sixteen-year-old, seemed star-struck by the presence of the good-looking man in their all-female abode. Brian spoke to Lynn as if she were a grown-up instead of a giggly, unsure-of-herself teenager, and she beamed whenever he was around.

There was no surprise, or opposition, when Brian proposed six months later, and Dani accepted. Marie Johnston's only request was that her daughter should continue with her education.

Shortly after her twentieth birthday, surrounded by her mother, her sister as her maid of honor, Brian's mother and their close friends, Dani married Brian Monroe in the small church she had attended all her life. Brian smiled lovingly at his radiant young bride as they said their vows, received congratulations from guests at the reception in the church hall following the ceremony, and Mr. & Mrs. Brian Monroe left on their honeymoon to begin life happily ever after.

Dani blossomed in her new role as wife and homemaker. She cut back on her classes and when, shortly after their second anniversary, she discovered she was pregnant, quit school altogether, much to her mother's dismay. Brian had a good job with an advertising company and they decided they wanted Dani to stay at home with their baby. When Brian's father and older brother had died in a boating accident when Brian was ten, his mother had gone back to work full-time. After Dani's father left them, she also knew what it was like to not have a full-time mother at home. Brian and Dani both wanted the fairy-tale yearnings of their childhoods: the picket-fenced yard around a happy little house where Daddy went to work and Mom stayed home, cared for the children, and baked cookies.

Shortly before Dani's twenty-third birthday Trace Andrew Monroe weighed in at seven pounds, two ounces, with wispy blond hair, and eyes that would turn an amazing hazel as he got older. Happily ever after was well on its way.

The small house with a picket fence turned out to be a brick-

and-cedar split level in a pleasant middle-class neighborhood. Brian's career advanced rapidly, tarnished only by increased required client lunches and dinners and golf games that took him away from his family more than he liked. And a little more drinking at those lunches, dinners and golf outings than Dani liked.

With the death of Brian's mother from a sudden heart attack, followed six months later by the auto accident that caused Dani's miscarriage and left Brian confined to a wheelchair, the fairy tale began to unravel.

". . . Penny for your thoughts." Brian reached out his hand to Dani.

"Oh, sorry. Just daydreaming, I suppose. What were you saying?"

"Just that things will get better. Let's work at it."

Determined to do just that, and hoping it wasn't too late, Dani gave his hand a squeeze and him the best smile she could manage.

The family room was cheery with carols playing softly in the background. Brightly colored wrapping paper lay strewn around the Christmas tree. Brian and Dani sipped eggnog while Trace filled them in on his new friends, classes and activities at school. A special sound crept into his voice when he mentioned a girl named Megan.

The holidays were the best they'd had in years, and the winter break ended too quickly for Dani. But this time Trace's leaving was a little easier. She concentrated on having things to look forward to—spring vacation and Trace being home for the summer. The heaviness in her heart lightened; her days became easier to manage. Brian shortened his hours and they worked harder finding things they could do together. They'd invited some friends over during the holidays, renewing relationships that had faltered in the past few years. They went to the movies, sometimes just the two of them, sometimes with friends, and even attended a high school play starring a neighbor's daughter.

Arriving home after the play, they found a message from Trace on the machine. "Hey, where are you guys? It's ten o'clock on a weeknight. Hope everything is okay. Call you tomorrow."

Dani laughed. "We've come full circle, I guess. Now we're out and he's worried about us."

"Guess we've all grown up, huh?" Brian said with a contented sound in his voice.

"Guess so. Want some hot chocolate before we go to sleep?"

"Sounds good. It was a nice play. I'm not ready to fall asleep yet."


Shouts and thundering applause from the television echoed over the crackling logs in the fireplace. Dani clapped as Coach Jackson hugged a grinning Michael Jordan. Cheering as the Bulls won another game, Brian said, "I think I'm getting to be a real Bulls fan."

Dani laughed. "With Michael playing, that's an easy thing to be."

Sporadic at first, Brian watched the ball games with increasing interest. Dani appreciated his company and struggled against memories of enjoying the games with Ray.

Sometimes, like a knife slash, she would recall Ray's words that had made her laugh, his tenderness and his touch that still lingered no matter how hard she tried to forget. As she fell asleep each night there was an emptiness in her heart like a chronic pain with which she'd learned to live.


Brian paged through the newspaper and glanced up to watch Dani dusting the coffee table. "Dani, do you mind if I go to the

Web conference in Texas next month?"

Holding a figurine in midair, Dani stared at him. "Of course not. I'm surprised. You haven't gone in years. It would be good for you to get out."

With a thoughtful look, Dani replaced the figure on the table. "Maybe I could go along too? We haven't been anywhere in a long time."

"I think that's a great idea." Brian smiled at her. "It will be a short trip. I won't have much time for sightseeing, but it would be nice to get away together."

"Great, it's settled then." She tossed the dust cloth on the table as they made plans for the trip.

# CHAPTER TWENTY

Dani peeked at her watch as the vet hurried into the barn.

"Sorry I'm late, Dani. Had a mare colic this morning."

"Is she okay?"

"Better, should be fine. Now, let's take a look at this guy."

Dani watched as Dr. Chris McCann examined Cash's left rear foot.

"He's looking good." The vet ran a hand along the bay's muscular rump. "Keep working him on the lunge line a few more days. You can start riding him next week."

"Thanks a lot, Chris." Dani rubbed Cash's muzzle and followed the vet out to his truck. "As long as you're here, do you want to schedule their spring shots?"

The vet paged through his appointment book. "Looks like I have several others here at the barn scheduled for six weeks from today. How about doing Cash and Chance then too?"

"Okay, that's fine. See you then."

A few days before their scheduled trip to Texas, Dani had received a call from Bud. Cash had gotten into a skirmish with a new horse in the pasture. In the course of the encounter, the horses broke through a section of fencing. Cash tore up his left rear foot as he struggled to fend off the rowdy newcomer and free himself from the tangle of wire.

"Dani, you know you wouldn't have a good time being away with an injured horse at home," Brian had said. "Besides this is a short trip and we wouldn't have much time to sightsee. Greg's been planning to visit his sister in Dallas anyway. He's agreed to go along and help me get around and see her too."

Disappointed, Dani agreed. Brian then suggested, "Why don't we go away for a few days when I get back. You think of someplace while I'm gone."

Again Dani glanced at her watch; she would barely have time to stop at the produce market on the way home. She scribbled a reminder about the vet appointment, tucked the note in her purse, and made mental notes for dinner as she pulled from the parking lot. Trace was coming home for spring break, and Brian would be back from Texas in a few hours. Eager to see Trace, and finding that she had actually missed Brian, Dani smiled to herself with a little sense of optimism about their future beginning to take hold.

Dani arrived home to find Trace's blue Camaro parked on the driveway. She pulled into the garage, collected her groceries, and hurried into the house.

Hearing the television, she dumped the bag on the kitchen table. "Trace, you're home early," she called as she headed for the family room.

Trace stood riveted before the television set, his face streaked with tears, white-knuckled fists clenched at his sides. When Dani entered the room, he rushed to her with outstretched arms. "Mom . . ."

A bowling-ball-sized lump plunged to the pit of her stomach as she held her son. "What's wrong?"

Trace pointed to the screen. Smoking wreckage lay strewn over a grassy field. Dani heard the words ". . . there appear to be no survivors in the crash of Flight #1109 shortly after take-off from Dallas International Airport."

"Mom, it was . . . Dad's flight." Trace's whisper was jagged with anguish. "I saw his itinerary sheet on the counter." He rubbed his hand across his face. "And . . . and he left a message . . ."

Trace turned to the answering machine on the table and punched the button beneath the red light.

Brian's voice sounded rushed. "Hi. Just wanted to let you know I'm at the airport, flight's on schedule. Looking forward to getting home. Love you and Trace. See you soon—bye."

Dead weight sagged against muscles no longer able to hold her upright. ". . . there are no survivors . . . are no survivors . . . no . . ." She swayed slightly, reached for . . . something . . . someone. Longed for the strength of Ray's presence and felt a stab of guilt that she should think of Ray now.

Trace held her, his tears hot against her icy skin. With a protective arm around her shoulder, he led her to the sofa. They sat holding hands and listening to the repeating news coverage.

Seized by a wave of vertigo, Dani scrunched her eyes closed and struggled to understand. Her brain searched the darkness for a place to hide. Trace tightened his grip on her hand. Dani heard his strangled sob through the throbbing behind her eyes and reached out to comfort him. She sucked in a deep breath, fighting against the dizziness that tried to engulf her.


Strains of "The Old Rugged Cross" floated through the small church filled for Brian's memorial service. Dani held Trace's hand in hers and stared at the flickering candle beside the framed photograph and plain gold urn. The overpowering sweet fragrance of the floral bouquets sent a queasy shiver through her stomach.

She struggled to concentrate on the minister's words as they faded in and out with slow-motion memories of her life with Brian.

In her mind's eye, she danced with Brian at their wedding. . . .

The minister said something about Brian's car accident.

She saw Brian proudly holding Trace as a baby. . . .

". . . fine man. Good husband and father . . ."

Brian lobbed a ball to Trace in the yard. . . .

The minister spoke of "strength and God's plan."

Brian beamed at Trace in his cap and gown at graduation. . . .

". . . the tragedies of our lives . . ."

Brian holding her hand as they waved good-bye to Trace as they left him at Notre Dame. . . .

". . . God's mercy . . ."

Brian's voice on the answering machine: "Love you and Trace. See you soon. Bye."

"Let us bow our heads in prayer," intoned the minister.

Dani obeyed.

"Our Father . . ." she whispered.

Trace's ashen face—there are no survivors, no survivors. . . .

". . . peace be with you . . ."

Through a distant haze, Dani's anesthetized inner being floated above her physical self. She moved in slow-motion numbness; felt hugs, hands clasping hers, words bouncing around in a fog. She heard her voice respond without recalling its words.

After the final mourners had left and a few last words with the minister, Dani's sister Lynn led Dani and Trace to the car.

*Everything seems . . . what? My brain feels fuzzy. Finally I can go . . . home. Home.* The word sounded strange to her now. Brian was . . . Brian was gone. Trace would be going back to school. People make a home. Am I enough people to make a home? Strange thought. Strange day. *I feel strange.*

Dani stared out the window, listlessly scribbling circles on a notepad.

Lynn reached out and touched her sister's hand. "Dani, we're about finished here, I think. I can put the stamps on these and drop them in the mail for you."

With a weary sigh, Dani looked over the table, scattered with thank-you notes and the memorial book from the funeral home. She gathered the stationery, pen, notepad, and tucked them into a drawer in her desk.

"Thanks for helping me, Lynn. I really appreciate it."

"Do you want to open these cards?"

An unopened stack of sympathy cards rested on the corner of the table.

"Oh, I don't think I'm up to that right now. I'll do it tomorrow."

Lynn tucked mountains of food into the refrigerator. "You sure have a lot of good friends, Dani. Everyone has been so nice."

Dani nodded.

"Well, I suppose I'd better get going. I'd like to get home before dark." Lynn hugged Dani and hesitated with her hand on the doorknob. "Are you going to be okay?"

Mustering up what she hoped was a convincing smile, Dani gave Lynn's hand a squeeze. "Yes, I'll be fine. Drive carefully and call me when you get home."

Lynn brushed a quick kiss on Dani's cheek. "Will do. Take care." And she hurried out the door.

*What do people expect me to do with all this food? There're only two of us here. I suppose I could . . . could . . .* The connections in Dani's brain seemed to short circuit. *Should have sent some of it home with Lynn.*

Dani shook her head and shuffled down the hall to her room. She kicked off her shoes, wiggling her toes in relief. She slipped out of her black skirt and jacket, leaving them crumpled on her bed.

Wrapped in a thick terry robe, she sagged onto the family room sofa, glad to finally be alone. She stretched her neck from side to side to relieve the stiffness and pain nagging at the base of her skull.

The house seemed wrapped in cotton. No sound came from Trace's room. The pendulum hung motionless behind the glass of the grandfather clock Dani had forgotten to wind. Her lungs pushed out a weary sigh that seemed to echo in the stillness.

Late afternoon shadows snaked across the room when Trace joined his mother. He flopped on the sofa and stretched his feet on the coffee table.

"Mom . . . I don't know what to do next."

She and Trace had rarely been alone since the accident.

"I know what you mean." She sighed. "After everyone is gone, it's so quiet . . ."

"I keep thinking," Trace hesitated.

Dani turned toward him. "Thinking what?"

He shook his head. "About how weird things are sometimes. I mean . . . you were planning to go with Dad. If . . . you would've . . ." His voice trailed off. He rubbed his arm across his face.

Reaching for his hand, Dani said, "It's hard to know how fate works."

His voice was shaky. "I'm glad you're okay, Mom," and he squeezed her hand. "Maybe . . . maybe I will stay here." He took a breath. "Not go back to school until next year."

"No, I don't think that's a good idea."

"But . . ."

In the twilight, Dani snaked her fingers through her son's and gave his hand a squeeze. "You only have a few more months. You can't throw away a whole year."

"I don't want to leave you alone and I'll only lose a semester."

"Trace, I'll be okay." Eyes deep with sadness flickered above a forced smile. "You have finals coming up, and it'll be good for you to be busy."

He nodded with a heavy sigh. They sat together, sharing the silence.

# CHAPTER TWENTY-ONE

With lethargic footsteps, Dani shuffled through the house. She paused at Trace's room—thoughtfully cleaned for her before he left—punctuated by the bare spots that once held his computer and CD player. Her bones ached with the oppressive emptiness of the house. Spurts of shallow, labored breaths pushed through the tightness in her chest.

Eager for a connection to a familiar voice, Dani turned on the radio. The teasing and laughter of the talk-show personalities filled the room. Feeling a survivor's guilt for whatever twist of fate that had spared her life and kept her son from losing both his parents at once, Dani hit the off switch. She gripped her hands against the edge of the countertop. Through the window over the kitchen sink she watched two small boys walking past the house, laughing, bouncing a basketball. In the yard next door a golden retriever barked at the boys, his tail wagging an invitation to play. The driver of a passing car honked at a young woman pushing a baby carriage. *Everything out there looks so . . . so normal.*

Dani shivered and went to check the thermostat. *Says seventy degrees—guess it's me.* She rubbed a hand against the back of her neck and shivered again. *Dammit, it feels cold in here to me.* She trudged to the bathroom and turned on the shower. Closed the door; locked it. Stared at herself in the mirror. *Great. Locking the bathroom door when you're all alone in the house.* She peeled off her clothes and left them in a heap on the floor.

The room filled with swirling steam. Dani tilted her head back and stood in the flow of hot water. The cascading drops pulsed against her skin like relentless needles.

*I'm so alone. The world seems too big, but I feel claustrophobic at the same time.* Dani frowned at the dichotomy of her thoughts and tried to sort it out. She closed her eyes, inhaled the steam; finally felt warmer.

An image flickered in her mind. Yes, that's it—claustrophobic, like being in a space ship, but adrift, alone, like in space.

Leaning against the back wall with a muffled cry, her tears mingled with the shower spray. Her knees sagged. She slid down the wall until she sat on the floor.

She rocked from side to side. *I'm so sorry, Brian . . . sorry you're gone . . . and about how hard your life was.* Dani clasped her arms around her legs and rested her head on her knees. *Now I feel warm.*

*I wonder—would we have become closer? Things were better. Still, there was Ray between us. Ray, I miss you so much. Will I ever stop missing you?* Dani strangled a sob. *I'm sorry, Brian. I'll miss you too.*

Eventually the water began to cool. Dani pulled herself upright, turned off the shower, and grabbed for a towel. Her ghostlike reflection rippled in the droplets sliding down the foggy mirror. Dani dried in a hurry, rubbed a towel over her hair, and pulled on a pair of flannel pajamas.

She crawled into bed. Lying in the darkness, Dani concentrated on deep, calming breaths, and fell asleep.

The covered dishes in Dani's refrigerator loomed before her like a mountain to be climbed. *Too much trouble to heat this up.* She closed the door; darkness closed over towers of Tupperware. She settled for peanut butter and jelly on crackers. What she ate, or if she ate, made little difference.

Unplugging all the phones except the one connected to the answering machine, Dani set it to pick up on the first ring. The days dragged by. She answered only calls from Trace and tried to ignore phone messages.

When Dani heard Bud's voice for the third time that day, she relented and intercepted the machine.

"Hi, Bud."

"I've been worried about you, Dani." Bud's voice was stern.

"Sorry. I should have called you back."

"How are you?" His tone softened.

"I've . . . had a lot to do." She glanced at the calendar with a frown as she tried to decide what day it was. "I'll send you a check for board tomorrow. And has Randy been out to shoe?"

"He was here yesterday. Chance was fine, but he trimmed and reset Cash's shoes." He paused. "Should I continue turning the horses out to pasture until you come out?"

"Would you, please? I'm not sure when I'll be there. I'll send you extra for that when I send my board check, and I'll send Randy a check today. Okay?"

"Okay, and Dani—take care and call me if you need anything."

The weeks slipped by without Dani caring. She returned phone calls to several friends when she knew they'd be out and left messages that she was fine, not to worry, she'd call when she felt like company.

Dani struggled to find a purpose, energy to do something— anything. "Maybe I should go out to the barn," she suggested to the empty room. Her voice sounded raspy and strange in the empty house. With thoughts of the horses came memories of Ray. Memories of Ray flooded her with guilt about Brian. She clutched her head in both hands. *Think of something else. Think of Trace.*

"I think I'll call Trace tonight."

The cavernous house had no reply.

Dani hesitated at the door to Brian's room. Her hand closed around the knob, slowly turned it, and pushed at the door. The room seemed cold. A dusty film had settled over his desk and the darkened computer screen. She ran her fingertips over the yellow legal pad and pens arranged neatly at the corner of his desk and shuddered. *Love you and Trace. See you soon, Bye. See you soon . . .* Brian's last words to them, saved on tape, wrapped in tissue and tucked away in her drawer—next to the letter from Ray. Too many good-byes.

Days, nights, weeks stretched endlessly without relief.

When she slept, her dreams were dark and confusing: Torrents of rain punctuated with vicious stabs of lightning and angry cracks of thunder whipped through onyx skies. Brian stumbled through dense woods, slipping in muck along an eroding creek bank. With torn, mud-spattered clothing and blood-streaked face, he struggled through the brush, chased by snarling animals and Ray in a wheelchair. The figures changed places. Their faces floated from one to the other. Dani reached out to help them. Brittle laughter pushed her away. Fiery horses ran in all directions with riders slipping and falling into turbulent waters. A spectral image of her mother floated above it all, shaking her head in dismay.

Night after night Dani awoke, drenched in the cold, clammy sweat of her nightmares. The desolate loneliness of her days and the terror of her nights fought for her soul.

The cold, congealing tomato soup sat untouched in a bowl at the edge of the table. Dani held the phone, listened, and doodled on a notepad in front of her.

"Um . . . uh-huh. Yes, I'll come in next week. Thanks for calling."

*Dammit! I hate lawyers; can't they leave a person in peace for a while? I just went through all this when Mom died. Ugh!*

Lawyers, insurance people, Brian's clients . . . the phone rang almost constantly lately. When she failed to return calls to clients, two of them came to the house. Dani tried not answering the door, but they were persistent. She did her best to be pleasant, referred them to the company for which Brian had worked before starting his own business. She'd also given records to the attorney for handling regarding contracts and money due. *My head is spinning with all these details to attend to. It's just too much to sort out. I'm so tired. . . .*

Dani reached for the stack of cards that had been collecting dust on the kitchen counter. She shuffled through them, opened the envelopes, tossed them in the garbage, and placed the cards in a pile before her. One by one, she quickly flipped through the expressions of sympathy from friends, neighbors, and business acquaintances. With a small gasp of surprise, she read a note handwritten next to the printed words of condolences. . . .

Mrs. Monroe,

We were so sorry to hear of your husband's death. Your family has been in our thoughts and prayers over the years . . . and we are saddened by your tragic loss. We will continue to remember you and your son in our prayers.

Bonnie & Roger Paterson

(Kyle's parents)

Dani read the card a second time, long-ago memories edging into her present pain, before placing it with the others. Nice people. They had seemed like nice people back then too, hurt and troubled by their son's behavior. And devastated by the accident he had caused to Brian and Dani. Thoughtful of them to write.

The jangling telephone broke into her thoughts. Dani reluctantly reached for the phone, then smiled when her caller ID revealed it was Trace.

"Hi, how are you? I was going to call you tonight."

"Doing okay, I guess. Have so much studying to do."

"Good. Keeping busy, that's best."

"Haven't talked to you in a few days. Are you okay?"

"Have a lot to do, things to settle. I'd rather be studying for your tests."

Trace chuckled. "I'll be glad when they are all over and I can come home for the summer."

"I'll be glad to have you here too."

Dani heard Trace call a greeting to someone on his end.

"Well, Mom, I have to go. Just wanted to talk for a few minutes."

"Sure. Do well on your exams. See you soon."

"Bye, Mom."

Dani broke the connection, but clutched the receiver to her chest for a moment before putting it back on the cradle.

*He sounds okay. Good for him to be at school. Miss him; wish he were here. Soon. He'll be home soon.* Dani groaned. *And he'll see me like this. This mess of a person; unable to cope. Tomorrow. Tomorrow I'll get myself together, get out, and see the horses. Do something. Yes, tomorrow.*

Dani curled up on her side, dragged the fleece throw blanket to her chest, and closed her eyes. Tomorrow. For sure.

# Chapter Twenty-Two

Dani's best intentions for tomorrow fizzled repeatedly with each new dawn. She did meet with her lawyer; he'd insisted on it and agreed to come to the house. She straightened the living room, made herself presentable—or so she thought—offered him coffee. Tried to listen, nodded and agreed, signed papers, and was relieved when he'd left.

She kept the door to Brian's room closed. Ghosts and memories—locked behind a door, except at night when the dreams came. Some days she sat for hours in Trace's room, comforted somewhat by high school memorabilia he'd left behind: school pennants, yearbook, and pictures on his bulletin board of ball games, clowning around with Ryan, senior prom. When the memories came full circle and collided with the present, she pushed them away and closed the door.

*Have to get myself together before he comes home from school. Tomorrow for sure.*

The bright morning sunlight flooded the window of Dani's room. She scrunched her eyes closed as the rays warmed her face. *How in the hell can the sun keep coming up? How can everything continue to exist?*

Dani awoke angry. It startled her; surprised her, to feel anything but emptiness. Even anger. Anger was better than the lethargy that had anchored itself somewhere just below her heart. Better than—than dead.

Her eyes flashed open. She squinted against the sunlight. Trace's photograph stared back at her from the nightstand by her bed. On the dusty table beneath the photo a handful of sleeping pills lay scattered beside an empty prescription vial.

The chilling memory of the night before engulfed her. For a brief moment, it had seemed the only solution—the only way out of the black hole of her life. Then, with her hand full of pills, Trace stared into her soul. Her scratchy eyes still felt the bitter torrent of angry tears that had followed. And then she'd slept. Slept well, free for the first time from the nightmares.

The sunlight felt wonderful on her skin. Dani took a deep breath, conscious of the oxygen filling her lungs, of her heartbeat. She felt—alive. And ashamed of herself for even entertaining the thought of a coward's way out. *What on earth could I have been thinking of? For whatever the reason, I wasn't meant to be on that plane. I've had enough of this . . . this self-pity. I have to get . . . get what?* She rubbed her hand against her eyes, trying to push through the fog. *Get on with my life. I'm sorry Brian is gone. Sorry Ray's gone. For some reason, I'm still here. I have Trace. And Chance and Cash. Dammit!* She realized for the first time, *I still have* me!

Dani hopped out of bed. She ripped the wrinkled stale sheets and blankets from her bed, tossed them into the hamper. Tugging off her T-shirt and underwear, she was horrified at the creature reflected in the mirror. Her hipbones looked sharp enough to cut meat. Her complexion beneath a shaggy mane of lifeless tangles was dull and splotchy. Bloodshot eyes stared out over protruding cheekbones.

Grabbing a robe, Dani trudged to the kitchen. Her stomach growled. The cabinets offered tuna fish, corn, green beans and cherry pie filling. The refrigerator still held an assortment of unidentifiable food brought by after the memorial service—shrunken, hardened, and covered with various stages of fuzzy growth.

A rush of frigid air grabbed at her bare feet as Dani yanked on the freezer door. Peering into the icy cavern, she discovered a deep-dish spinach and mushroom pizza. *Heaven.*

As the oven heated, Dani slid her treasure onto a pizza pan. She tossed it in to bake, set the timer, and hurried off to take a shower.

She washed her hair in billowy mounds of green-apple–scented shampoo. Rinsed and applied conditioner until it dripped in citrus smelling globs on her shoulders. Scrubbed her body with strawberry shower gel, careful not to slash her wrists on her hipbones.

With her head wrapped in a thick towel, she slathered cherry-and-almond-scented Jergens lotion over her squeaky-clean body. She inhaled the plethora of scents swirling through the steam. *I smell like a fruit salad.* Laughter gurgled in her throat. The foreign sound made her smile at the woman in the mirror. *I can't remember the last time I laughed.*

Though in serious need of a cut, her hair bounced in shiny copper clouds around her shoulders. Dani slipped on the Notre Dame T-shirt Trace had brought her from school and khakis that needed a belt to keep them from slipping over her hips.

Bare feet dug into the plush carpeting as she hurried down the hall to the kitchen. The tinny-bell sound of the timer heralded the finished pizza. Dani poured Pepsi into a large glass of crushed ice. Watched it fizz. Listened to it crackle. Turning on the radio, she settled down with her pizza in front of the large bay window.

A few names in the news broadcast Dani didn't recall; the discussion afterwards about news stories seemed out of context.

She studied the calendar, trying to decide what day it was. *I don't even know what week it is, let alone what day.* She shivered as she swirled the ice in her glass. *Don't know what's going on in the world. I feel a little like Rip Van Winkle.*

The house had been quiet for too long. Dani cranked up the volume on the CD player and listened to the dulcet tones of George Strait float through the house as she dusted and vacuumed. A load of laundry sloshed around in the washing machine while another tumbled in the dryer. *Sounds. Sounds of life.*

She filled a large trash bag with the old food in the fridge, cleaned the kitchen, and washed the floor. Dani wiped her damp forehead with the back of her hand, reveling in a sense of accomplishment.

After weeks of inactivity, she was suddenly tired and her muscles felt twitchy. She ate an apple, brushed her teeth, went to bed; and slept through a peaceful and dreamless night.

Squaring her shoulders, Dani sighed and opened the door to Brian's room. She slid the large box next to the closet. *This is so hard to do. Seems like I just finished doing it for Mom.* She folded a shirt, tucked it in the box, and reached for another. *I wasn't alone before. I had Ray to help me.*

Dani rubbed her hand over Brian's favorite sweater. *I wish things had been better for us, Brian. If they had been . . .* she shook her head. *How can I ever be sorry Ray came into my life?*

*Won't these memories ever go away?* She remembered Ray helping her clean out her mother's house. Beautiful memories, but they hurt so much.

Dani finished packing the closet; closed up the box. She hesitated at the dresser. *It's been a pretty good day. A little bit at a time. I'll do more tomorrow.* This time, she knew tomorrow she would.

Dani carried the box to the garage then checked the front door lock. A faint crying sound caught her attention. Tucked into the shadows of the entryway was a cardboard box, top taped shut with holes cut in the sides. The rough cement prickled against her bare feet as Dani stepped outside for a closer look. With pitiful cries, a kitten scratched against its cardboard prison.

Dani carried the box inside, turned on the hall light and tugged at the tape. A fuzzy black kitten jumped to freedom. It let out a howl, turning toward Dani with a defiant glare. A white splotch over one eye topped off by three white paws and a fuzzy tail that looked as if it had been dipped in a can of paint gave it a comical look. The kitten backed up, surveying Dani through squinted eyes. Dani sat on the floor and held out her hand. The kitten stood its ground, but poked its head forward in curiosity. It sniffed Dani's hand twice, looked into her eyes, and climbed onto her lap. Dani murmured as she stroked the bundle of fluff. Within a few minutes the kitten was crying again. "I'll bet you're hungry, aren't you, sweetie?" She carried the kitten to the kitchen and heated a saucer of milk in the microwave. Eating so fast she got hiccups, the kitten kept a watchful eye on Dani.

When the bowl was empty, the kitten washed her face.

She took a look around, strode to the crescent-shaped throw rug by the kitchen sink, curled up and went to sleep. Dani laughed. "Well, I guess you plan to stay."

Leaving the sleeping kitten, Dani dashed to the store for kitten food, dishes, kitty litter and a litter box. With renewed sense of purpose, she tossed items in her cart like the Russians were on Main Street.

The kitten greeted Dani as she opened the door. She smiled

at the inquisitive creature. "Looks like you've made yourself right at home."

Dani placed the food and water dishes on a placemat under the bay window in the kitchen. She filled the litter box in the laundry room and carried her new friend in for a lesson.

"I suppose we have to think of a name for you." Dani thought about it as she watched the kitten. "I know, I think Patches would be a good name. How do you like that?" The kitten rubbed gently against Dani's ankle. "Okay then, Patches it is."

All of its basic needs met, the fuzzy feline began to explore her new home and get acquainted with this human she now owned.

While Dani enjoyed a lighthearted movie, Patches poked 'round the house, stopping now and then to stare at Dani. When Dani shut off the TV, turned out the lights and headed for her bedroom, Patches trotted along beside her. Dani placed her new friend on a fluffy towel in a large wicker basket in the corner of the room.

Minutes after Dani crawled into bed and snuggled beneath the comforter, Patches joined her. The kitten circled a few times, curled up next to Dani's shoulder, and purring like a Mack truck, Patches fell asleep.

Dani felt comforted by the purring kitten snuggled beside her . . . and she too drifted off into a peaceful sleep.

# CHAPTER TWENTY-THREE

Bud Morgan smiled as Dani slid into his parking lot. He led a black stud colt to the paddock before catching up with her on the way to Chance's stall.

"Sure is nice to have you back, honey." He draped an arm around her shoulders. "How're things goin'?"

With a slight shrug, Dani replied, "Some days are better than others." Chance reached out to nuzzle Dani's hand. "But I've had more good days than bad this past week."

Bud nodded.

"Had a lot to catch up with around the house." She rolled her eyes and grimaced in aggravation. "Legal matters to attend to."

Her tone brightened as she continued, "And I had a call from my former boss. The secretary he hired hasn't worked out and he wondered if I wanted to go back to work a few days a week. I decided I might as well. I need to fill up my time somehow."

"What type of business is it?"

"Interior decorating. I really enjoyed working there. Small office, just the three of us."

"Good for you to keep busy." Bud chuckled. "And you can't ride horses all day."

Cash whinnied at her and rocked in his stall. As Dani reached out her hand, the bay stretched toward the bag of carrots.

"Looks like they're glad to see you too." Bud laughed.

The bay's muscular neck rippled beneath Dani's touch.

"Thanks a lot for everything and for turning them out to pasture for me. I appreciate it."

Bud dismissed the thanks with a wave.

Her voice cracked slightly. "Bud, have you . . . ?"

In answer to the unfinished question, Bud shook his head. "No, I haven't heard a word. Sorry." He cleared his throat before continuing. "I drove by his house the other day when I was running errands. There's a for-sale sign on the lawn."

Dani nodded with a sigh.

"You've been through a lot the last few years, but time does heal, Dani." Bud's voice was soft and his eyes hinted of a long-ago pain.

"I suppose . . . I just miss him so much. He's such a special person . . ."

"Yes, that he is. I've known him a long time. Hate to think of him hurting too."

Dani merely nodded before she brushed a hand against his arm and headed toward the tack room. *It's in the past; get over him. Move on. Look forward.* Brave words that stung like shrapnel in her gut.


By the time Trace came home for summer vacation, Dani had some semblance of a life again. She'd gained a few pounds and her clothes no longer hung on her frame like a scarecrow flapping over a cornfield. The dark circles under her eyes had faded to the point they could be concealed with a little makeup. She was able to smile and laugh without feeling guilty.

Life settled into a routine. Working three days a week, riding and caring for the horses, gave her a sense of focus and a structure to her life. Ray had done a fine job calming Cash; his manners were now impeccable. Though Dani felt safe with him, she always chose Chance for trails. Alone in the woods with

Chance was where she found peace; like a therapy session for her soul. It was still difficult to ride with anyone other than Ray; but occasionally Dani accepted an invitation to join friends at the ranch on a ride, knowing she had to get past the pain of being without him.

At the end of each day Patches ran to greet her. The kitten's playful antics brought some life to the house and kept Dani company.

Having Trace at home for the summer filled up some of the lonely spaces in Dani's life, even though with his full-time job and friends, the house seemed to have a revolving door. He and Ryan spent equal amounts of time at each other's homes, and Dani liked having them around, especially enjoying their company at dinnertime. Ryan's girlfriend was vacationing with her parents, and with Megan living in Michigan, Trace also had a lot of free time. Some days it seemed as if high school had never ended. When she saw Trace and Ryan clowning in the backyard, it was easy to push back the time, pretend it was a day before the plane crash, before . . . before Ray. . . .

Missing Brian. Missing Ray. The pain and twinges of guilt were still there, but she had to stop pushing them inward. Accept them, the good feelings along with the bad. Stop agonizing over what might have been, what was, and what she'd lost. She needed to treasure what she'd had and forgive herself for loving Ray.

She'd finally decided to put her house up for sale in the fall when Trace went back to school. Her moods teeter-tottered as the ghosts and memories followed her from room to room in the empty house. She wanted a change, a place where she could keep her horses with her instead of boarding them.

Shortly after leaving the ranch, Dani screeched to a stop, checked her mirror, and whipped into a U-turn. She pulled onto a gravel driveway next to a real estate sign. *I don't believe this place is for sale.* She fumbled around for a pen and jotted down the number of the sales agent.

Dani gave one more glance around the yard, and pulled back onto the street. *I have to take the plunge sometime. Might as well be now.* The red-brick ranch house nestled on wooded acreage at the end of a winding gravel driveway had always caught Dani's attention. *At least I can finally see what it looks like inside.*

The real estate agent remained silent as Dani strolled through the house a second time. *Okay, try not to show too much excitement here. They'll double the price if they know how much I want the place.*

The U-shaped ranch house with full basement for plenty of storage was as lovely as she'd imagined. Two bedrooms and a bath, plus a laundry room comprised the left wing. A large country kitchen looked out over the wooded backyard, and a two-sided fireplace divided the living and dining rooms. The right wing held the master bedroom with private bath, a half bath off the family room with another fireplace and sliding glass doors opening onto a stone patio. A path running through a privacy hedge led to a four-stall barn. The barn needed some work inside but was dry and sound. Stall doors accessed a large sandy arena and paddock, with lush green pastures stretching beyond. The property, a total of ten acres, was heavily wooded and private. Dani fell in love with it immediately and escalated her moving plans.

Dani shook hands with the real estate agent.

"I'll be in touch with you. My son—he's in college, but he's home for the summers—I'd like him to take a look at it with me."

"Would you like to make the appointment now?"

*Be cool. Not too eager.*

"It'll probably be in a day or so. I'll call you."

Dani took a few steps toward her car before she turned and asked, "Are . . . are there any other serious prospects right now?"

The agent smiled. "I don't think so, but of course that could change any minute. It is a beautiful home."

"Yes, yes it is. I'll call you tomorrow." *Transparent as glass, Dani. Good thing I don't play poker.*

Trace sat quietly as Dani described the house to him.

"Would you like to go with me tomorrow to see it?"

"Sure, I suppose I could." His voice held little excitement.

Dani's enthusiasm faded a bit. "I know it'll be hard for you to leave this house. You grew up here." Dani searched her son's face. "It's difficult for me too, but soon you'll be on your own, and I need to make a fresh start."

Trace was silent.

"Do you understand?" Dani twisted a strand of hair around her finger.

"Sure. Sure I do." He smiled at her. "We can go tomorrow."

Dani drove in silence, letting Trace sort out his feelings about the house.

Trace glanced toward his mother. "It's quite a place. I can see why you're so excited about it."

"I think it's a good investment too."

Staring out the window, Trace merely nodded.

"Do you think you'd like living in the country?" Dani probed.

"Uh . . . I suppose. I really won't be there much. It's your decision."

They rode on past farmhouses, pastures full of grazing horses and sleepy cattle. Ahead lay a new development, upscale homes on two- and three-acre plots. A decisive sigh preceded Trace's words. "I think it's a good place for you. I can see you there with your horses. I'd say go for it, Mom."

With a smile, Dani reached over to give his shoulder a squeeze.

Dani made a bid on the house by the end of the week. After a few minor negotiations with the owners, her offer was accepted, and she listed her house for sale. Excited and eager to share her news, she pulled the phone onto her lap and dialed her sister.

"Lynn, it's Dani."

"Well, you're sounding pretty chipper. You didn't sound so well the last time we talked, I've been worried . . ."

Touched by the concern in Lynn's voice, Dani continued, "I'm sorry to worry you. I am doing much better. Been working with the horses, went back to work—oh, I told you that. Anyway, I sold the house and bought a place in the country where I can have the horses with me instead of boarding them."

"You're going to live in the country all by yourself?"

"Well, it's not Siberia, Lynn, just a little bit country." Dani laughed.

"My little-bit-country sister," Lynn quipped. "Bet you'll be driving a pickup soon too."

The camaraderie with Lynn felt good. "You never know. Hope you can come to visit when I get settled."

"Just let me know when. I . . . I . . . well, I started a new job and I may be moving soon too. I'll call and let you know."

Dani sighed. With the way Lynn changed jobs, she should just work for a temp agency.

"Okay, I'll call you soon. I have a lot of work to do."

"Bye, Dani."

Holding the receiver against her chest, Dani shook her head. *Someday I hope she'll settle down.*

★ ★ ★ ★ ★

Leaning against two pillows, Dani sat in the middle of her bed with her sketchpad, planning her new tack room and making notes. *I can't wait to have the horses at home with me . . . to wake up each morning and know they're there—right in my very own barn.* Her mind buzzed with plans. *Ummm . . . I've got four stalls and only two horses. Maybe I could board a horse or two . . . have someone else around to ride with.* Patches scratched at the sketchpad and stared at her. Dani rubbed her eyes, glanced at the clock. "Okay, bossy cat, it's time to get to sleep."

Dani rinsed her toothbrush and plopped it into a glass. The woman staring back at her in the mirror bore little resemblance to the mess she'd been not too many months before. *I can take care of myself, and I'm going to be okay. One day at a time.* She smiled. *I think I like the new me.*

Trace left for school on a Sunday with only a few tears from Dani. Their house had sold within a week. Trace spent the last few weeks sorting through his belongings and helping his mother pack.

Two weeks earlier Dani had driven by Ray's house and noticed a "sold" banner slapped across the real estate sign in the grass. So much for him coming back. *You have to stop doing this to yourself. He's gone. Get over it.* She sighed, squared her shoulders, and drove on.

Surrounded by boxes in the middle of her living room, Dani wiped a wisp of hair from her forehead. Patches played with bubble wrap under the dining room table. The photo album resting on Dani's lap showed three-year-old Trace splashing in a backyard pool—a red-and-blue, star-speckled Band-Aid on his knee and blue swim trunks sliding over his butt. In the next photo he grinned and waved from a green-and-white helicopter at Kiddyland. Another photo, taken shortly before the car accident, showed Dani and Brian dancing at a friend's wedding.

Fragments of her life with Brian and Trace had been flickering through her thoughts all day. It was the last night she would spend in the house; the movers were scheduled for nine the next morning. The young couple buying the house had two children—a boy, nine, and a girl, seven. *I hope they'll be happy in this house. I'll try to remember only the good times.*

From somewhere in the cardboard mountain range of her living room came the incessant jangling of a telephone. Dani scrambled to find the cordless phone. On the fourth ring, she located it between two boxes marked Miscellaneous Kitchen and Books.

"Hello," she answered, slightly out of breath.

Bud Morgan's voice boomed at her from across the miles. "Dani, glad I caught you. Didn't know when your phones would be disconnected."

"There's nothing wrong with Chance or Cash, is there?"

"Oh, sorry, no. They're both fine. I . . ." he hesitated.

Dani held her breath; the back of her neck prickled.

"Ray's home. His house was sold—forgot to tell you. Anyway, he stopped by to say hi and asked about you."

The silence stretched as Dani waited for him to continue, her thudding heart punching against her ribcage.

"I told him about Brian . . . and that you were moving." Bud paused to clear his throat. "I hope that's all right, hon."

"Sure, that's fine." Dani hesitated, her mind a jumble of conflicting emotions. *Do I want to see him now? Am I strong enough? God, how I've missed him.* "Well . . . thanks for letting me know, Bud. I'll talk to you soon." She disconnected the call.

There was a nervous flutter to her heartbeat. *I wonder . . . No, after this much time, he probably won't call.*

Patches snuggled beside Dani. Stroking the cat, Dani tried to sort out her feelings about Ray. Though she tried not to think about him, he was never too far away from her thoughts. Memories had a way of creeping up on her when she least expected them. *What do I say if he does call?* She looked at the boxes stacked around the room: a reminder of the new and improved Dani Monroe, strong, on her own. Dani Monroe, survivor. *I don't have to talk to him; I can just let the machine pick up the call.*

She stretched out on the floor with Patches, listening to the purring cat and trying not to think of Ray.

When the doorbell rang, Dani knew it would be Ray. She sat against a box full of books, debating whether to answer the door. *No use pretending I'm not home. The car's parked on the driveway.* The doorbell chimed again. She ruffled Patches' fur, pulled herself up, and sucked in a deep breath as she opened the door.

Boots, blue jeans, red western shirt and the black Stetson; the air around him seemed to tingle. Her reaction was visceral. Words stuck in the dust-storm dryness of her throat, leg muscles faltered and her pulse thundered in her ears. She searched his face—a deeply tanned face that looked older than the year he'd been gone—and tried to read the blue eyes beneath the Stetson's shadow.

Patches howled at being ignored and darted through the open door. Ray caught the cat just before she hit the lawn.

"Well, who is this?"

Dani reached for the squirming pet. Currents rippled through her as she brushed against Ray's arm. *After all this time, he still has this effect on me. . . .*

With the cat held tightly against her chest, Dani said, "This . . . this is Patches."

Ray ruffled the kitten behind her ears and held the door open. He hesitated in the doorway. Dani nodded to the unspoken question in his eyes; he followed her into the house.

Clearing a spot on the sofa for Ray to sit, Dani settled in a chair across from him, with the cat on her lap.

Ray leaned back, crossed an ankle over his knee, and rubbed a hand against the edge of his boot. "You don't seem surprised to see me."

"I'm not. Bud called earlier and told me you were home," Dani said, her voice calmer than she felt.

"Ah . . . I supposed he would."

The silence stretched.

"I'm really sorry about Brian. It was quite a shock."

Dani bit against her lower lip and nodded.

His eyes searched hers. "Are you all right?"

"I'm getting there. Each day . . ." she trailed off.

"And Trace?"

"He's fine. Doing well at school." She smiled. "He has a new girlfriend."

Ray swallowed hard. "Dani, I'm sorry you've been dealing with this alone. If I had known . . ."

"If you'd known . . ." Angry sparks flashed in her eyes. "I seem to remember a long time ago after my mother died—and I told you I felt disconnected—that you said I wasn't disconnected anymore and that we would get through whatever we had to together." Distressed by the change in Dani's mood, Patches jumped to the floor. "Well, I'm getting quite good at handling things and being alone, thank you." *As if I had a choice in the matter.*

As Ray moved toward her, Dani raised a hand to hold him away. In spite of her brave words, she felt as fragile as the fall leaves. *If he touches me, I'll crumble into a thousand pieces.*

"Don't," she said.

The word stopped Ray like a wall.

*I shouldn't have let him in. I can't handle this.*

202

"You'd better go now," Dani whispered.

"Dani . . ."

"No, please don't say any more."

"We need to talk, honey."

"You can't just stroll in and out of my life and leave me to pick up the pieces. I can't . . ." She shook her head and looked away to keep from yielding to the sadness in his eyes. "It hurts too much," she whispered.

"Hurting you is the last thing I ever want to do."

Dani glared at him, "How did you think I would feel when you left . . . with no explanation . . . walked out without saying good-bye . . ." She dragged her fingers through her hair and rubbed her neck. *Dammit! Do you know how much I loved you? Still love you?*

"Let me explain."

As Ray rose from the chair and reached out to her, Dani pulled away, shook her head sadly, and said, "No, Ray, it's too late for explanations now."

Ray closed his eyes, rubbed his forehead with the palms of his hands. "Do you want me to go?"

She couldn't say the words, lowered her eyes so he wouldn't see the tears, and gave him a nod.

He slid his hat over his creased brow. Pausing a moment, he gave her a sad smile before he opened the door.

Dani held a fist against her mouth to strangle the scream in her throat. Her eyes felt like pools of liquid fire. Her heartbeat ticked away the passing minutes. She waited to hear the sound of his truck pull away. *I love you so much, I don't know if I can let you go again.*

She ran to the door, hands pressing against the oak panel that separated her from Ray. In a flash, love conquered pride. Dani grabbed the doorknob.

Ray's truck sat on the driveway next to her car. He stood

leaning against the entryway wall, head bowed, hands stuffed into his pockets, the sole of one boot resting against the planter box.

With his head still lowered, he raised his eyes to hers, giving her that special smile that had always quickened her heartbeat and made her knees tremble.

Dani's lip quivered. "I—I don't want you to go." She opened the screen door and he followed her back into the house.

Standing amidst the boxed clutter, Dani hesitated. *Now what do I say?* Ray stepped close behind her, circled his arms around her, nuzzling his face in her hair. Moments passed before she turned in his arms to face him. Their anger, hurt and loneliness melted away as they held each other. No words were needed; just spirits reconnected through love undiminished by time spent apart.

Dani turned on the only lamp still unpacked. Ray settled on the couch and beckoned to her. "Come here."

She hesitated slightly before stretching out with her head on his lap. He smiled and smoothed a strand of hair from her face.

"So, are you going to tell me where you've been and what you've been doing?" Dani asked.

His voice was brittle. "Well, I've been in hell, to tell the truth. Other than losing Kathy, this has been the worst year of my life." He traced his fingertip along her lips. "Life without you is unbearable. Dani, time goes so fast. Life's so short. I don't want to spend another day of mine without you."

Apprehension flickered through her stomach. "Ray, all this time not knowing where you were . . . or how you were doing . . . whether or not I'd ever see you again . . ." Dani swallowed hard. "Living each day without you, and then losing Brian . . ." Her voice trickled off with a shuddering sigh. "It's taken a lot of work to get myself together, to know I could be alone and be okay."

"I'm so sorry." He cleared his throat. "Had the situation with Brian improved any?"

"Somewhat." Her eyes clouded. "We both tried a little harder. He worked a bit less. Yes, it was . . . better. It's comforting to know that he seemed happier and more at peace before . . . before he died."

Ray brushed away the tear lingering at the edge of her eye. "I'm glad for that too, honey." He held her face and looked into her eyes. "Dani, I promise you this: I will never leave you alone again." He shook his head. "I didn't know what else to do for you. I thought since I hadn't heard from you in a week, you were trying to break it off between us. Thought I'd help make it easier."

He told her about the magazine article he'd seen on panic attacks and the conversation he'd overheard in the tack room.

Dani's groan caught in her throat.

"Ray, I had the flu. I was in bed for over three days. Trace was in Arizona with Ryan. I think Brian unplugged all the phones except his office line. When I finally felt well enough to be up, I called you several times but got no answer." Her lip trembled at the memory. "The day I went out to the barn and got your note from Bud, I'd called and got a recording saying your phone had been disconnected. I thought I'd dialed wrong."

Ray shook his head. "We really screwed things up, didn't we?"

Dani was silent.

He continued, "Or maybe not. Maybe you and Brian needed that time—and you needed not to feel so guilty."

She nodded.

The silence lingered—but it was a comfortable-with-you type of silence.

"I was in Montana," Ray began.

Dani's eyes flashed with surprise.

"An old friend owns a cattle spread there. I helped him out and lived at the ranch. I worked hard, rode hard and tried my best to be too exhausted at night to think about you."

Her eyes asked her unspoken question.

A lopsided grin reached the twinkle in Ray's eyes. "It didn't work—I always think of you."

Dani stretched. Her head ached and a pain nagged at her side. Beside her on the carpeted living room floor, Ray slept with his arm resting around her waist. He rolled to his back and groaned. Sitting up, he rubbed his lower back. "Sleeping on the floor is for kids, honey. I ache worse than being in the saddle all day."

They had stretched out on the floor, talking deep into the night before they fell asleep. Dani reached for his hand to check his watch. "Great, it's seven-thirty. The movers will be here at nine."

Ray struggled to his feet. "You get ready; I'll run out and pick up something quick for breakfast. Okay?"

"Thanks." She ran back, gave him a kiss and a smile before rushing to change clothes.

# CHAPTER TWENTY-FOUR

The heavy doors of the moving van clanged shut on the last of Dani's belongings. She tossed some odds and ends into her trunk and watched as the movers drove off.

"Hard to believe almost everything I own is packed into that one truck. My whole life . . . just boxed up and loaded on a moving van."

Ray gave her hand a squeeze.

"I'm glad you're here with me now. This's really hard to do. So much of my life is connected to this house. There were a lot of good times along with the unhappy ones." Dani took a deep breath and locked the door for the last time. After dropping her key with the real estate agent, she would meet the movers at her new house.

Ray draped his arm around her shoulders as they walked to her car. "I hate to let you go, but I have things to do at my house," Ray said. "I'll meet you at your place about . . ." he glanced at his watch. "How about four?"

"That's fine." She reached for a hug. "I'm so anxious for you to see the house. I know you'll love it," she said.

He touched a fingertip to the end of her nose. "I love anywhere you are." He walked toward his truck, stopped, and said, "Don't go moving or lifting anything heavy. Wait for me to help you."

Dani nodded, too emotional to trust her voice.

★  ★  ★  ★  ★

When Dani heard Ray's truck, she rushed to the door.

He gave her a kiss and handed her a bouquet of pink sweetheart roses he'd held behind his back.

"How sweet, thanks."

"Great driveway, darlin'. I'll bet you can hear someone coming a mile away. Plenty of time to put on the coffee . . . or load the shotgun."

She laughed. "I have a coffee pot, but no shotgun."

"We'll have to do something about that. Can't live out here all by yourself without a shotgun."

Dani looked skeptical as she plunked the flowers into a plastic drink container. "I don't think so. I don't really like guns very much."

Boxes cluttered the floor space around the tentatively arranged furniture, but Dani's eyes sparkled as she led Ray on the grand tour. Patches followed closely at Dani's side, making nervous little cries as they moved from room to room.

"It's beautiful. But I'm dying to see the barn."

Laughing, Dani took his hand and pushed open the sliding glass doors. Burning bushes and brilliant yellow and russet mums nestled at the far edge of the patio. Rising above a tangle of vinca vines and ajuga in a flowerbed, the delicate purple, pink, and white cosmos petals held onto summer. A spattering of leaves dotted the lawn and collected at the base of the hedgerow. Two blue jays squawked and abandoned the feeder that sat atop a cedar post.

"First thing next spring, I'm going to get a swing for the yard. I saw one—a double with a canopy top—I just loved it."

"Umm, sounds nice." Ray's gaze swept over the yard as they headed toward the barn.

Unused for quite some time, cobwebs and birds' nests filled

the rafters of the faded rusty brown structure. The air inside was musty and damp. Scrap pieces of lumber, a broken feeder bucket, old flowerpots and a coffee can full of rusty nails littered the wall just inside the large sliding door. Ray poked and prodded. He rubbed his chin and nodded his approval at the four twelve-by-twelve stalls, two on each side of a spacious aisleway.

"All right already." Dani stomped her foot. "What do you think?"

"I think it's a great little barn." He grinned. "Needs some cleaning up, but it's in good shape. Nice and solid, big stalls. I hope you'll let me help you."

"Of course you're going to help me." She tilted her chin. "After all, half of your horse will be living here." Dani stretched out her arms and paced off a section toward the back that she planned to enclose for a tack room.

"And look what I found." Her excited voice bounced around her as she scurried to a darkened corner of the barn. "Two big, heavy rubber mats. Look at these. They're in great shape. I'm going to use them in the aisle between the stalls, put up some crossties." Her hands gestured to emphasize her words. "Great place to groom the horses or when the vet or shoer comes—plenty of light—as soon as I replace those bulbs overhead."

"Whoa there, darlin'. You're making me dizzy." He hugged her. "Sounds great. Good ideas. I love to see you so excited and happy. And I'm glad to hear I still have half a horse." He ruffled her hair. "To go with this sweet whole new woman I love." Ray secured the latch on the barn door. "Now, why don't we take a walk in the woods and relax before you bust at the seams?"

Ray kicked a stone in the path and listened to Dani ramble.

"And I thought about getting a boarder—or two—but that was before . . . before you came back. Thought maybe it would be nice to have someone else around, to ride with, help each other out if I took a vacation, or . . . or whatever . . ."

Ray pulled her close and kissed her in midsentence. "So glad to see the walk calmed you down."

"Okay, okay." Dani laughed. "I'll shut up. It's just that I'm so excited. I was excited before, but now that you're here to share it . . ." Dani met his tender look with one of her own. "It's so much more special," she whispered.

With the sun resting just above the horizon, a sudden crispness nipped at the air as Dani and Ray finished their walk.

Ray reached into his jacket pocket. He tossed a set of keys in his hand.

"Okay, I give up. You're about to tell me something."

He dangled the keys in the air. "Keys to *my* new place."

Her eyes filled with surprise. "What?"

"When I came back it was to clean out my house. I had planned to sell what I could and give the rest to charity. I was going back to Montana."

Dani searched his eyes and asked, "Were you going to leave without seeing me?"

"That's why I went out to Bud's . . . to see how you were." He hesitated. "If you were happy, then I would have gone back without seeing you."

"And now . . . ?"

"And now I'm here—to stay." He tilted his head, his eyes teasing. "If you want me to."

Her only answer was a smile.

He tossed the keys back into his pocket. "On the way to the house, I noticed that apartment complex on Waverly Street had been finished. The sign near the office said there were vacancies. I stopped in, liked what I saw, and rented a two-bedroom on the second floor."

"You don't waste any time, do you?"

"I've wasted enough as it is."

"Why did you wait so long to tell me?"

"Well . . ." He chuckled. "I couldn't get a word in edgewise."

"I guess I have been a little . . . uh . . . animated."

"Animated, hell. You're a real Road Runner cartoon."

Dani motioned with her hand across her lips that she was zippering it up and shoved her hands in her pockets.

"Wonder how long this is going to last." He reached for her hand. "I made arrangements with the movers. In two days the new owners close on my house, and I move into my new apartment."

Dani pursed her lips together to keep quiet and merely nodded.

Ray walked Dani to the door of her new house. The sun had set and she shivered in the evening chill. As she unlocked the door, she turned to him. "So what do you do for the next two days?"

He pulled his Stetson low on his forehead, shrugged his shoulders inside his denim jacket, and drawled. "Well, ma'am, I'll probably bed down in the barn next to m'horse."

Dani laughed. "Seems to have gotten a little chilly this evening. I could really use some help finding my sheets and blankets. Might be cold tonight without them."

"Honey, I'd be happy to help out such a pretty lady in a time of need."

Dani slid the dead bolt closed behind them, tossed her purse on the floor. She navigated through the maze of boxes toward the master bedroom. She glanced at him over her shoulder. "Still remember how to ride a bike?"

The house echoed with his throaty laugh. "You betcha, darlin'."

# CHAPTER TWENTY-FIVE

The unseasonable chill stretched into morning. Dismal skies and a steady drizzle settled over Dani's little ten acres of paradise. With one glance through the rain-speckled windows, she snuggled against Ray's chest and went back to sleep. He murmured softly and drew her closer to him.

After several attempts to get some attention, Patches let out an angry howl, jabbed an angry paw against Dani's side and stared into her face.

"What 'n the hell . . . ?" Ray opened his eyes and glared at the intrusive feline.

"I think she's had enough of our being lazy. She wants to eat," Dani mumbled as she scratched the cat's head. She grabbed her robe, followed the cat to the kitchen. Scrunching her bare feet against the chilly tile floor, Dani scooped a handful of Meow Mix into the dish.

Back in her bedroom, Dani stared down at Ray; his eyes squinted closed to hold off the morning. A smile stretched across his face; he opened one eye and reached for her.

"Come here, woman. I missed you while you were gone."

Dani sat on the edge of the bed. A giggle rumbled in her throat. "I've only been gone a few minutes."

"Ah, seemed like an eternity to me." He coaxed her back into bed and nuzzled her neck.

"We really should get up. I have to start unpacking." There was little enthusiasm behind her words.

He rolled onto his stomach and buried his face in the pillow with a groan. "Haven't you ever heard it's bad luck to unpack a new house when it's raining?"

"And what is it good luck to do in a new house when it's raining?" Dani knelt beside him and massaged his shoulders.

He peeked up at her from the pillow, grinned and grabbed her arm. "Here, I'll show you."

Dani stretched in luxurious satisfaction. Ray smiled at her with loving eyes. She kissed him firmly on the forehead and forced herself to get up. "Umm, sure am glad you didn't turn out to be a serial killer." She tossed her pillow at him. "Now, we really do need to get busy. I'm going to take a shower and you'd better be up when I get back."

"Hold on, babe, I'll go with you." He kicked against the tangle of blankets. "I think it's also bad luck to shower alone the first time in a new house."

Dani's mouth twisted into a smirk. She shook her head. "I never knew cowboys were so superstitious. How many other bad luck theories do you have?"

Ray pulled two fluffy blue Egyptian-cotton towels from the box Dani had opened the night before and tossed one to her. "Oh you'd be amazed, honey."

"You never cease to amaze me." Throwing the towel over her shoulder, Dani headed toward the shower. She crooked a finger at him, "Well, come on. I definitely don't want any bad luck in my new house."

Surrounded by cardboard boxes and opened cabinet doors, Dani tried to organize her new kitchen while Ray sorted through a tangle of wires to hook up her television and entertainment center. Patches climbed in and out of boxes, scattering crumpled newspaper in her wake. Smiling with contentment, Dani arranged spice jars in a cabinet as Ray muttered to himself.

Ray rummaged through a box of CDs. "Ah-ha. Here it is." He popped the disc into its tray. "Honey, come here." He held out his arms as Randy Travis's twang filled the air. Happy tears pooled in Dani's eyes as they danced to "Forever and Ever, Amen."

"Do you remember when we danced to this at Congress and I said it was our song?"

Dani could only manage a nod. When the song ended and they held each other amidst the half-opened boxes, she eased the words out from around the lump in her throat. "Whenever the song played on the radio I had to turn it off. It hurt too much."

Ray brushed a kiss against her cheek. "Me too, honey." He sighed, gave her hand a squeeze and replaced the CD on the shelf. "No more hurt—only happiness from now on."

"Aye, aye sir. I agree." Dani gave a mock salute and went back to her work in the kitchen.

In the middle of her family room Dani pondered the furniture arrangements. She placed a floral watercolor painting on the small wall next to the fireplace, nodded to herself, pleased with the effect. In two days the essential boxes had been unpacked, put away and the house felt somewhat like home. Ray'd moved the miscellaneous boxes to the basement and garage to be unpacked later.

Ray wiped his hands against his jeans and gave her a thumbs-up sign. "Okay, all the boxes are on one side of your garage. I think we've done enough for today. How about you?"

Dani shoved the vacuum in the closet. "I agree. Why don't we go to the store and get some food to stock this kitchen, and I'll cook for a change?"

"Sounds good to me. Let's have steak tonight. I need

something to replace my energy."

"Men . . . you're all alike." Dani laughed. "A little red meat to boost the testosterone level, huh?"

"I resent that remark. I'm not like any other man you've ever known."

"You've sure got that right." Dani slid her arms around his neck. "And I love you just the way you are."

Ray kissed her and gave her a pat on the butt. "Let's get to the store."

The ringing telephone postponed their departure. Dani grabbed the extension by the back door.

"Hi, Mom. How's everything going at the new house?"

"Hi, Trace. Fine. Getting unpacked and settled in."

"You sound out of breath."

"Oh, well . . . I was just going out to the store for some groceries."

"Okay, I won't keep you then. Mom?"

"Yes."

"Are you okay?"

"I'm fine. Why?"

"You sound . . . different."

Dani smiled. "I'm just busy, honey. How are things at school?"

"Busy too. Workload is harder this year. But I'm doing okay. Well, I won't keep you. Talk to you soon."

"Okay, hon. Bye." Dani hung up the phone.

"What was that all about?"

"Trace. He said I sounded . . . different."

"You do. You sound happy."

She nodded. "I am happy. I'm very happy."

He opened the door for her. "Well, let's get going. If I'm going to keep you happy, *I need food.*"

"You know, it really surprises me." Dani tossed her napkin on the table. "Things I've been doing automatically for so long—like grocery shopping—all of a sudden aren't quite so boring."

He nodded with a smile. "Everything is changed. More fun because we have each other to share things with." Ray pushed his plate away with a groan. "That was a wonderful dinner, honey. You're a great cook . . . among your many other talents."

"Thanks. Don't go getting too relaxed there. You get to help me with the dishes."

He clutched his chest. "Dishes?"

"By all means. This is an equal opportunity household. If I can clean stalls, you can do dishes." There was a mischievous twinkle in her eyes. "And things are so much more fun when we share. Right?"

"I walked right into that one, didn't I?"

"Sure did." Dani carried dishes to the sink. "Didn't you do dishes at home?"

Ray helped her clear the table. "Not much. I ate out a lot and heated up a lot of frozen stuff."

"Ugh. You'd better get used to home cooking now."

"Swell, we'll both be waddling around here like a couple of prize pigs at the fair."

"We'll work it off. Remember, tomorrow we have to tackle your new place."

Ray groaned. "Getting to feel like a professional mover."

"We have to get the biggest part of this work done this week. Next week, it's back to work for me."

"I wish you didn't work, that you were here with me all the time."

"I like my job. It was difficult to leave when Mom was sick, but then I couldn't handle it all. I'm glad it worked out so I could go back."

"I'm sure I'll find lots of things to do while you're gone. Don't worry about me here pining away for you." Ray pulled a sad-looking face that made Dani laugh.

Dani and Ray woke early the next morning, fed Patches, and drove to Ray's apartment.

By early afternoon, with the furniture arranged to Ray's satisfaction and pictures hung on the wall to bring the rooms to life, Ray surveyed his new home with a nod.

"Well, glad that's done." He shoved an empty box against the wall and wiped his face along his sleeve.

Dani stared at the canned goods Ray had just arranged in a cabinet.

"This is kind of creepy, Ray."

He glanced in the cabinet. "Creepy?"

Dani waved a hand toward the cans. "It's like in the movie *Sleeping with the Enemy*—remember with Julia Roberts? Her husband was such a neat freak—all the canned goods lined up perfectly with the labels all facing front."

"I like it neat like that, don't you?"

"Well . . . yes, I suppose. I just never took the time to be that precise. Sure am glad you didn't see Trace's dorm room the first time we went to visit. I think the best description would have been 'early crime scene.' Looked like the place had just been ransacked."

Dani flopped on the sofa in the cozy living room.

"I'm really getting tired of unpacking. How about you?" Ray groaned.

"Yep, sure am. Although it sure took us less time to do your apartment than my house."

"That's because I don't have nearly as much junk . . . I mean stuff . . . as you do." He slouched next to her, resting his feet on the coffee table. "Gals sure do like a lot of doodads and knick-knacks, don't they?"

She laughed. "It's all those little doodads, as you call them, that give a house its unique personality and make it home."

Ray stretched his arm around her shoulders. "All I need to make a place feel like home is you."

Dani smiled at him and reached for the five-by-seven walnut picture frame on the end table. Holding onto the reins of her paint mare and a trophy almost as big as she, the young girl with curly dark hair grinned for the camera.

"How old was she in this picture?"

He took the photo of his daughter from Dani and gazed at it for a few moments before he answered. "About twelve. Yes, that's just after her birthday. She had a real good time at the show that day, won in two classes and placed in a third." He slid the photo gently back on the table.

Dani glanced at her watch. "Guess I'll head for home."

"Why don't you stay here tonight?"

"So you'll have good luck . . . first night in the new place and all that?" Dani joked.

"You catch on fast, darlin'."

"You should have warned me. I don't even have a tooth-brush."

Ray pulled himself off the couch. He gave her a sly smile and left the room. He returned with one hand tucked behind his back.

Dani tilted her head at him. "Okay, what are you up to now?"

"I want you to feel as much at home here as I do at your house." He grinned and tossed her a plastic Wal-Mart bag.

Dani plucked items from the bag: a medium-bristled toothbrush, toothpaste, hand lotion, strawberry-scented soap, shampoo and deodorant . . . all her favorite brands. Her hands closed around the items in her lap as if they were priceless treasures.

"You are without a doubt the sweetest and most thoughtful man I know."

His face lit up with delight at her response. He pulled her off the couch. "Come help me decide what to fix for dinner. *This* is an equal opportunity household too."

Dani laughed. "You sure learn fast too."

# CHAPTER TWENTY-SIX

Dani slipped the carpenter's apron over her head, tying it around her waist. She tucked a hammer in the loop at her side and grabbed a box of nails.

Ray grinned at her. "You sure do look cute playing carpenter."

"I've never done anything like this before. It's really fun." She stepped back to survey the studs that framed out the new tack room.

"We can afford to have this work done, you know," Ray said.

"I know we can, but it gives me such a sense of satisfaction to see it taking shape and doing it ourselves." She turned toward him with a puzzled look. "Aren't you enjoying it too?"

"Of course I am. It feels wonderful to be building something together." He placed his hand against the back of her neck to pull her close for a kiss. "Let's get to work. I'm in a hurry to get this barn ready so we can move the horses in. Then we'll be a family together."

Smiling at the thought, Dani reached for her hammer and nailed up the plywood sheet Ray held in place.

Above the dying screech of the power saw, the cordless phone rang.

Dani spoke briefly and disconnected the call; an anxious look clouded her face.

"Something wrong, hon?"

"Uh . . . no. Not exactly." She leaned against the newly hung stall door. "That was Trace. He's on his way home for the weekend. He stopped at the store for a few things. Wanted to know if I need anything."

Ray looked puzzled. "And that's a problem?"

A sudden look of understanding crossed his face. "Ah, I see. You haven't told him about me, have you? He doesn't know I'm back and . . ." His hand trailed off in the air with his words. He leaned next to her and took her hand. "Why not?"

Dani closed her eyes and shook her head. "I don't know how. I'm not sure what his reaction will be. He lost his father and I sold the only home he's ever known. This place isn't home yet. Maybe it never will be to him."

"Maybe I should run a few errands so you can talk to him alone." Ray gave her hand a squeeze. "How soon will he be here?"

The crunch of tires against the gravel drive and a few snappy beeps of the car's horn answered his question.

Dani took a deep breath and scrunched up her face. "How about right now."

"Okay then. We'll deal with it together. Unless you want me to leave?"

"No, stay. I need the moral support."

"Hey Mom," Trace called out as he strode through the barn door. "Don't tell me you bought a pick-up truck . . ." The teasing sound in his voice trailed away at the sight of Ray standing next to his mother.

Dani stepped forward to hug her son. "I'm so glad you're home." She gestured toward Ray. "I, uh . . . I don't think I had a chance to mention Ray was back in town."

"No. No you didn't." Trace reached out to shake the hand Ray extended toward him. "Nice to see you again, Ray. How are you?"

"I'm fine, Trace. Just giving your mom a hand with her new tack room. How's school?"

"It's okay." He turned in a circle to admire the changes in the barn. "Didn't know you knew how to build anything, Mom."

"I didn't. But I'm learning and Ray's helping."

Trace glanced at the new wood flooring, then turned toward them. "You two did all this by yourselves?"

"We sure did." Dani beamed. "Isn't it great?"

"Yeah, it is."

Dani linked her hand through her son's arm. "Hey, why don't we take a break and get you settled. The house is fairly organized and your room is ready. Come on."

"I'll work out here and let you two visit a bit," Ray said.

Trace headed toward the house without a word. Dani shot Ray a worried glance before following her son.


Dani held the door while Trace grabbed his backpack and a duffel bag.

"So much for having less laundry," Dani teased as Trace tossed his bag next to the washer.

"Oh, I don't expect you to do it," Trace mumbled.

"I was just kidding you." Dani led the way to the kitchen. "How about some lemonade? Made fresh this morning." Dani tumbled ice cubes into a glass and poured before he could answer. She placed the glass on the table and fixed another for herself.

Trace took a long gulp. "So, how long has Ray been back?"

Dani wiped the counter, avoiding his gaze. "Oh, uh . . . a few weeks now, I think."

"Is he staying around long?" A touch of irritation floated around his words.

"Yes . . . yes, he is. He sold his house and rented an apartment. You know that new apartment complex about a mile south of the high school?"

Trace nodded and sipped at his lemonade. "So he's helping

you out here, huh?"

"After all, he's half-owner of Cash. Remember?"

Trace's eyes hardened. "I thought when he left that he said Cash was yours."

"He did . . . but now he's home and . . ." Dani brushed her hand through her hair. "He's home and he owns half the horse . . . so that's that." She tossed the dishtowel over the chair and sat next to her son. "Does it upset you that he's here?"

"I . . . I suppose not. You need the help . . . and friends to share the horses with."

A rueful smile tugged at her lips. "That I do." She finished her lemonade, rinsed the glass, and poured another for Ray. "Let's go see how the project is going, okay?"

On the way to the barn Trace paused beside the lounge chair in the shade of the giant oak tree. "Mom, I'll be down in a while okay? Going to crash for a bit." He positioned the lounge flat and stretched out, eyes closed, arms flung over his head.

Dani ruffled his hair and bent to kiss his forehead. "Take a nap if you'd like."

Trace took a deep breath. The woods were alive with squawking blue jays and the melodic exchanges of cardinals. High overhead a sleek silver jet cut through billowy clouds, leaving contrails in an azure sky. The aircraft's engine silenced in the whine of the power saw from the barn. Steady hammer blows followed the faint sounds of his mother's voice.

Ray rubbed his hand against his jeans and reached for the lemonade. "Ah, that's good, honey." He wiped his mouth with the back of his hand and nodded his head toward the hay bale in the corner. "We've got some visitors."

Two gray tiger-striped kittens sat closely together on the hay, watching them. "They're so cute. Where'd they come from?"

"Don't know. I was just taking a break and they wandered in."

"Seem kind of young to be just wandering around."

"That's a thing you have to learn about being in the country. A lot of people don't care for animals as well as you do. Barn cats have litters and they just roam, searching for food and shelter."

Dani cooed soft little greetings as she knelt beside the hay bale and reached out for the kittens. They rubbed against her hand and licked her fingers.

"They're probably hungry. Maybe we should give them a home, let them live in the barn."

Ray laughed. "That would be a good idea. I saw a mouse while you were gone."

"That settles it. We have two barn cats if they want to stay. You can name them."

Ray studied the kittens. He pointed to the larger of the two. "That's Tiger." He paused. "And the other is Tiger Two."

"I guess that's easy to remember," Dani laughed, "and when we call one, they'll both come."

Ray sat on the hay bale beside her. "How's Trace?"

"I don't know." Dani gave a slight shrug and waved her hand in the air. "He seems uptight. I wish I'd had a little warning that he was coming home."

Ray nodded with a sad sounding sigh. He reached over to unplug the saw. "Why don't we call it quits for today. I'm going to take off so you can spend some time together."

Dani pressed her head against his chest. His strong arms reached tightly around her, pushing away the world and making her feel protected.

"I'm sorry. We planned to get so much done today."

"This is more important." He kissed her lightly and let her go. "Call me later, okay?"

"Sure." Dani closed the barn door and walked Ray to his truck.

Dani sorted Trace's laundry and threw a load of dark colors into the washer. With a new Stuart Woods novel she'd started the day before, she slipped out into the yard to read while Trace slept nearby.

Dani watched her son doze on the shaded lounge chair. As the leaves floated in the breeze, shadows and light danced around him, and his child's face flashed off and on with his handsome grown-up face. *You're not a little boy any longer, but I still want to keep you from being hurt. I suppose that will never change no matter how old we are.*

"Um, smells great in here. I've sure missed your cooking, Mom."

Dani perched on a kitchen stool and watched her son slide a pan of garlic bread into the oven and then begin to slice cucumbers and tomatoes for the salad.

"You're looking more at home in the kitchen lately," she said.

One year in a dorm had been enough for Trace. This year he'd rented a house along with three other friends from school.

"It's a matter of survival," he laughed, "unless I wanted to live on pizza and donuts for an entire year."

"There were times I thought you could do just that," Dani teased.

"It got old even for me. Ben and Rick are totally lost in the kitchen, so Steve and I took over cooking. Steve had to help cook at home so he knows a lot and I'm learning. We don't do anything fancy and sometimes our schedules clash, but several times a week we all eat together." Trace placed the salad and bread on the table next to the lasagna.

"It has its upside too. Since Steve and I cook, Ben and Rick have to do all the laundry."

"Ah, the plot thickens." Dani ruffled his hair and pulled out a chair at the table.

After dinner Dani and Trace moved out on the patio under an incredibly clear and star-studded night. An owl hooted a greeting from the woods, and in the pasture a bullfrog accompanied a chorus of crickets. Dani sipped at a glass of wine. She nodded toward the beer bottle in Trace's hand.

"Hope you don't drink a lot at school."

"Don't worry, Mom. I only have a few, mostly weekends. And I never drink and drive. Learned my lesson on that one. Steve—I told you he had to help out a lot at home—it was because when he was about fourteen, his Mom was killed by a drunk driver." Trace squeezed Dani's hand. "We've talked a lot about how accidents with drunk drivers have impacted our lives. Guess it's made us both more responsible about alcohol."

"I'm glad to hear that. How are your other roommates?"

Trace paused. "You know, I hadn't thought about this much. One night Rick came home. He was watching TV. Steve and I were outside on the porch talking about drinking and driving. The next day Rick asked me some questions about Dad's accident and what had happened to Steve's mom—that's how come I knew he had been listening to our conversation. Rick kind of drinks too much. He doesn't have a car at school, but one night he was walking home and passed out in the park." Trace was silent a minute. "I was just thinking, lately he doesn't seem to be drinking as much . . ."

"I hear so much about binge drinking at colleges. It worries me. Maybe if you and Steve talked about your experiences it would get through to more kids."

Trace sighed. "Don't see myself as . . . as the preacher type, Mom."

"I didn't mean that. There are groups of kids against drunk

driving. I've heard . . . I think it's called SADD—Students Against Drunk Drivers. Hearing stories from other kids probably has more effect than listening to adults preach about drinking."

"Yeah, I've heard about it. Maybe you're right."

A mournful howl echoed through the night.

"What on earth is that?"

Dani laughed. "It's a coyote."

"You have coyotes here?"

"Sure, this is the country, you know."

"Wow, never heard one before. Cool." Trace listened as other howls answered the first call. "They aren't dangerous, are they?"

"No, but I don't let Patches outside unless I'm with her."

"Any other wild animals around here?"

"Sure, I saw a fox the first week I was here, deer, raccoons, skunks, lots of great birds. I love it."

Trace glanced at his mother's face in the moonlight. His voice was soft as he replied, "I can see that. You look . . . happy."


Folding clothes from the dryer, Trace thought about the evening he'd spent with his mother: peaceful and relaxing, their conversation comfortable. His relationship with Megan had developed into a serious one, and his mother seemed pleased when he'd told her. Glad to see her happy and getting on with her life, Trace tried to sort out his feelings about Ray. It wasn't that he didn't like Ray; he did. He worried about his mother being alone. Just didn't know how he felt about her with another man.

He would soon be on his own. Sometimes the thought scared him and he wanted time to slow down, to go back before the accident. Wished he could have been closer to his father and things could have been better for his mom. As much as he resisted, he knew that as he made his way in the world, it was time for his mother to do the same.

Trace tossed the duffel bag aside. On the desk in his room—his furniture, but it didn't really feel like his room—Dani had placed a photograph of Brian and Trace taken the Christmas before Brian died. She'd caught them off-guard and snapped the shot—one of the few photos of Brian in the last years of his life. In the living room a formal family portrait shot taken around Trace's sixth birthday—and just before the accident—was tucked in among Dani's favorite photographs on a shelf.

A headache nagged at Trace's temples. He searched the medicine cabinet for some aspirin, but found none in the powder room or the guest bathroom. He crossed the hall and tried Dani's bathroom.

His hand tightened against the cabinet door. Next to a toothbrush holder containing two toothbrushes was a razor, shaving cream and a bottle of Stetson After Shave. Moments ticked by before his eyes left the aftershave and located the aspirin. He swallowed two with a gulp of water and closed the cabinet.

In the center of his mother's room Trace stared at the mirrored sliding doors of the two closets. Through the partially opened door closest to him he could see Dani's blouses and jeans hanging neatly above a shoe rack. The other door mocked him from across the room. Did he really want to know?

He turned and started from the room, stopped and strode back to the closet. He slowly slid open the door. Several western shirts, jeans and a denim jacket hung above two pair of cowboy boots. Trace quickly left the room.

Trace threw his backpack and duffel bag in the trunk. He glanced up as Dani jogged up the driveway.

"Good morning." Dani waved. "I needed to go for a walk. You were still asleep so I left you a note on the table."

He nodded and closed the trunk. "Yeah, I saw it. Sorry I wasn't awake, I would have gone with you."

"I didn't want to wake you. We could go for a walk now if you'd like. It's a gorgeous day."

"Nah." He avoided her eyes. "I think I'm going to head back to school. I have some studying to do anyway."

Dani's forehead wrinkled in a frown. "So soon? I thought you were going to stay for the day."

"It just seems . . . weird . . . being here. All our furniture is here . . ." He shrugged. "It doesn't feel like my room . . ."

Dani draped an arm across Trace's shoulders. "Oh, Trace. I'm sorry. I know it doesn't seem like home to you. It will take some getting used to. It felt strange for me too for a while."

Trace leaned against the car door.

"I guess. I have a headache anyway and probably wouldn't be good company. I'm sure you want to get back to work on the tack room."

"There's no hurry. Do you want some aspirin for your headache?"

"I found some. Thanks." Trace opened his car door. "I'll call you later. Okay?"

"Honey, is there something wrong? Stay awhile and we can talk." Dani reached a hand up to his shoulder.

"Nothing's wrong, Mom. I just want to go back to school." He brushed a kiss against her cheek and slid behind the wheel.

"Okay, be careful. You call me tonight so I know you got back safely."

Trace nodded, slipped on his sunglasses, and pulled away.

Dani watched her son drive away with a puzzled look and an ache in her chest. When he was out of sight, she turned toward the house. Patches met her at the door, howling for breakfast. Dani scratched the cat behind her ears, fed her and headed to change clothes.

Pulling off her sweatpants and T-shirt, Dani kicked her Reeboks next to her bed. As she straightened, her glance caught the opened closet door across the room. Ray's shirts hung like evidence at a crime scene. Dani hurried to her bathroom, yanked open the cabinet. The opened aspirin bottle stood, guilty as charged, beside the Stetson After Shave.

"Oh, hell." Dani slammed the cabinet shut. Her reflection stared at her from the mirror over the vanity.

"Dammit. I have no reason to feel so guilty. I'm a grown-up. A damned grown-up, widowed woman."

She reached for the phone beside her bed and dialed Trace's car phone: no answer. Dani flung herself on her bed. A stream of hot, angry tears ran over her face. She punched a fist into the pillow. "Dammit."

The phone rang just as Dani and Ray came in the kitchen door. Dani balanced a bag of cat food against her hip and reached for the phone.

She made a surprised face toward Ray and shoved her purse onto the counter.

"Hi, Mom. How are you?"

"Just fine. How about you? I've been calling you all week."

"Uh, I'm okay. Been really busy. Sorry I didn't get back to you sooner."

"You were supposed to call me when you got back to school on Sunday . . . remember?"

Silence.

"Trace?"

"I know. I just didn't want to talk, that's all."

"That's fine, but you could have let me know you got back okay."

"Okay, okay. I'm not a baby anymore, you know. I'm a grown-up."

"Yes, Trace, and so am I."

"What in the hell is that supposed to mean?"

"You just think about it. We're going to have to sit down and have a talk one of these days."

With an exasperated look, Ray waved his hand in the air and went outside.

"Yeah, well I'm pretty busy right now, so it will have to wait. Just wanted to see how you were doing."

"I'm fine . . . and I'm busy too." Dani fought to keep the irritation from her voice.

"Okay, I'll let you go then." Trace's voice sounded petulant.

"Trace, I don't want to have bad feelings between us over anything. Let's not end this conversation with either of us being angry."

His voice softened. "I don't either. I'm sorry for not calling. And . . . and we'll talk soon. Okay?"

"Okay. Take care and let me know when you can come home."

"Bye, Mom." He hesitated slightly. "I love you."

"I love you too, honey. Don't forget it."

Dani held the phone in her hand a minute after he disconnected the call.


The barn was redolent with smells of new lumber mingled with the rich scents of leather and fresh hay. In the tack room bridles, reins, and lead ropes hung neatly from horseshoe hooks on the wall. Freshly cleaned saddles rested on the padded racks Ray had just finished.

Ray and Dani stood back to admire their finished project.

"I can't believe it's done. It looks just wonderful."

Dani leaned against his shoulder. "I'm very proud of us. We did a great job," she said.

"We sure did. Let's say we hook up the trailer and go get the horses. I can't wait another day."

"Sounds good to me. I was hoping we could do it today."

Ray pulled into the large sandy arena. Dani jumped from the truck to close the gate while Ray unlocked the trailer doors. He untied Chance's lead rope and eased him out of the trailer. Cash pranced in place, his ears pitched forward. Dani spoke softly to calm him as she backed him down the ramp.

Leading the horses to the small grassy corral between the arena and the pasture, they gently unhooked the lead ropes and stepped back against the fence. Both horses stood side-by-side, ears pitched forward, heads high to sniff the air, surveying their new home. Cash made the first move: bucked, and circled the corral in a dead run. Chance followed closely behind.

They let the horses graze for about half an hour before introducing them to their new barn. Chance and Cash nosed around the fluffy fresh wood shavings in stalls almost twice as large as those at the boarding barn. Dani measured out their grain, filled water buckets, and secured the door latches before they left the barn.

"We are now officially home." Dani tucked her arm through Ray's as they strolled to the house.

Ray stopped in the middle of the yard and reached for Dani's hand. "Dani, I love you. One thing would make everything perfect."

She searched his eyes for a hint. "What would that be?"

"If I were young enough to ask you to marry me."

Wide-eyed, Dani opened her mouth to reply.

Ray held up a hand. "I'm sorry if I startled you. Forget I said that."

Dani linked her arm through his. "You know the age difference doesn't matter, Ray."

"Not now," he sighed, "but someday it will, and I don't want you tied to a feeble old man."

"I'm with you for the long haul, whether we're married or not, Ray," Dani whispered.

He reached his arm around her waist and they walked toward the house in silence.

# CHAPTER TWENTY-SEVEN

The gray sky swirled with fast-moving clouds. Dani pulled up the hood on her sweatshirt and locked up the barn. In typical midwestern fashion, summer had ended on a beautiful, balmy seventy-eight-degree day. Fall came on a Thursday and lasted four and a half hours before an angry wind blew in and the temperature dipped to a chilly thirty-six. *Buckle up for your first winter in the country. Let's see how much of a pioneer you really are.* Dani smiled to herself at how far she'd come and what she'd accomplished. *Okay, so I didn't do it all alone. But I know I could have. Having Ray to share it with me just makes it . . . special.*

Dani filled the birdfeeder and hurried toward the house. *Okay, Laura Ingalls, time to get the turkey in the oven.*

Her hands submerged in hot sudsy dishwater, Dani stared through the kitchen window into the shadowed backyard. From the family room she heard rumblings of the football game with occasional comments from Trace and Ray. Dani chuckled. *A Little House on the Prairie Thanksgiving*—with football.

Thanksgiving had been strange—their first holiday without Brian. Trace had not been home in over a month. While they'd had brief phone conversations, Dani and her son had not had their heart-to-heart talk. When Dani asked, Trace had said it would be fine for Ray to have dinner with them. The Monday before Thanksgiving, her sister Lynn called to invite herself to dinner and to see Dani's new house.

Lynn's flirty giggle floated in from the family room. A moment later she hurried into the kitchen. "I'm going out for a while. Don't wait up for me. I may be late." She rolled her eyes in a dreamy expression. Without waiting for any comment from Dani, she rushed out to her car.

*Just like her. Invites herself to dinner. Doesn't offer to help with anything. Lets Ray and Trace help clear off the table while she chats on the phone with old friends. Who has the time on Thanksgiving to talk with her, anyway? And now she's off to meet someone.*

Ray put his arms around Dani's waist and kissed her cheek. "I thought they were all going in the . . . the machine. How about if I dry these for you?"

"They won't all fit in the dishwasher and there are some I do by hand anyway. No need to dry, but you can keep me company."

"Um . . . my pleasure." Ray nuzzled against her ear. "I heard Lynn go out. Where's she going?"

An exasperated sigh escaped before Dani could muffle it. "Oh, who knows? I heard her on the phone, then she said she was going out and may be quite late."

Ray brushed a hand against her hair. "You two are so very different. It's difficult to believe she's your sister."

"I keep hoping she'll begin acting like a grown-up. Maybe our relationship would change, we'd be closer—become friends." Dani shook her head sadly. "Other than Trace, Lynn is the only family I have left, and yet she doesn't feel like family at all."

She wiped her hands on the dishtowel and turned to him. "Were you and your brother very much alike?"

Ray looked thoughtful before he answered. "Well, in a lot of ways, yes, we were. Since he died very young, who knows if we would have remained alike as we grew older." He laughed slightly. "Of course, my sister was the best, a real sweetheart. Very gentle and kindhearted."

"Not much different than you." Dani placed a damp hand against his cheek.

He kissed her hand. "Let's go in and join Trace. The game is almost over."

"You seem to be getting along well." Her words sounded hopeful as well as questioning.

"Yes, I think we are. He seems less resentful of me anyway."

Dani stretched out on the bed and watched Trace fold his clothes. "I wish you weren't leaving so soon. I thought you'd be here through the weekend."

"I wanted to spend some time with Megan and her family too. I guess I should have told you earlier. Hope you don't mind."

"No, I understand." Dani gave him a lopsided smile. "It's rough getting used to you being all grown-up and independent."

Trace yanked on the drawstring of the duffel bag. "Uh . . . I feel better about you being out here with . . ." He looked embarrassed as he mumbled, "I worry less about you now with Ray around."

A sudden lump in her throat kept Dani from a reply. She reached for Trace's hand. "We never had our heart-to-heart talk, you know."

"I don't know if we need to. I've thought a lot about things since I was home last. I remember how things were with Dad. I never really thought about how difficult it was for you, and how lonely you must have been." He tightened his hand around hers. "I like Ray, Mom. He's a super guy and I can tell he . . . he loves you very much." A flicker of concern clouded his eyes. "I wish he wasn't so much older than you."

"Why does that bother you so?"

"Because . . . I don't want you to be left alone again."

She reached out to hug her son. "That's very sweet, Trace. I hope that doesn't happen for a very long time." Her voice was husky as she continued. "Every day is precious, you know that. We have to make all of them count."

He nodded. "I dreaded the holiday, but it turned out better than I thought. Even with your goofy sister here." He smiled at her. "How long is she staying?"

"Who knows?" Dani groaned. "Not too long I hope."

Trace laughed. "Well, I guess I'd better get going. Promised Megan I'd be there this afternoon." He gave Dani a hug and grabbed his bag.

Dani walked Trace to the car, gave him a kiss as he slid behind the wheel.

"Have a save trip and say hi to Megan."

"I really like having Trace here." Ray stretched his legs in front of the sofa. "I hate having to go back to my apartment alone every night."

"Well, he's gone to Megan's for the weekend. So . . ."

"But *The Weird One* is still here . . ."

Dani laughed at the funny face he made when he spoke of Lynn. "But *The Weird One* doesn't live here. It's *my* house and I'll do as I please whether she's here or not."

"Good for you. One down and one to go." Ray slapped a hand against his thigh. "Need to advise them of the Mortgage Rule."

With a slight squint and a tilt of her head, Dani asked, "What is the Mortgage Rule?"

Ray chuckled, "The one who pays the mortgage, makes the rules."

Dani punched him playfully against the arm before he pulled her close for a kiss.

"Didn't you get milk and bread at the store?" Dani called to Ray from the kitchen.

No answer.

"Ray?" she poked her head into the family room.

Ray skimmed through the latest *Quarter Horse Journal.* "Oh, I guess I forgot. Had so many . . . uh many . . . so much to do." He tossed the magazine onto the coffee table without glancing at her. "I'll get them in the morning."

"That's okay. I can stop when I'm in town tomorrow. Just surprised me, that's all." She brushed a kiss against his cheek. "You never forget anything," she teased.

Ray pulled her on his lap and hugged her closely. "I never forget what's important. Like I love you."

Dani had just finished folding laundry when her sister shuffled into the kitchen. *Well, princess, aren't we up early? It's only ten-thirty.* Dani raised an obvious glance at the clock, but the gesture was lost on Lynn as she rummaged through the refrigerator.

It had been over a week since Thanksgiving with no indication from Lynn as to how long she planned to stay and Dani's patience with her sister was running thin.

"All out of yogurt, I see. Mind picking some up when you go to the store next time?" Lynn poured corn flakes into a bowl. "Strawberry or raspberry is fine."

*Steady, girl, and keep me away from sharp objects.*

Dani took a deep breath before joining her sister in the kitchen. "Lynn, we need to talk." She pulled out a chair and sat down. "Uh . . . don't you have to get back to work?"

Lynn raised a hand in a just-a-minute signal. She munched her cereal. "I've been meaning to talk to you about that." She dragged butter over her toast with deliberate care. "That was a real dead-end job. I just got fed up. So about two weeks ago, I quit. I'm looking for something better."

*Like CEO of Microsoft maybe?* Fighting for control of her temper, Dani bit against her lip and waited for Lynn to continue.

"Since I've been . . . home . . . I've been thinking. Maybe I'll stay around for a while. Look for a job here, you know?" She glanced at Dani. "You have more than enough room so I thought . . ."

Tolerance reached its limit. "Stop right there, Lynn." Dani raised her hand. "I'm always glad to have you visit, but . . . but you and I cannot live in the same house. It wouldn't work."

"Why not?"

"Why not? Because every time you're here, you treat me like your personal maid. It's 'pick me up some yogurt, Dani,' 'Dani would you mind throwing these clothes in when you do a load?' " Dani shook her head. "No, Lynn. You're an adult and you need to start behaving like one. You flit from job to job and place to place. You need to be on your own, and I don't want to have you here on a permanent basis. I'm getting used to being on my own and I like it."

Lynn interrupted with a loud grunt. "Yeah, sure, you're really 'on your own.' The cowboy is here most of the time. Noticed he didn't go home last night either."

Dani pushed her chair back so hard it almost fell over. "Dammit, Lynn. What I do in my own home is none of your business. This is *my* house. I pay the bills and I take care of myself."

"Well, you're lucky you can pay all your bills. You sure have enough money. You'll probably get a damned good settlement from that airline . . ."

Standing with her hands gripping the counter for control, Dani whipped around to face her sister. *"Lucky?* Lucky that my husband was paralyzed in a car accident? Lucky that ten years later my husband is killed in an airplane crash? That's what you call *lucky?*" She strode next to Lynn and glared into her stunned face. "I have more than paid my dues over the years, so don't you throw anything I have in my face."

Dani took a deep breath. "I think it would be best if you left today, Lynn." She picked up the empty cereal bowl and juice glass from the table and carried them to the sink.

Lynn sat quietly at the table for a few minutes. Finally, she said, "I don't have any money."

Dani grabbed her purse; counted out all the cash she had—$250—and threw it at her sister. "Now you have some money. I suggest you get some kind of a job fast before it runs out."

"You're kind of heartless, you know that, Dani?" Lynn ran her hand over the bills scattered on the table. She gathered them together and stuffed them into the pocket of her robe.

Dani's shoulders slumped with exasperation. "No, I am not heartless. But you are irresponsible." Dani threw the dishtowel against the chair. "I can help you get on your feet one more time, but then you have to make some better decisions and be responsible for your actions." She pushed open the back door and jogged down the path to the barn.

Ray parked his truck on the drive next to Dani's car. He balanced a case of pop against his hip and reached for the screen door. Lynn knocked against Ray as she pushed through the partially opened doorway.

"Whoa there. What's the hurry?"

"Ask your girlfriend," Lynn snarled.

"Where is Dani?"

Lynn fastened an angry stare on Ray, her voice heavy with sarcasm. "The lady of the manor is down at her stables."

Ray placed the pop on the counter and faced Lynn. "I don't know what happened here, but I don't care for your attitude."

"Well, well, well . . ." Lynn's voice was filled with scorn. "My big sister finally has a daddy to take care of her."

In two steps Ray reached Lynn's side. With a glacial stare, his blue eyes commanded her attention. "You had better watch your mouth, young lady. *I* don't have to put up with you . . ."

"And neither do I." Dani burst through the door. "I heard your smart remarks, Lynn. You've got five minutes to get out of this house."

"That's five minutes more than I need, sister dear." Lynn grabbed her purse from the table and stalked through the door.

Dani leaned against Ray, listening to the car door slam and wheels spinning in the gravel seconds later.

Ray rubbed his hand over her shoulder. "What 'n the hell is going on with her?"

Waving her hand in the air with an exasperated sigh, Dani filled him in with the ongoing saga of the world according to Lynn.

# CHAPTER TWENTY-EIGHT

The twinkling lights of the Christmas tree lit the room in soft puddles of color. Patches stretched in front of the fireplace, tucked into a ball, and went to sleep. Curled next to Ray on the couch, Dani stared into the snapping fire. Christmas carols floated in the background.

The house had been hectic and noisy with Trace home from college. Megan came to spend Christmas with them, and Dani smiled at the easy way she fit in and the tenderness that passed between Megan and Trace. Two days after Christmas they left to visit with Megan's family in Michigan and then head on to Colorado for skiing with a group of friends.

Dani enjoyed the laughter and fun with so many of Trace's high school friends stopping by. Now she enjoyed the peace and quiet alone with Ray. His breath was soft and warm against the back of her neck. She felt his strong and steady heartbeat against her shoulder.

*I have so much to be thankful for.* And her thoughts turned to Lynn. Three days after the Christmas card she'd sent her sister had been returned, Dani had received a card from Lynn. A generic Christmas card—Best Wishes for a Merry Christmas and a Happy New Year—signed only "Lynn." Postmarked from Tampa, Florida. Dani tried calling the last phone number she had for Lynn, got a recording; number had been disconnected with no new number available. *Wherever you are Lynn, I hope you're happy and having a nice holiday.*

Gentle flurries during the day had increased into a heavy snowfall. Strong winds swept a drift against the patio door. Weather, both good and bad, was more intense in the country. Winds, thunder, and lightning seemed much angrier without other houses and buildings close to buffer the sounds and the fury. The darkness was profound; stars breathtakingly beautiful without artificial lights to mute their brilliance.

When winter had first settled in, Dani groaned as she pulled herself out of a warm bed in the morning darkness to feed the horses—until she stopped to appreciate the absolute stillness and serenity of the countryside still asleep around her. It was as if Mother Nature had the world on hold while she pondered the weather for the day.

Bundled up against the cold, Dani loved the crunch and squeak of her boots in the crusted snow. Loved to see what nocturnal visitors had left tracks in her yard while she'd slept. Smiled at the two tiger-striped cats that wandered through shortly after she'd moved in, decided to stay and now greeted her each morning as she opened the barn door. Met by the sweet scent of hay, hearty knickers from the horses and a soft nuzzle from Chance was a wonderful way to start each day.

If Ray stayed over, sometimes he'd get up in the morning, but more often than not Dani had grown to love her early-morning commune with nature.

Ray tightened his arm around her waist. Feeling loved and contented, Dani closed her eyes and drifted off.

Dani shivered in the sudden coldness, her body warm only where she snuggled against Ray and where Patches had curled up around her feet. Dying embers of the fire flickered in the blackness of the room. The Christmas tree lights were no longer twinkling.

Dani touched Ray's shoulder. "Ray, wake up."

"Umm . . . what . . ." he mumbled.

"The power is off." She sat up and slid her feet into the cold slippers beside the couch. Welcome to winter in the country— real life behind the Currier & Ives print.

Suddenly chilled, Ray was instantly awake. "Whoa. I guess it is. Damn, it's cold in here."

Lit only by a sliver of a moon, the raging storm swirled in fiendish gusts. No longer fluffy, the wet globs of snow clung to the tree branches and coated the drifted banks that changed the topography of the ranch.

Dani found the battery-operated lantern and placed it on the table. Using a flashlight, she rummaged in the hall closet for sweatshirts. With Patches following closely at Ray's heels, he stoked the dying embers in the fireplace, got some kindling wood going and threw in a giant white birch log.

"I'm glad I brought in a supply of wood before the . . . the . . . before it snowed. Looks like we spend the night in here by the fire," Ray said.

Dani knelt before the hearth and opened the screen.

"What are you doing, honey?"

"Squaw heating water to make hot cider."

Ray laughed and sat beside her. "I can't think of anyone I'd rather be stranded with in a . . . storm than you." He kissed her cheek. "Sure am glad I didn't go home. You'd be out here all alone."

Dani and Ray curled up with blankets, pillows and Patches in front of the fireplace. The crackle of the blazing fire sang along with the howling winds in an eerie winter duet.

Morning brought no letup in the storm. Ray watched Dani pull her heavy parka over a sweatshirt and ski pants. "You look like an . . ." Ray bent to pull on his boots. "Uh . . . an . . ."

Dani glanced at him. "An Eskimo?"

"Yeah, that's it . . . an Eskimo." He laughed and threw gloves to her.

"It's a good thing you thought to fill all these jugs with water," Dani said as they each grabbed two plastic containers and headed toward the barn barely visible through gusting winds that spun the snow in a whipped-cream frenzy.

High-stepping through drifts and buffeted by strong wind, they struggled through the snow. Off-balance by the two water containers, Dani fell twice on the way to the barn. Each time, Ray laughed as he put down his own water jugs and pulled her out.

"Good thing I wear this red jacket."

"Why's that?"

"If I'm here alone and fall in the snow maybe someone would spot the red glob in the snow and call for help."

"Guess I'll have to stay here until . . . it gets warm."

"If it keeps on snowing you may not have a choice. You'll be here until the spring thaw."

By the time they reached the barn, they were winded and crusted with snow. Dani dropped the water jugs on the barn floor and sank onto a hay bale. Chance whinnied his delight at seeing them; Cash spun in his stall and snorted his disapproval at being kept indoors.

Ray dug the heavier blankets from the box in the tack room and covered both horses while Dani measured out their grain, gave them fresh hay and filled water buckets. The cats peered over the top of their straw-filled box, waiting to be fed. Working quickly against the cold, Dani and Ray each cleaned a stall, gave the horses a final pat and prepared for their trek back through the snow.

The wind had died down a bit and the snow had stopped falling. Ice daggers hanging from the gutters shimmered like diamonds in the bright sun glaring through the frigid air.

"Do you think we should plow out the drive?" Dani asked as she looked longingly toward the house.

"I'll do it. You go on in."

Ray stomped his boots and brushed the snow from his jacket. Dani met him at the door with dry clothes. "Hurry up and get changed into something warm." She patted his cherry-red face with a fluffy towel.

"Your first winter in the country is sure turning out to be a rough one, honey."

"Come on by the fire and get warm." Dani took his hand. In the family room she had pulled the coffee table close to the fire. She made sandwiches and heated soup in the fireplace.

"Um . . . that sure smells good." Ray rubbed his hands in front of the fire. "You make a good little pioneer, pretty lady."

Dani smiled, poured him some soup, and sat next to him on the floor. "It's kind of fun, actually," she grinned.

Ray raised an eyebrow at her as she sipped at the steaming mug of vegetable soup.

"If it doesn't last too long, that is," Dani finished.

But the rough winter lasted until late March: heavy snow, wind and ice storms, power outages. Ray stayed with Dani most of the time, reluctant to let her be alone, and she was grateful for his presence. Several days he'd gotten up early to feed the horses and plow the driveway so she could get to work. As winter dragged on, Dani wondered at her decision to move to the country alone. What if Ray hadn't come back? What if she had been alone to care for the horses and dig out after each blizzard? *I would have coped, that's what. I would have found a neighbor to plow the drive and I would have taken care of the animals because I had to.* She felt good about life, her newfound strength and knowledge that she could take care of herself.

"These times are rough, but they make you stronger, Dani," Ray had whispered to her one night, as they lay snuggled together during another power outage.

"I'm about as strong as I care to be right now," she'd answered. "Right now I need a break."

He'd kissed her softly and said, "Okay, let's sleep and dream of spring and twenty-second pole runs."

Dani laughed, and did just that.

The dreams of spring became a welcome reality. Ray worked Chance daily, having consistent clean runs and shaving time gradually. Dani began teaching Cash the pole pattern and eagerly looked forward to having two horses for Ray to compete with at horse shows.

As they walked the horses around the arena to cool them down, Dani was strangely quiet.

"Something wrong today, darlin'?"

Despite the warmth of the bright sunshine falling on her shoulders, Dani felt a chill.

Her voice was soft and sad as she replied, "It's been a year today that . . . that Brian died."

Ray reached out to squeeze her hand.

"Sometimes it seems like yesterday, but when I think of all that has happened, all we've done, it seems like longer."

He nodded. "When Kathy died, I couldn't believe how the world just went on about its business like nothing had happened. Everything had changed for me, but the sun kept coming up in the morning and going down each night."

He glanced at her. "When did you last talk to Trace?"

"Last night. He realized the date and called to talk."

"He's such a fine young man."

"Thanks." Dani smiled. "I think so too."

"Let's put these horses away and take it easy the rest of the day."

Dani sighed and pulled Cash toward the barn.

# CHAPTER TWENTY-NINE

Ray pushed Chance through the poles as Dani rooted them on from the fence line. As Chance slid past the timing light in a cloud of dust, the loud speaker crackled with the results: "That's a clean run and the time is . . . 22:225. Getting better, Ray."

At the smattering of applause and cheers, Ray doffed his hat in the air and nodded his head toward the announcer.

The sorrel horse bobbed his head and snorted as he sucked in air. Ray hopped from the saddle, loosened the saddle cinch, and rubbed his hand along Chance's sweaty neck. "Good run, big guy. We're goin' places."

Ray and Dani watched another rider push his horse through the poles, weaving, changing leads, last pole ahead. Damn, pole down. Spoiled run.

"See? Doesn't matter how fast you are. If you get a pole down, it's over. Chance has consistent clean runs, and we're increasing speed a little at a time. He's going to be a good pole horse." Ray slid the bridle off and hooked on a halter, tied the lead rope to the trailer. He gave Chance a final pat on the rump.

"Worked up an appetite, babe. Let's get some . . . uh . . ."

"Chili?" Dani finished for him.

"That's it. Chili."

The Triple R Horse Show concession stand was famous for its thick, spicy, homemade chili; and Ray and Dani always finished off Ray's last run with a hot bowl as they watched the rest of the events.

The evening was picture perfect for an outdoor event. The sparkling stars and full moon brightened the deep velvet sky. With the setting sun, a mild breeze cooled off what had been a muggy day and brought whiffs of fresh alfalfa from a new-mown field nearby. The pungent aroma of leather and horseflesh mingled with the night air was an intoxicating mixture for those who loved horses and horse shows.

From the speed-event riders in dusty roper boots and jeans, to the neatly groomed pleasure-class riders in colorful shirts, some in jackets and chaps, hats to match, the atmosphere was relaxed and friendly.

"I just love horse shows," Ray exclaimed as he balanced his bowl of chili in his lap and took a frosty Coke Dani held out to him.

"Me too. And they are even more fun being with you and having my horse compete."

"So when are you going to bite the bullet and get out there and run him yourself?"

Dani shook her head. "Oh, no. You enjoy it so much, and I love to watch you both. Love how he responds to you, gives everything he has when you ask him. Training him at home is okay with me, but I'm just not aggressive enough to get out there and let him fly."

Ray tilted his head back and closed his eyes. "I love when he flies."

"A successful run for me would be if I didn't fall off or throw up."

That brought a hearty laugh from Ray. He tousled her hair and said, "You're such a sweetheart. I'll gladly ride your horse and you cheer us from the fence."

"Deal."

The summer was a whirl of trail rides on the days Dani didn't go to her office; horse shows on the weekends; and plenty of hot, dusty work around the ranch. Somehow they managed to plant a small garden spurred on by Ray's casual comment, "How about if we put in a few tomato plants?" A few tomato plants expanded to include lettuce, green onions, cucumbers, green beans, and just for the heck of it, a watermelon vine.

"Always wanted to grow a watermelon," Ray revealed at the nursery where they bought their plants and seeds. So they tried a variety of watermelon suggested for the area.

Ray weeded and watered the garden and puttered around in the barn when Dani was at work; and on her off-days, she cleaned stalls while Ray swept up the barn and played with the cats.

They'd made no definite arrangements, but three or four times a week Ray stayed overnight. They sensed each other's needs and moods, when they needed to be together or when they needed some time alone. They worked together like they'd been doing it all their lives.

One morning when Dani was alone after she'd fed and watered the horses and barn cats, she stopped on her way back to the house to pull a few weeds in her flowerbed. A small shower during the night had left the ground soft and easy to work. When Ray arrived sometime later, he found Dani still working in the flowers. Dressed in shorts and a T-shirt with her hair pulled back in a ponytail, she knelt in the damp earth, pulling weeds.

She smiled at him as he reached out his hand to pull her to her feet. She was more tanned than she'd ever been, and the summer sun had splashed her copper hair with golden highlights. Her face and knees were smudged, and her hands covered with dirt.

"You look about twelve years old, playing in the dirt like that," Ray said.

Dani shook her head and gave him a kiss, holding her dirty hands out to her sides.

"I can't believe I've been out here this long. I fed the horses and it seemed just too beautiful to go back indoors. I stopped to pull a few weeds and . . ." she pushed the back of her hand against his wrist to see his watch. "Wow, I've been out here an hour and a half."

Ray turned on the faucet by the back door and held the hose while Dani washed the dirt from her hands and knees.

He brushed away the smudge from her cheek. "Missed a spot here," he said.

"Put up the umbrella on the table while I get us some juice, okay?"

"Yes, ma'am."

Dani was thoughtful as she sipped her cranberry juice and watched the blue jays and cardinals at the bird feeder. "I just realized something."

"What's that, honey?"

"When I was a little girl, I remember my mom working out in her garden really early in the morning on weekends and sometimes a few times before she went in to work. I couldn't imagine why she'd be up working that early. Now I know. It's such a glorious time of the day." She took a drink and continued. "I noticed in the winter it's so still and kind of peaceful. In the summer, it feels different. Like . . ." She thought a minute. "Like everything can hardly wait to get the day started. I hear the birds just about sun-up. And the roosters and cattle down the road."

Ray ran his finger around the wet ring his glass had left on the table and smiled.

"And I can't stand to waste a minute of the sunshine by being indoors," Dani finished.

"Turned into a real little country girl," he teased.

"Guess I have." Dani pulled herself out of the chair with a groan. "Country girl's back kind of hurts from kneeling so long. Think I'll go in and get dressed. Oh, by the way, did you miss something this morning?"

"You mean besides waking up without you next to me?"

"Yes, besides that. Like your wallet, maybe? You left it here yesterday."

"Ah, that's where it is. Looked all over the house last night," he mumbled.

"Good thing you didn't leave it somewhere else. With all that cash, someone would be having a really good time today."

"Yep, sure would."

"It's in the kitchen by the phone."

Ray nodded.

"I almost forgot. Trace called last night . . ."

Trace and Megan had got jobs at a resort in Vermont for the summer. Dani had finally come to grips with the fact that her son was grown-up and would soon be on his own. He'd be home for two weeks and then back to school to start his junior year.

Although he was at ease now with Ray, Dani knew Trace would probably never feel as though the ranch was his home, and it had surely been a factor in his deciding to take the summer job out East. It would have been a different summer if Trace had been home. Ray would have gone home alone to his apartment each night, and Dani would have missed falling asleep with his arms wrapped around her.

Dani glanced at the calendar.

"Ray, I was thinking the other day, I've been here almost a whole year."

"Uh-huh." He turned the page of his newspaper.

"And that means your lease is about up for renewal."

"Uh-huh."

"You sure are gabby this morning. Something wrong?"

"Nope."

"News must be pretty interesting this morning."

Ray grunted. "Says here there's a meteorite heading for earth."

Dani threw her hands in the air. "Well, guess we should cancel our plans for this afternoon."

He glanced at Dani; her expression made him laugh.

"Okay, what's on your mind?"

Wiping her hands on a towel, she took a chair beside him at the table.

"I was thinking . . ."

Ray folded the paper in his lap and gave her his attention.

"Thinking of how silly it is for you to pay rent on the apartment in town, when . . . when you're here most of the time anyway."

"You thinkin' I'm here too much? Just say so."

Dani almost heard her chin hit the floor. *What in the hell has gotten in to him lately? Comes out with some of the darnedest things.* She reached for his hand.

"Of course, that isn't what I meant. I was thinking you should just move out here." She smiled with a little self-conscious smile. "If you want to, that is."

"Don't need an old coot like me here all the time."

"Old coot?" She moved over and sat on his lap. "I love you, you old coot."

"Wouldn't look good, me living here with you and us not being married. And I'm too old to marry you, much as I want to."

"For goodness sake, Ray. We're not married and you sleep here half the time anyway. Who cares?"

"The boy would care, that's who."

"The . . . ? Trace?"

"Yep."

"I've already crossed that hurdle. I talked to him the other day to see how he felt about it. He said it's fine with him. He just wants me to be happy."

Ray slapped the paper on the table and pushed Dani to her feet.

"So glad you have a kid's approval to lead your life. Happy you discussed it with him before talking to me. What if he'd said no?" Ray tilted his head and raised an eyebrow at her.

Dani forced out an exaggerated sigh. "Forget I even mentioned it, okay? Renew your damned lease if that's what you want."

"It's not what I want. I want you, all the time, forever." His eyes squinted with a sadness Dani hadn't seen in a long time.

"Then . . . what's wrong?"

"I love you, I love the animals, the ranch. Every day you grow so vibrant, so full of life, so precious to me."

"So what's the problem?"

He pulled her to him, holding her so tightly she gasped for breath.

"I'm so aware of time running out. I'm . . . getting old and I don't want to leave you alone."

A sudden alarm bell rang in Dani's head. "You aren't sick or anything, are you? You feel okay?"

"I feel fine."

If Dani noticed the answer came a little too quickly, she pushed it aside.

"We can just go on with things the way they are if you want."

"Sure it was okay with Trace?"

"If you moved in?"

"Yes."

"Yes, I'm sure. He likes you, and he worries less about me

when you're here. He told me that a long time ago."

"Okay."

"Okay, like you'll move in?"

"Yeah." He smiled his lopsided grin and looked like his old self again.

In a cloud of dust, Ray spurred Chance past the timing light and slid to a stop just short of the gate. As the crowd cheered, the announcer boomed, "Twenty-one seconds flat. And that's good for second place, Ray."

Ray had ridden Chance at horse shows all summer, taking an occasional third or fourth place in pole bending where tenths of a second separated the winners. This was his first second-place run.

Dani jumped to her feet and ran to greet Ray when he left the ring. She brushed a hand against Chance's muzzle, patted his sweaty neck and threw her arms around Ray as he eased out of the saddle. "Great ride! Best ever."

Ray grabbed his hat from his head, rubbing the dust from his eyes. "It was, wasn't it? Felt just . . . just right all the way."

They led Chance back to the horse trailer where Cash danced in place and pawed a hole in the turf. Dani loosened the saddle cinch while Ray haltered Chance and tied him to the trailer. "Fantastic run, big boy," Ray whispered. Chance bobbed his head and pushed his head against Ray's shoulder.

Sliding the dusty saddle onto the rack in the trailer, Ray searched for a brush in the tack box. He reached for the bottle of cold water Dani held out to him.

Still wired from his run, Chance shifted back and forth as Ray ran the soft brush over his sides before covering him with a sheet blanket.

After rewarding Chance with a sliver of apple, Dani strode around to the other side of the trailer to check out the baby—as she thought of one of the newest acquisitions to the menagerie. A sleek black gelding with a white diamond on his forehead stood nibbling at his hay bag. Two months before—and shortly after Ray had moved to the ranch—Dani bought the calm three-year-old, named Magic, from a distraught husband whose wife—and the owner of the horse—had been killed in an auto accident. Dani ran her hand along the black's lean body. He twitched his ears and glanced toward her. "You're doing pretty well, Magic. Don't seem bothered by all the noise and confusion at all."

Another member of the family, a honey-colored year-old Lab puppy strained at a leash attached to the bumper of Ray's truck. The Lab came into their lives compliments of an idiot who felt the best way to dispose of unwanted pets was to dump them along a country road. Ray had been driving back to the ranch one afternoon and saw a car slow slightly and push the pup from the car door before he sped away. The puppy stood beside the road, looking confused. As Ray eased to a stop and opened his door, the dog perked up his ears, giving Ray a long, appraising look. With a sudden wag of his tail, and a "woof" of a greeting, the orphaned canine bounded to Ray's side. Ray scratched the luxurious butterscotch-colored fur and mutual admiration was formed on the spot. The dog jumped into Ray's truck and had been his adoring companion ever since, earning him the name—uncreative as it was—of Shadow.

"Okay, Shadow," Dani bent to unhook the snap. "You stay with me now." Shadow jumped against Dani, licking her face. Dani placed her hand on the dog's head. "Sit. Sit, Shadow." The dog immediately obeyed. "Good boy." She slapped a hand against her thigh and commanded, "Come." Shadow trotted along and sat beside her as she eased into a lawn chair beside Ray. She wiped the perspiration from her forehead with the back of her hand. The evening had brought no relief from the daytime temperature; even the nightly cricket chorus sounded lethargic in the field nearby. In spite of the unseasonably humid night, Ray had pulled on a blue cotton windbreaker.

"Are you okay, Ray?"

"Yeah. Why?"

"What's with the jacket?"

"I'm just a little . . ." He raked his hand through his hair and slid his hat lower on his brow. "It's cool, that's all. Okay?"

"Sure." Dani gathered up the rest of their gear and stashed it in place in the truck. "Hey, I'm kind of tired. Why don't we get this circus loaded up and go home. I don't really want to stay for the last classes," she said.

In the lights from the arena, Dani glimpsed a look of irritation along with the set of his jaw. "Fine with me," he mumbled.

Without any conversation, they loaded the horses in the trailer. Dani opened the door of the truck for Shadow.

"Want me to drive home?"

Exasperation sounded in Ray's exaggerated sigh. "No, Dani. I'm not too old and feeble to drive home."

Shadow settled on the seat between them with his head in Dani's lap. She ran her hand over the puppy and stared into the dark country sky. She bit against her lower lip as she thought over the last few months, of the moments of irritation and short-tempered outbursts in Ray's normally easygoing manner.

*I wonder if he's sorry he moved in with me. Maybe he doesn't feel at home there. That's silly. He was there most of the time before, anyway.* Dani stole a glance at Ray, both his hands gripping the wheel and staring straight ahead at the traffic. What if he's sick and doesn't want to tell me? I think I'll get him to go in for a check-up.

They worked so well together, unloading and putting the horses in the barn took only minutes to do and required no conversation. "I'm just going to leave this rig in the arena. I'll put the trailer away in the morning."

"Fine. That's okay."

When Dani had finished brushing her teeth, Ray was already in bed facing away from her side, his breathing slow and regular. *I know you're not asleep.*

She slipped into bed beside him, his naked body warm and soothing next to hers. She snuggled close against his back with her arm across his waist. He reached his hand to hers and gave it a squeeze.

"Ray, are you all right?"

He turned toward her and held her tightly. "I'm fine, sweetie. Just tired." He tilted her chin and brushed his lips against hers. "I'll always love you, Dani."

Dani lay quietly in the dark, listening to him fall asleep. Despite the warmth of his body next to hers, she felt chilled.

Ray was already up and at the barn when Dani awoke the next morning. She hurried into her clothes and jogged to the barn. Ray whistled as he hung bridles and lead ropes in the tack room. He smiled when he saw Dani. "Finally up, sleepyhead."

"You certainly seem chipper this morning. Sleep well?"

"Like a . . . a baby. Yep, just like a baby."

"Me too. Think I'll clean stalls before I take my shower."

"No need. I've already cleaned them." He folded the sheet blanket and tucked it in the trunk. "Go get ready for work. I'll be in as soon as I park the trailer."

"No work today. It's Sunday."

"That's right. Sunday. No work today."

Stepping from the shower, Dani draped a large towel around herself. She stood in front of the mirror and aimed the dryer at her hair. She smiled at her reflection, thinking of Ray's words before he'd fallen asleep: "I'll always love you, Dani." Deep within her mind came the response, "Someday you won't even know my name."

A shiver flickered down her spine. The air around her suddenly felt heavy and the walls seemed too close. She gazed at herself in the mirror and sucked in a deep breath. *Where in the hell did that come from? Why would I think something like that?*

In slow motion, with automatic movements, Dani finished drying her hair and got dressed. Moments later she found Ray in the kitchen making toast.

*Don't be so melodramatic. It didn't mean anything.* Dani tucked away her thoughts and poured him some juice.

"Trace will be home today," Dani said.

"Uh-huh."

"Wish he could stay longer, but he has to go back to school in less than two weeks."

Ray frowned. "Why can't he?"

"He needs to be back at school. He's an SA this year."

"SA?"

"Student advisor. He's going to help incoming freshmen get settled in—just like someone helped him his first year."

"Ah. That's nice."

Rinsing the soapsuds from his car, Trace glanced over his sunglasses at his mother and Ray working in the yard.

Ray looked annoyed as he rummaged through the toolbox. "Damn. Where is that . . . ?"

"Hammer? Are you looking for the hammer? I saw it on the workbench in the garage a little while ago."

"Umph. Yeah, that's it. That's where I left it."

"I'm going in the house to check the dryer. Clothes should be almost finished by now. Okay?"

"Sure," Ray mumbled.

Carrying a basketload of towels, Dani headed toward Trace's room.

Trace sorted through the clothes he was taking back to school and paused to watch Ray tack up a new fence board on the arena. "Mom?"

"Yes, what is it?"

"Uh . . . how long has this been going on?"

Dani glanced toward her son as she sorted Trace's towels from the rest and put them on his bed.

"How long has what been going on?"

"You finishing Ray's sentences . . . filling in his words."

With a nervous little laugh Dani replied, "That's the way people get when they work closely together and can almost read each other's minds."

Trace placed both hands on his mother's shoulders. "Mom, that's not what I mean. *You* fill in *his* sentences. He doesn't fill in yours."

Dani stared past Trace to where Ray worked along the fence line.

"Mom, there's something going on here. I don't think Ray is . . ." Trace hesitated. "Has he had a check-up lately?"

Dani shook herself loose from Trace's grasp. Her sigh sounded frustrated as she flopped onto the bed.

"I've suggested he go in for a check-up. He hates doctors. Says he's fine."

"I think you need to insist, Mom." Trace sat next to her, his voice soft and concerned. "There's something wrong."

"I know," she whispered. "I know."

# Chapter Thirty

Dani and Ray sat hand-in-hand on the couch in the family room. Neither spoke. Patches curled up next to Dani, the cat's face buried against Dani's side. Shadow's chin rested on Ray's knee, sad, questioning eyes searching his master's face. Dani heard the drumbeats of her heart. Felt hot. Felt cold. The oxygen in her lungs seemed too heavy for her bloodstream. A raw, acid taste stung her throat. *What can I say to him? How does he . . . how does he feel? How can I make it less frightening for him?*

"Ray?"

He shook his head. "Don't. Don't talk right now, honey."

It had been a rough two weeks. They argued. She cried. He yelled. She cried more. He gave in and finally agreed to a check-up.

"Don't have a doctor to go to," he'd argued.

"My doctor is very good. I think you would like her . . ."

"Her? Oh no . . . not going to any woman doctor."

"Okay, I'll find some grizzled old curmudgeon you'd feel comfortable with."

"You do that. I'll probably be in better shape than he is."

Dani's doctor recommended a colleague specializing in geriatrics, a compassionate young doctor who, despite his age, worked very well with his elderly patients.

Geriatrics. Elderly patients. Words Dani couldn't think of in context with Ray.

Ray insisted Dani talk to the doctor with him. "I don't know what to tell him. What should I say I'm here for? Anyone can tell by looking at me, I'm in great shape," he'd said to her.

So they waited together in the exam room with all the usual interesting things to look at while one waits for the doctor: blood pressure apparatus, glass jars of Q-tips, cotton balls, tongue depressors, colorful anatomy charts on the walls so one can visualize and wonder what parts of their insides might have gone haywire. Of course everything's spotless and all the framed university degrees hanging on the wall are there to instill confidence that *this* doctor can fix whatever it is that has gone wrong.

Ray flexed the doctor's card in his hand. "Geri . . . whats?"

"Geriatrics," Dani said. "It's a physician specializing in . . . in older patients."

"Umph." He crumpled the card and stuck it in his shirt pocket.

A snappy knock preceded the entrance of Dr. Marshfield, slim, athletic, sandy blond hair, twinkling blue eyes, early forties.

Extending his hand in a firm handshake, he said, "Mr. Crowley, Gary Marshfield. Nice to meet you."

"No need to Mr. Crowley me, you can call me Ray." Ray shook hands. "Look kind of young. What would you know about getting old?"

"Ray," cautioned Dani.

As Dr. Marshfield glanced toward Dani, she extended her hand. "Dani Monroe. I'm afraid he isn't too pleased to be here."

The doctor shook Dani's hand and glanced over Ray's chart. "You are . . . Mr. Crowley's . . . uh, daughter?"

Ray gave an irritated snort. "I'm not old. I'm not sick. And she's *not* my daughter. She's my girlfriend."

Marshfield didn't miss a beat. "You sure as hell don't sound sick . . . or old." He glanced at his chart. "Certainly don't look your age, and you're a very lucky man."

Dani closed her eyes and felt her face flush.

Ray grinned and nodded. "So you can tell her I'm fine and I can get home and ride my horses."

"Ride horses, do you?"

"Yep. Show quarter horses—speed events. Ever ride a horse, Doc?"

"No . . . well, yes, but it's been a long time ago. Now I ride a motorcycle."

Dani stifled a sigh and wondered how long this pissing contest was going to last.

Dr. Marshfield nodded to Ray. "Ray, strip down and put on this designer gown and I'll be right back."

"Ms. Monroe, why don't you have a seat in the waiting room? I'd like to examine Ray and have a little talk. I'll have my nurse call you when we're finished."

After Dani spent a half an hour fidgeting in the waiting room, trying to read, the nurse called her back into the exam room.

With a smug look on his face, Ray buttoned his shirt and folded his arms across his chest.

"Ray seems to be in good health. Heart sounds good, great blood pressure. I'm going to order some routine tests since it's been . . ." he winked at Ray, ". . . quite a while since his last physical. See if there is anything causing these 'little problems remembering sometimes,' as Ray put it." Handing Dani the order for the tests he wanted, he said, "Just call the hospital and ask for Outpatient Scheduling." He shook hands again with Ray and Dani. "I'll see you when we get all the results."

"Thank you."

"Thanks, Doc."

When they were seated in the car, Dani looked at Ray with an exasperated scowl. "Why were you so belligerent? He seemed very nice."

Ray laughed. "Just checking him out. See how he responded if I needled him a bit."

"And?"

"He did fine. Just fine. I like him."

"Good. How did the exam go?"

Ray sat straighter in his seat. "Fine. I could tell he was impressed."

Dani sucked in a breath and burst out laughing.

Ray grinned and watched Dani try to gain control of herself. Finally he grabbed her, and kissed her hard.

Breathless, Dani said, "Why wouldn't he be impressed? I sure as hell am impressed with you too."

"Good. Let's get home. I have horses to ride."

Complete blood workup. Routine tests. Stress test. Neurological tests. MRI. Ray mumbled and grumbled about them all, but left a memorable impression on the hospital staff. Refusing to be "just another patient in one of these dumb little get-ups with my ass exposed to the world," he insisted on wearing his Stetson and cowboy boots along with the hospital gown. The nurses and techs all flirted with him and everyone called him Cowboy. As much as he hated the tests, he loved the attention.

They waited for results and tried not to worry; life continued around the ranch as usual. Dani found it difficult to concentrate at work, breathing a sigh of relief when she got home to find Ray snoozing in a lounge chair under his favorite tree with Shadow close to his side.

Then finally the call came from the doctor for them to come into his office. Dani tried to make small talk on the drive to the clinic. Ray turned on the radio. "Why don't we just listen to music, okay?" he'd said.

Once seated in the waiting room, Dani held Ray's hand. She could feel his tension. She stared into the tropical fish tank that ran the length of the smaller wall of the room.

"I enjoy watching the fish," she said.

"Guess they're supposed to make people relax," Ray grumbled.

"I think they do. Don't you feel relaxed watching them?"

"Nah. All that water just makes me need to pee."

Dani scrunched her eyes and shook her head. Just as she glanced at him and whispered, "Behave," the nurse called his name. Dani was relieved to see Ray's grin and know he was just working through his tension.

The nurse tucked Ray's chart in the wall slot as she ushered them into the doctor's private office.

Ray rested his hat against his knee and stared at the framed diplomas above the large oak desk. Dani folded her hands in her lap to keep from fidgeting, glanced at the stack of medical journals on the corner of the desk next to a framed photograph of a smiling young blond woman holding a baby. From the hall came muffled sounds of closing doors, coughs, and a nervous laugh. Ray tapped his boot against the floor and sighed. Dani glanced at the clock and reached out to hold his hand. Hands on that clock seem glued in one spot. *We've been here—*she glanced at her watch—*oh, fifteen minutes. Feels like at least an hour.*

Chart in hand, the doctor eased into his office and softly closed the door behind him. He gave Dani's shoulder a pat and shook hands with Ray. "How're you feeling today, Ray?"

"Guess you should tell me, Doc." Ray's voice was low, with a slight tremor.

The doctor sat in the large leather chair behind his desk. He paged through Ray's chart. "You're in remarkable physical health, Ray. Most routine testing is within acceptable levels." He cleared his throat. "Through a process of elimination, we've ruled out other possibilities for your memory problem."

Dani swallowed hard and held her breath at the sad look that flickered in the young doctor's eyes as he explained the findings of the MRI.

*Diagnosis: Alzheimer's Disease.*

Ray sat still, hands folded in his lap, and stared at a spot just above the doctor's head.

Trying to breathe normally, Dani bit against her bottom lip, afraid to glance at Ray. The words, in bold, capital letters flashed through her mind like the repeating sign at the bank: TIME—TEMPERATURE—NO-FEE CHECKING—NEW CD RATES—ALZHEIMER'S DISEASE.

Dr. Marshfield rose from his desk and handed Dani some pamphlets. He sat against the corner of his desk, wrote out a script for *Aricept.*

"You need some time to talk about this. Why don't you come in to see me next week so we can answer any questions you may have."

Ray slid off his chair, shook hands with the doctor, and walked to the door.

"Make an appointment at the desk, and don't hesitate to call before if you need to." Dr. Marshfield held the door as Dani followed Ray down the hall.

Yesterday they didn't know. Concerned. Something minor, manageable. Small stroke. High blood pressure. Change in diet, prescribed medication to make everything better. Now they knew. Books on the coffee table: "Coping with Alzheimer's

Disease—A 36 hour day." Pamphlet from a drug company: "ARICEPT—Help for Early to Moderate Alzheimer's Disease."

Yesterday, the sun rose on a normal day. Today, their world tilted out of its orbit. Two words had changed their lives.

# CHAPTER THIRTY-ONE

Dani drove home from work through light afternoon traffic, pondering the feeling there seemed to be a barrier between them and the rest of the world. Devastating news has a way of making you feel isolated from everyone else—like it's *us* and *them*. Their lives are okay, normal; ours has changed. We're suspended in time, hung on a hook, watching others go about their business while we figure out how in the hell to go about ours.

The air didn't smell or feel the same; the sun didn't seem as warm against her skin. She was at a loss as to what to say to Ray; didn't know how he felt—he'd shut down, stopped sharing his feelings with her. She no longer feared "being alone" but she was afraid of "being without Ray."

Dani pulled into the garage, shut off the engine, and sat for a few minutes. She never knew what Ray's mood would be from day to day, sometimes from hour to hour. With a smile and an air of determined cheerfulness, Dani pushed open the back door. Shadow greeted her with a half-hearted wag of his tail. The dog had become her barometer of Ray's moods. She reached out to stroke the butterscotch fur, her own frame of mind slipping a notch at the look in the canine's eyes.

"Ray?" Dani called out as she slid her purse on the kitchen counter.

"In here . . ." came his gruff reply.

Ray tossed a book on the coffee table. "I shouldn't have moved in with you." He pulled himself out of the recliner and strode out of the house. Shadow whined and followed Ray to the door. With a glance toward the table, Dani saw one of the Alzheimer's books Dr. Marshfield had given her. Opening to the bookmarked place, Dani scanned the page. ". . . in the later stages of the disease . . ." She sagged onto the sofa with the book in her lap.

"Dammit. Shouldn't have left this lying around." Dani paged through the book to one of the how-to-handle sections, reinforced herself while giving Ray some time to be alone.

She again summoned a cheerful attitude as she joined Ray in the barn. After retrieving the brush box from the tack room, she hooked Chance in the crossties. She balanced Chance's left front foot against her knee and cleaned out his hoof, methodically—like it was brain surgery—picking and brushing against the horseshoe. Focused on her task, as if she went about her life in a normal manner, things would be normal.

She tossed the hoof pick into the box and stole a glance toward Ray as he secured Magic in his stall.

"Dammit, Dani. I can't stand this any longer. You look at me like you expect me to start sucking my thumb and drooling like a baby any minute." Ray threw the brush in the tack box and stalked from the barn.

Seconds later Dani heard his truck start, tires scrunching too rapidly through the gravel driveway. Dejected, she slumped to a bale of hay. Tiger Two jumped into her lap. *Does he really feel that way? Am I treating him differently?* She scratched the cat behind its ears and wondered. She'd read all the books, thought she knew what to expect. Told herself she'd be strong and patient, make it easier for him. Let him know she still loved him, always would.

Dani turned up the volume on the radio, hoping the jabber

of the talk show would drown out her thoughts. She cleaned stalls, put in fresh bedding, and measured out the evening ration of grain into each bucket. An hour ticked by, the news came on. *It's okay; he hasn't been gone that long.*

Dani sliced an apple and divided it among the three horses. The sound of crunching gravel in the driveway brought a sigh of relief.

Ray eased behind Dani and slid his arms around her waist.

"I'm sorry. Shouldn't snap at you," he whispered.

"Why did you say you shouldn't have moved in with me?"

"Pretty damned obvious, honey. You don't need another invalid to take care of, now do you?" He spun her around to face him.

"And where were you all day?"

"Where . . . ?" She looked confused. "What do you mean where was I? I was at work."

"Yeah, right. All those good-looking young guys you work with. Pretty soon they'll be lined up down the block."

Her mouth dropped open and she stared at Ray. "What in the hell is . . . ?"

"What in the hell is the matter with me?" Ray snapped. "I guess we both know the answer to that, don't we?"

"Ray, don't . . . please don't." She reached out to hold him.

He slumped against the stall and held her. "Dani . . . my dear Dani. I love you so much. I don't want to lose you to somebody else."

"I know, and that's not going to happen. I love you, too."

"I've taken good care of myself all my life, been proud of being healthy, trim and active. Now . . . now this damned disease . . ." His voice trailed off in anguish.

"It won't happen overnight. It's . . . it's gradual. And the medicine will help. A year ago they didn't have anything, now there's Aricept. Who knows what tomorrow will bring? A cure, or something to stop the progress of the disease."

Ray looked in Dani's eyes and shook his head slightly. "My sweet little dreamer." He kissed her cheek. "Someday there will be a cure, but I doubt it will be in time for me."

"We don't know that." Dani reached for strength. "What we do know is that we have today. And for whatever tomorrows we have, we need to make them count."

"I hate that you have to go through this. You're too young to be saddled with me."

"I don't ever want you to say that again." Dani stomped her foot. "I love you, and we are going through this together. You've been here for me, and I'll be here for you. And for the record, there are no young guys at work." Dani touched her hand to his face. "Even if there were, I wouldn't trade you for one."

"One. You could trade me for two or three."

Dani grinned. "Nah, it would take at least six to replace you." She slid the stall rake against the wall. "Now let's get on with living. Dammit, we could both be hit by a bus tomorrow." Dani reached out for Ray's hand. "Come on. We need to go for grain and bird seed."

"Okay. You drive." Ray laughed. "And watch out for buses."

# CHAPTER THIRTY-TWO

Hot, sudsy water tickled against Dani's chin as she wiggled lower in the large oval bathtub. Dead tired and aching in every bone, she took a sip from the wine glass on the tub's edge and closed her eyes. Patches perched precariously near her feet, batting at puffs of soapsuds.

*Is this winter ever going to end? I don't think I can stand another snowstorm.* She'd had a hectic day at work, slid into a ditch on the way home avoiding a car out of control in front of her, and finally arrived home to find the snow plow had blocked her driveway—again—cranky horses and frozen water buckets.

Her second year in the country was proving to be more difficult than the first. One snowstorm after another kept the ranch buried in ever increasing drifts of white, conjuring up scenes from *Doctor Zhivago* as she looked out over mountains of snow and ice that more resembled winter in Russia than Illinois.

Between snowfalls there'd been several severe cold snaps that were even harder to deal with when it came to caring for the horses. Blanketed against the cold, Chance, Cash and Magic grew restless and irritable being confined to the barn. They were reluctant to drink since the water froze on contact with their skin. Dani found she could coax them into drinking by patting their muzzles dry with a towel after they finished. Chance and Magic caught onto the routine right away. Cash seemed to think she was trying to smother him and took a little time to get the picture. Ray and Dani worked hard at keeping the stalls cleaned, fresh water in the buckets, and plowing out the driveway.

Dani eased herself out of the tub and grabbed for the thick, fluffy towel she had placed on the floor near the heat vent. The hot towel brought a weak smile of pleasure to her lips. *Such wonderful little indulgences.* She pulled on a cozy flannel nightgown, thick socks, and her favorite old terry robe.

Ray was sound asleep, lying on his side with one hand tucked under his cheek. In the soft nightlight burning in the bedroom, his peaceful sleep softened the lines around his eyes that were so evident lately when he was awake. Dani's heart ached. *You don't deserve this, Ray. I wish I could take it away.* She softly closed the door and let him rest.

Shadow slept in front of the fireplace, his head propped against one of Ray's shoes. He raised one eye when Dani walked by, sighed, then went back to sleep. As Dani settled in the recliner with a book, Patches snuggled in her lap. With one hand wrapped around the unopened book, the other scratching absently at the cat's fur, Dani stared into the fire.

Winter seemed to be taking a toll on Ray this year. He tired easily and bursts of irritability replaced his easy-going nature and energetic zest for life. The disease seemed to be progressing more quickly than Dani'd imagined, or maybe she just blamed everything on *the disease* lately.

Trace spent Thanksgiving with Megan's family, but stopped by in the evening to visit. A surprise letter from Lynn—short, but a letter, all the same—came the day before Thanksgiving. The postmark was still Florida. Almost a year in the same spot? Close to a record. And to Dani's surprise, a Christmas card "To a Special Sister" arrived just before Christmas.

Trace and Megan spent three days with Dani and Ray at

Christmas. There'd been a slight break in the weather, and Ray had a good spell. Yet Dani could see the concern in Trace's eyes, both for her and for Ray.

Content with her animals and with having Ray nearby and safe for now, Dani opened her book and between the pages of the mystery novel found escape from the cares of her world.

The morning light filtered in the bedroom window. Again the dreaded night was over; Ray breathed a sigh of relief, but couldn't remember why he was so frightened by the darkness. His heartbeat slowed and he felt less afraid. He lay awake, watching Dani sleep, willing a place deep inside himself to remember her.

"It's been cold for a long time," Ray grumbled as he stood by the kitchen window and watched the birds pecking the ground around the feeder.

Dani stood behind him, her arms around his waist, her head nestled between his shoulder blades. His warmth penetrated from beneath a thick flannel shirt. "Um, but we're warm and cozy in here."

"I don't want to think . . . uh . . . of you being cold when I'm gone."

"You're not going anywhere for a long time."

Ray turned and placed both hands on her shoulders.

"You have to stop thinking like that. I need to know you'll be okay." With pained eyes, he continued, "You're too young to be alone. Much as it hurts to think of you with someone else, don't close yourself off."

"Ray . . ."

"Promise me."

"Most people don't have one soul mate in their lives, I can't think of finding two."

"Maybe not, but someone to share things with, not to be alone. Promise."

Dani sighed. "I promise I won't shut myself off from life." She snuggled against his chest. "Besides, you'll always be with me. And whenever I think of you I'll have beautiful memories."

"Memories don't keep you warm."

"Um, memories of you will keep me warm," she teased.

She felt his tears on her cheek as he murmured, "My sweetheart."


Dani trudged along the path toward the barn. Peeking through the earth and around scattered leaves, tulip and daffodil tips struggled to secure their grasp on spring. The air had the unmistakable feeling that winter had lost the last hand and was out of the game for a while. Tiny green nubs strained at the tips of the hedges around the edge of the yard. *Thank goodness spring is finally on its way.* Dani gently touched her fingers against the budding branches and hurried in to feed the restless horses.

Sitting on a hay bale, Dani closed her eyes and listened to the barn sounds. Each horse had his distinct noises. Chance nuzzled his oats, making soft little swishing sounds against the bucket. Dear Cash, always bursting with energy, banged his bucket against the wall with each bite and danced in his stall as he ate. Magic rooted and played with his hay first, tossing it around, munching his oats in between.

Tiger ravenously attacked his food, while Tiger Two ate a few bites and curled up on Dani's lap, enjoying being cuddled and petted first before he ate.

Her barn felt like a sanctuary, where she could let down her guard, cry when she needed. She buried her face in the cat's fur and let the tears come. Ray had been listless all week, and his moods were more and more unpredictable. He complained about eating foods he'd always liked, and preferred sweets to anything else.

Dani considered quitting her job to stay home with him full-time, but realized she needed some time away. Dr. Marshfield reminded her that she must think of her health too. Often caregivers suffered health problems from the constant stress and strain of the daily routine of caring for an Alzheimer's patient.

Magically, as if spring could barely wait any longer, it grabbed the country and shook it to life. Overnight tender new shoots of grass teased the horses, and leaves filled in the spaces between the bare tree branches. Dani found the barn cats eager to go outdoors after their breakfast rather than return to the straw-filled box nestled among hay bales.

Dani stood by the kitchen window watching Ray clean out the stock tank in the paddock. Chance munched grass nearby and poked his head around from time to time to see what was going on. Shadow, true to his name, sat close to Ray's side, content to be there should he be needed, and to enjoy a pat on the head whenever Ray reached out to oblige.

Stretching her hand to the window, Dani felt the warmth of the glass and smiled. The sunshine fell on Ray's face and seemed to melt away the lines the harsh winter had put there. *How many more quality springs and summers does he have? Please help me to make* this *one special for him.* Constantly aware of the ticking clock, Dani treasured all the good days, the tiniest bits of happiness, and tucked them away to remember and draw on for strength when she'd be without him. She searched for ways to make each day special for him now while making memories she hoped would last her a lifetime.

Ray reached out a hand to stroke Chance's muzzle. Jealous of his master's attention to the horse, Shadow nipped at the horse's heels. Chance swung his head around in his patriarchal way and fixed his stare on the canine. Shadow eased back on his hind legs and barked playfully at his equine friend. Chance spun and chased the dog in circles around Ray. The animal antics and Ray's laughter brought joy to Dani's heart and a smile to her face.

Ray hummed as he strode into the kitchen and kissed the back of Dani's neck. She smiled and turned to snuggle against him, marveling at the transfusion of energy and joy that his closeness brought. She kissed him softly and stepped back. She eyed his new jeans, black western shirt and the silver belt buckle and dressy Dan Post boots he hadn't worn in a long time.

"What are you all dressed up for?"

"I'm going into town. I have an appointment."

Dani tucked the dishtowel over the handle of the stove. "Give me a minute to get ready and I'll ride along. I have some errands to . . ."

"Not this time. I need to go alone," Ray interrupted.

A look of apprehension flickered through her eyes.

"Don't worry, I won't be gone long . . . and I'm okay." Ray brushed a hand across her shoulder. "I love you."

"Okay, then . . . drive carefully."

"Always do." He reached for his keys on the hook by the back door and headed toward his truck. As Dani watched, a small trickle of perspiration snaked between her breasts. *How long should I let him continue driving? He seems so much more . . . more like his old self lately. The winter was difficult for me, too. Maybe that was more his problem lately than an escalation of the . . . the Alzheimer's.* It was difficult to say—or even think—the word. Usually she referred to it as the disease. She read and reread the books in order to spot the changes and give him the best care. She hadn't suggested that he not drive, and he hadn't argued when she'd fallen in a routine over the winter of doing most of the driving.

As the spring eased into summer, he seemed stronger, renewed along with the season. Last week while she was at work, he went to the feed store for grain and supplies. Apprehension about his safety as well as that of others on the highway fought with her desire that he be self-sufficient and independent for as long as possible.

Cleaning stalls, scrubbing water buckets, Dani tried to keep busy and avoid glancing at the clock. He'd been gone all morning, and she found herself listening for the crunch of gravel in the driveway. Her work finished in the barn, she headed for the house to do some laundry.

As she tossed a load of clothes into the washer, she heard the back door, and sighed with relief. In the kitchen Dani found Ray seated at the table, his fingers tracing the edges of a large envelope in front of him. He tossed his hat on the chair beside him. "Sit down for a minute, okay?"

Worry lines edged her eyes as she took a chair and waited. Ray reached out to hold her hand. "Don't look so . . . so . . . can't think of the word." He shook his head. "Dammit, I hate this."

"I was just getting a little concerned, that's all. You've been gone a long time."

"Legal . . . stuff takes time." He pushed the large envelope toward her. "I figured I'd better do this now . . . while I could."

Dani ran her hand across the envelope and noticed the legal firm's sticker on the corner.

"Go ahead, open it up," Ray urged.

"Ray, I . . ." Dani's voice squeaked.

Sighing heavily, Ray slid his finger under the flap, reached inside and slid three documents toward Dani.

Without a word, Dani read the large bold letters on the individual documents—LAST WILL AND TESTAMENT.

POWER OF ATTORNEY—HEALTH CARE, and POWER
OF ATTORNEY—PROPERTY.

She lowered her head and tears slid down her cheeks.

"Don't cry, darlin'. I needed to take care of this now. To
make it easier for you later." She saw her sadness mirrored in
his eyes.

"If it wasn't this . . . this disease, something else would get
me, sweetie." He smiled at her. "Just because you make me feel
like a young man doesn't mean I am." He slid his chair back
and motioned to her. She sat on his lap and buried her head on
his shoulder.

"I love you, Dani."

He tilted her chin and looked into her glistening eyes. "I
know I say it a lot, but I'm afraid I'll forget to tell you and long
after I do, I always want you to remember that I love you."

His words brought a watershed of tears. He held her until the
tide eased.

"I'll always . . . remember you . . . and that you love me."
Dani smiled through her tears. "And someday we'll be together
again."

"Don't know how I feel about a hereafter but I hope you're
right about that, darlin'." His lips against hers were soft and
tender. "I'll surely be waiting for you if there is."

# CHAPTER THIRTY-THREE

"Mom, you have to make some decisions soon." Trace dragged a coffee cup in circles on the kitchen table. "You can't be with him twenty-four hours a day, and it isn't safe for him to be alone anymore."

Two different companions Dani had hired had both quit. Ray was so belligerent to them; the first stayed two weeks, the other, only one.

"I know . . . it's just . . ." Her voice faltered. "It's just so hard to think of putting him in a nursing home."

"You can't take care of him by yourself. Remember in the book where it said sometimes caregivers are lost before the patient. It's too much strain, Mom. You need help."

Their summer had been bittersweet. They went to horse shows without their horses, just to watch and visit with friends. They took day trips into the city to museums, the zoo, the aquarium and planetarium. Had picnics and short trail rides with Ray now always riding Chance. Magic, and especially Cash, were both too much for him to handle.

There had always been a special sort of connection between Ray and Chance, the big sorrel eager to give Ray his best. Lately, when Dani watched, she was aware of a different dynamic in the relationship between the horse and rider. Where he had always been in command before, Ray was now a passenger astride the gentle quarter horse that knew there was a difference in this man and was taking care of him. Experiencing the amazing awareness of the horse she loved with the man she loved made Dani feel blessed.

"And he needs professional care so he'll be safe," Trace continued.

Dani knew he was right. She worried whenever she was away from home and Ray was alone. She'd taken the keys to his truck and always kept her car keys hidden. He'd been angry and sulked for days.

The incident that precipitated her taking his keys happened when he told her he was going for grain and hurried off before she could protest. Moments after he left she remembered they needed birdseed and called the feed store to ask that they add it to her order when Ray came in. As the morning stretched into afternoon, Dani's apprehension turned to alarm. She checked with the store and was informed Ray had not been there. Another hour passed, and just as Dani debated calling the police or going to look for him, she saw him turn into the driveway.

Trace listened as Dani related the incident to him. "There was a desperate look in Ray's eyes. Then he saw me and looked so . . . so relieved." Dani shivered. "I remember that look, Trace. When you were about four, you got lost in the grocery store. When I found you moments later, you had that same relieved look in your eyes."

"What did he say?"

"I asked him where he'd been. Said they were too busy at the feed store, so he came home." Dani ran her hand through her hair. "He had no idea he'd been gone for hours. I'd just had the oil changed in the truck the day before and we hadn't driven it since. I checked the mileage when he got home—he'd driven sixty miles, Trace. I have no idea where he went, or if he was just driving around lost."

"Oh, Mom . . ." Trace sighed and reached for his mother's hand. "And soon it's going to be worse for you than for him."

Dani coped with incidents—annoying but not as yet dangerous. Horses put away in the wrong stalls, blankets not secured properly, forgetting to clean stalls or fill water buckets. She'd let Ray putter around, doing what he felt like doing and always checked and rechecked. When she found him giving the horses grain after she'd already fed them, she put a lock on the grain bin.

In the house, she looked for dangers as she had when Trace was a toddler. Kept the medicine cabinet free from anything that could cause confusion and harm. Cleaned up the mess when he put a carton of chocolate ice cream in the refrigerator instead of the freezer. Changed the shower nozzle to a hand-held type when showers suddenly became frightening. Closed the drapes and shades at dusk and kept lamps on in all rooms because he was apprehensive in the dark.

Yesterday the screeching of the smoke alarm woke her. Suddenly aware she was alone in bed, Dani grabbed her robe and ran down the hall. In the kitchen she found an empty pan on a red-hot burner. The back door stood wide open and in the yard sat Ray, barefoot and in his pajamas. Shadow draped a paw across Ray's knee and whined.

"Ray, come in the house. It's cold out here." Dani reached for his icy-cold hand and led him back into the house. Shadow followed closely at Ray's heels, looking confused and forlorn. Patches avoided being in a room with Ray unless Dani was also there.

"Is it ready yet?"

"Is what ready?" Dani asked.

"My . . . I was making . . ." He shuffled to the counter and held up the hot chocolate mix.

"Sit down, I'll finish it for you."

Ray rinsed his hands under the bathroom faucet, stared into the mirror above the sink, and hurried back to the kitchen. "We have to get rid of that guy."

Dani frowned. "What guy?"

"That guy that lives here with us. I don't like him being here anymore."

Weak in her knees, she took a chair next to him at the table. Her voice trembled, "Where is he, Ray?"

Ray took her hand and led her to the bathroom mirror.

"See?"

Ray's reflection stared back at her. Dani stepped close to him and pointed to herself beside him in the mirror. "Who is that, Ray?"

He smiled. "That's you."

"And this," she touched the mirror, "is you."

His brittle chuckle mocked her. "Nope. Not me." Ray pointed to the mirror. "That's an old man."

# CHAPTER THIRTY-FOUR

Dani struggled with the inevitable nursing home decision. Trace and Megan, now engaged and planning their wedding, helped Dani investigate available facilities. Megan's grandfather had suffered from Alzheimer's, and she was a source of comfort and strength to Dani and Trace as they evaluated the pros and cons of each residence.

The sight of vacant-eyed lost souls bound in wheelchairs sitting alone in dreary hallways where there seemed little attempt to cleanse away the stench of urine caused Dani several sleepless nights. No matter what she had to do, Ray would never end his last days in such a place.

The Meadows—a peaceful country retirement village— serenely settled on wooded acreage with a separate Alzheimer's residence, and not too far from Dani's house, was just as pictured in the brochures. After a few unscheduled visits at different times during the day and evening, chatting with employees and residents alike, it was the choice she finally made for Ray.

With his hands folded in his lap, Ray sat quietly beside Dani on the couch. Dani pointed to the glossy color brochure.

"It's a beautiful place, Ray. I've talked to several people living there and they're all quite happy. Their families say they are well cared for . . . all the staff seem cheerful and friendly . . ." Her voice trailed off; she glanced at Ray for some reaction.

"I can't stay here with you?" His words held a tremulous squeak.

Dani barely heard her voice above her heartbeat. She took a deep breath. "I wish you could." And she reached for his hand. "You just can't be alone and I can't be with you all the time."

Ray stared at the brochure and nodded his head.

"Okay."

Only one word, but it spoke of sadness and defeat, and broke Dani's heart.

"It's not far away, and I'll see you every day." She held both his hands in hers and wondered how much he comprehended.

While Megan hung shirts in the small closet next to the bathroom, Trace pushed the ottoman in front of Ray's favorite chair and surveyed the room. He slid an arm around Dani's shoulders.

"Mom, if you don't need us for anything more, we'll let you spend some time alone with Ray, and see you back at the house later."

Dani kissed her son's cheek. "That's fine. Thanks for helping."

Megan held Ray's hand in both of hers as she spoke quietly to him and then bent to kiss him good-bye. Dani was touched at the tears glistening in Megan's eyes as she turned away. Dani hugged Megan and walked to the door with her and Trace.

"Thank you both for everything," Dani said.

Megan's voice cracked as she spoke, "He's such a sweet man. I hate to see this happening to him." She brushed away a tear. "He . . . he thinks I'm Kathy."

"I appreciate you being so patient with him. The doctor says at this point it's best not to argue with him. It just upsets him and makes him irritable."

"I know. Gramps got us all mixed-up too."

Trace waved to Ray from the doorway.

"See you later, Ray."

"Sure thing, buddy. Remember we have a game tonight."

Ray sometimes thought Trace was a friend on his basketball team; other times he believed the young man was his son.

Trace nodded, squeezed Dani's hand, and followed Megan down the hall.

Surrounded by his television set, recliner, clothes and personal articles that he didn't realize were his, Ray sat calmly on the bed and watched Dani place clothes in the dresser.

"Where are your . . . clothes going to go?" Ray asked in a voice low and shaky.

Dani closed the drawer, placed her hands against the dresser top, and took a deep breath. "No, Ray, this is going to be your room."

"Oh." His response was barely audible.

She placed photos on a shelf beside his bed: pictures of his daughter, herself, Trace and Megan, and all the animals.

"Ray, do you remember when Trace and I talked to you yesterday?"

"Trace is such a good boy. We've done a good job raising our son, haven't we?"

*Give me strength.* She nodded. "Yes, Ray, we have."

Ray looked around the room. "Where did he go? Did he take Kathy with him?"

"Yes, they had some things to do."

With hands folded in his lap, a look of fear crept into Ray's eyes. "Will I ever see you again?"

*My God, how can a person hurt so much without ripping apart and bleeding all over the damned floor?* Dani clutched her hand against her stomach as if she feared she might do just that.

"Of course, Ray," she answered. "I love you, and I'll come to see you every day. And on days I don't have to work, you can come home with me for a while to see the animals."

Ray smiled. A childlike smile—easily placated for the moment.

Sitting beside him on the bed, Dani held his hand, searching for words of comfort. She rubbed a hand against her throat, expecting to feel the golf-ball-sized lump straining against her windpipe.

"I love you, Dani," Ray whispered.

"I love you too, Ray."

"I hope I don't forget that . . ."

Dani blinked against the fiery tears that blurred the room and stung like molten lava. *What on earth do I say to him?*

"I hope not too."

Ray turned a childlike gaze toward her.

"You can remember for me."

Somehow the words whispered past the lump, "I'll do just that."

They sat quietly together until a knock came on the door summoning Ray for dinner. Dani walked with him to the dining room, gave him a kiss, and hurried to her car before she started to cry.


Dani draped her jacket over the kitchen chair as she carelessly shuffled through the day's mail. A Florida postmark caught her eye—this time with a return address in the upper left corner. A letter from Lynn. Dani tapped the envelope on the table. *This day has been difficult enough. Do I really want to read her letter now?* With a weary sigh, she slid her finger inside the flap and pulled out two sheets of pale blue stationery. Dani quickly scanned the letter, pulled out a chair, and reread Lynn's words.

Dear Dani,

It's taken me a long time, but I've finally gotten my life

in order. I've lived in Florida since I left your house. I stayed with a friend for a while. It took me a few weeks to find a job and an apartment. I work in an insurance office, and like it a lot. Got a promotion and a raise about six months ago. I'm studying to get my agent's license. Never had a job or stayed in one place this long.

I was angry with you for quite a while—until I realized you were right. I'd like to apologize and thank you for all the times you've helped me and for finally forcing me to grow up. I hope we can be closer sisters now.

Now, for my other news: I'm getting married. His name is Steve—he's a great guy. We've been seeing each other for over a year and last week he proposed. We're getting married in the spring and I would like you to stand up at my wedding. I'll call you soon—maybe we can get together. I want Steve to meet you, Trace and Ray.

Hope all is well.

Love,<br>Lynn

Patches rubbed against Dani's ankle, impatiently reminding her it was dinnertime. Dani slid the letter back in its envelope. Trace and Megan. Lynn and Steve. Bright new beginnings for the people she loved. With a heavy sigh, she got up to feed the cat.

Dani pulled on her barn jacket and went out to care for the horses and cats. Shadow trailed along, stopping occasionally to look around, his brow knitted in a frown and a confused look in his dark eyes.

"You miss him too, don't you, Shadow?" She sat on a bale of hay and cradled the dog's head in her lap. Closing her eyes, Dani listened to the horses rattle grain buckets, heard the cats crunching their dinner, and the sad whine in Shadow's throat.

The barn gave her a solid feeling of security, caring for the animals, a sense of purpose in knowing they needed her.

*You've given me so much, Ray. I'm stronger because of you. I won't fall apart this time.*

After a final check of the barn, Dani secured the door latch and headed to the house, Shadow hugging closely to her side.

Dani pushed the last crate of Trace's belongings toward the stairs. "He is officially a grown-up now," she announced to the basement rafters. Trace and Megan were getting married in two months and had bought a house. Trace was stopping by to move his things to the new place. "No need to have your basement cluttered with my junk," Trace had said to his mother. Dani insisted there was no hurry. Having mementos of his childhood stored in her basement made her feel less alone somehow.

As Dani reached for the light switch, other boxes in the corner caught her eye. Forgotten belongings Ray had stored there when he'd moved in. Several minutes dragged by as she stared at them, nagged by the thought that somewhere he must have someone—a niece, nephew, cousin maybe—someone who would want to know about him.

She knelt beside the dusty cardboard box, hesitated, and then tugged at the flap. Treasured keepsakes from a daughter loved and lost were carefully packed away. Dani touched a small wooden case. Folded in pink tissue paper were ribbons from horse shows, photos of Kathy, carefree and innocent, smiling next to a paint pony. Dani's heart ached for Ray and for a little girl she'd never known. Beneath lay a stack of letters, envelopes addressed to Ray in a young girl's careful hand and tied together with a gold cord. Dani felt her shallow breath against her hand as she held the letters, pulled at the cord, and opened the first envelope. The note began *Dear Daddy,* and spoke of a first day at camp. *I can't read these.* Dani shuddered and quickly folded the page and tucked it away.

A large brown envelope with Ray's name in bold black letters and Austin PD stamped below caught her attention. Dani glanced through a brief official statement, Kathy's driver's license, miscellaneous personal effects returned to Ray after Kathy's death. Goosebumps rose on her arms, she shivered and returned them to the envelope.

As she placed Kathy's letters back, a folder fell to the floor, spilling a photograph, a letter, and a folded and yellowed newspaper clipping. Dani picked up the photo. A dark-haired young man with hard and angry eyes sat astride a motorcycle, his arm clasped firmly and defiantly around Kathy's waist.

Dani's hand shook. Her eyes closed to shut out the young man's mocking stare. *It really can't be.* She held the photo closer for a better look. The back of her neck prickled. With the other hand she reached for the letter. Apprehension crept along her spine.

Postmark: Austin, Texas.
Name in the return address: Crowley/Paterson.

*Please, God.*
Dani stared at the photo, placed it on her lap, and unfolded the letter. The creased paper shook as she read:

Dear Daddy,
    Sorry I haven't written in a while. Hope you're not still made at me. Kyle and I . . .

The air whooshed from Dani's lungs. She felt the throbbing of her pulse in her head; a chill plunged clear to her toes. No, no, *no!* Burning lungs grasped automatically for oxygen. She sucked in a breath, held the letter with both hands, and continued to read.

Kyle and I are getting married. Don't be mad . . . he's got a good job, we're clean—no more drugs, he's promised—

Love you Daddy.
P. S. Will call you soon.

Dani read and reread the letter, stared at the photo, and forced herself to breathe. Placing the letter and photo on the floor, she unfolded the newspaper clipping. Dated one month after the postmark on the letter, it read:

Austin, Texas.

The bodies of twenty-year-old Kathy Crowley and twenty-five-year-old Kyle Paterson were found Tuesday in an apartment they shared on East Bay Street. The medical examiner ruled the deaths were from a drug overdose. Toxicology reports showed cocaine and alcohol present in both bodies. Neighbors stated the couple had moved in about three months before and said they were from Illinois. Crowley worked as a waitress and Paterson tended bar at The Lonesome Cowboy Bar & Grill.

The clipping fluttered to the floor. Dani sat on the cold basement floor and stared at her hands. Icy fingers wrapped around her spine. The thick, damp air pressed against her like a body cast.

Kyle Paterson.

Dani closed her eyes. Did Ray know? Could he have possibly known and never told me? No. *No!*

Kyle Paterson. Kathy's boyfriend: responsible for her death—and the auto accident that had paralyzed Brian.

# CHAPTER THIRTY-FIVE

Dani listened as Trace told of his visit with Ray the night before.

"It was so sad, Mom. I don't think he recognizes anyone now."

"I know. I'm never sure how he'll react to my visits. I don't think I'll suggest he come out to the ranch today. It seems to upset him lately. Besides, I have someone coming out this afternoon to discuss boarding a horse, so I need to get home early."

"Okay, I'll let you go. Hope the boarder works out. You need someone else around the place to talk horses with."

With a feeling of distraction, Dani said good-bye to her son and left for the nursing home.

"Don't want to go away." Ray's voice was petulant. He slouched in his recliner and held his hands tightly against the armrests.

Kneeling beside him on the floor, Dani reached for his hand. "It's okay. We aren't going anywhere. We'll stay here and visit."

His eyes narrowed, vacant and confused. He tilted his head slightly. "Who are you?"

The day was bound to come, the day when he no longer recognized her. She knew that. Knew it, but dreaded it all the same. Dani recalled the time she'd just got out of the shower, remembering when Ray had said, "I'll always love you, Dani," and a voice inside her had said, "Someday you won't even know my name."

She shuddered at the memory of that premonition. For the past month there had been days he didn't recognize her, and then suddenly he'd smile at her. He never called her by name anymore, but he seemed to be glad to see her. Sometimes. Often he pulled back when she kissed his cheek or held his hand, leaving Dani with a hollow space in her gut and a loneliness that cut like a knife with each breath.

He felt uncomfortable leaving the nursing home, didn't ask about the animals. He liked to see Trace, but thought he was a buddy on his basketball team. Last week he introduced Dani to one of the nurses as his daughter.

Dani stopped to see him every day. He tired easily and sometimes wouldn't talk at all. She kept her visits short. She supposed now she was going for herself instead of for him. But she needed to know he was okay. Wanted to be there in case her visit might coincide with one of his moments of clarity. As time went on, she expected it to happen less and less.

Dani searched his eyes, wondering if locked away with all his fading memories was the knowledge of how Kyle Paterson had impacted not only his and his daughter's lives, but Dani's family as well. Some nights she couldn't get to sleep for thinking about it. They'd been too close for him to keep such a secret, but how do any of us truly know another's thoughts and the secrets they harbor?

She'd kept the information from Trace. Afraid of how he'd react if he knew. Secrets. Secrets kept out of fear, secrets kept to spare the others we love from pain.

Fragments of conversation drifted into the room through a partially open door. Stretching her shoulders, Dani sat straighter in the chair, turned a page and continued to read from her favorite book of poetry. Beside her, Ray sat quietly in a large wooden rocker, gazing vacantly out the window. Hands once strong and tanned, now thin and pale, rested listlessly in his lap. Dani finished the poem, softly closed the book and placed it on the table. She adjusted the blanket around his frail shoulders.

He took no notice of her or her comforting words, but continued to stare through the window at the swirling snow that blanketed the world beyond his grasp.

Curling up in the chair beside him, Dani glanced out into the winter panorama—and she remembered what he no longer could . . . that once he loved her, passionately, unconditionally, unselfishly . . . and that she still loved him.

She heard him laugh. Saw him tan and healthy, sitting straight in the saddle, confidently working his horse through training patterns. She remembered peaceful summer rides through wooded trails . . . late night drives home from horse shows . . . lazy drives through the country with the fragrance of new-mown hay drifting through open windows . . . picnics . . . dancing . . . long walks . . . movies . . .

Dani pulled her sweater tightly around her, smiling to herself with memories of laughter shared, tears shed, loving and being loved that made them both whole. She had felt cherished, protected and secure.

Shadows crept into the room, loud voices from the hall intruded on her reverie. Glancing at her watch, Dani was startled at how long she'd been daydreaming. She helped Ray to his bed, covered him with a blanket, gently kissed his forehead and wished him a good night.

Dani waved to the staff as she hurried from the nursing home, shivering inside her heavy jacket. She fumbled with the key in the door, and slid behind the wheel. Giant, sloppy snowflakes splashed against the windshield as she started the engine and waited for the car to warm. She reached for the radio, her fingers cold without the gloves she'd forgotten to wear. As Randy Travis crooned "Forever and Ever, Amen," the tears she'd held firmly in check all day finally flowed with an ache so deep, nothing could reach to ease the pain.

She clicked off the radio and eased into traffic. Impatiently she wiped away the last of her tears and concentrated on the slow-moving traffic. Her thoughts turned to the animals at home needing her care and the meeting with a prospective boarder. Until tomorrow, when she would visit Ray and yearn for a flicker of recognition behind gentle blue eyes.

# CHAPTER THIRTY-SIX

Dani traced a finger around the date on the calendar. Two years. Two years since Ray had gone to live in the Alzheimer's Unit at The Meadows Nursing Home.

She'd been distracted all day, unable to concentrate, even had trouble focusing on her visit with Trace and Megan when they stopped by with the baby. At six months old, Joshua was a friendly, happy little boy, and developing his own personality. Usually the thought of spending time with her grandson filled Dani with joy and anticipation. But today she felt somehow disconnected from everyone. Memories of Ray and the time they'd had together had been unusually vivid—bringing comforting feelings of being loved along with the pain of missing him.

Shadow usually followed her to the barn, but when she called to him tonight, he stretched his head out on his front paws and closed his eyes. Chance seemed out of sorts as she closed up the barn for the night. He left most of his oats untouched and stared into the corner of his stall. *Sure hope he isn't about to colic.* She removed the oat bucket as a precaution, checked him several times before she went to bed, and set the intercom so she could hear any sounds of distress during the night.

Dani shivered as she pulled on one of Ray's old flannel shirts, still warm from the dryer, and crawled into bed. Patches snuggled at her feet and Shadow curled in a ball at the foot of the bed. Dani murmured her prayers, rubbed a hand through Patches' silky coat, and closed her eyes.

Dani slept peacefully, her face softly lit by the moonlight through the bedroom window. Dreams came like a kaleidoscope of memories . . . riding trails with Ray, horse shows, of happier and healthier times they'd shared.

Patches stirred, let out a screech, and ran from the room. Shadow whined, moved around in a circle and followed the cat into the hall.

On the nightstand, the illuminated dial on her clock read three a.m. A cool breeze settled over Dani's face. A gentle moan escaped her lips as she tugged at the blanket. She felt a faint movement flicker against her cheek.

Beside the bed, the silver-haired man stood watching her with loving eyes. Suddenly, Dani awoke. She touched her cheek and smiled. "I was having such lovely dreams of riding trails together." A tear slid down her cheek. "I knew you wouldn't go without saying good-bye," she whispered.

"Don't cry, Dani. You're much stronger than you used to be. You'll be fine."

Dani nodded.

"I'll always be with you." He smiled. "And darlin', you were right . . . and I'll be waiting for you."

Dani sat up and reached out for him.

"Remember me," he whispered, touched a finger to his lips and he was gone.

Shadow howled from his hiding place down the hall. Patches cried, leapt onto the bed and snuggled against Dani.

Closing her eyes, Dani went back to sleep until the telephone rang an hour later. The Meadows telephone number shown on her Caller ID. Dani answered the phone and listened as the director identified herself.

"Dani . . ."

"I know, Margaret. I know. What time?"

After a slight hesitation, Margaret continued, "About an hour ago, just before three, dear."

Dani nodded and hung up the phone.

# EPILOGUE

Dani Monroe tucked the package into the travel bag behind Chance's saddle. She fastened the buckle and rechecked all the straps.

Shadow raced circles around Chance. The sorrel horse stood strangely quiet and ignored him. Dani grabbed the dog's collar and led him to his pen. "Not this trip, Shadow. We won't be gone too long." Shadow sat in the corner of his pen and sulked.

Running her hand along Chance's neck, Dani eased into the saddle. She nestled her feet in the stirrups and urged Chance toward the gate.

The bright sunlight spilled around cumulous puffs in a clear blue sky. The air was calm and the sun warmed Dani's face. From time to time she grazed her fingers against Chance's shoulder and felt the horseflesh quiver beneath her touch.

They rode through the forest preserve to the valley where she had shared a picnic lunch with Ray on their first trail ride. And where he had first kissed her. Dani pulled Chance to a stop beside the creek and slid from the saddle. She dug the container from the saddlebag and held it tightly to her chest, a momentary reluctance to say a final good-bye. Chance pushed his muzzle against her, his warm breath tickling her arm.

As Dani opened the container, a breeze flickered in a single tree overhead. Chance crow-hopped and nickered. Dani smiled and stroked his face. "Easy, boy." Chance bobbed his head up and down and nickered once more.

With a deep sigh, Dani sprinkled Ray's ashes in the wildflowers along the water's edge. "I'll always remember you, Ray Crowley," she murmured. One final swoosh through the treetop, and the air fell silent again.

Dani replaced the empty container, patted Chance on the rump and climbed back in the saddle.

"Chance, let's go home."

# ABOUT THE AUTHOR

*Remember Me* is **Sandra Tatara**'s first novel. She has had short stories published in three anthologies by Whitney Scott's Outrider Press, and in *Detective Mystery Stories,* Issue #23, 2001. In 1997, she won second place in a writing contest sponsored by NOW. In 2003, her story "Change of Command" appeared in *Chicken Soup for the Horse Lover's Soul,* and most recently, she has had a story accepted for *Chicken Soup for the Dieter's Soul,* due out in January 2007. She is currently working on her second novel, a mystery/thriller.

While she has been an interior designer, Emergency Medical Technician and is presently an office manager for a landscape firm, Sandra finally decided what she wanted to do when she grew up was to write. She also paints in several mediums and is a hospice volunteer. She loves spending time with her horses, cats, and her family, especially the two newest joys of her life, Jonathan and Lily.